Even before Corinne saw the dark hump on the bed, she sensed the presence of something awful. She quelled the scream that rose in her throat and took a step closer. She saw the arm dangling over the edge of the cot and the lifeless hand, with the fingers frozen in a curved position, and the scream could no longer be restrained.

The banshee wail caused Luten and Coffen to leap, stare a moment at each other in alarm, then run down the hall to the open doorway. Luten just touched Corinne's shoulder in passing, as if to ascertain she was all right, before he hurried on to the bed.

"She did this," Corinne said, in a small, angry voice. "She killed him. . . ."

By Joan Smith
Published by Fawcett Books:

THE SAVAGE LORD GRIFFIN
GATHER YE ROSEBUDS
AUTUMN LOVES: An Anthology
THE GREAT CHRISTMAS BALL
NO PLACE FOR A LADY
NEVER LET ME GO
REGENCY MASQUERADE
THE KISSING BOUGH
A REGENCY CHRISTMAS: An Anthology
DAMSEL IN DISTRESS
BEHOLD, A MYSTERY!
A KISS IN THE DARK
THE VIRGIN AND THE UNICORN
A TALL DARK STRANGER
TEA AND SCANDAL
A CHRISTMAS GAMBOL
AN INFAMOUS PROPOSAL
PETTICOAT REBELLION
BLOSSOM TIME
MURDER WILL SPEAK
MURDER AND MISDEEDS
MURDER WHILE I SMILE

MURDER WHILE I SMILE

Joan Smith

FAWCETT CREST • NEW YORK

A Fawcett Crest Book
Published by The Ballantine Publishing Group

http://www.randomhouse.com

Library of Congress Catalog Card Number: 97-94398

ISBN 0-449-22494-5

Manufactured in the United States of America

First Edition: January 1998

10 9 8 7 6 5 4 3 2 1

Chapter One

Countess deCoventry, Corinne to her *intimes*, sat tapping her dainty fingers on the arm of a striped satin settee in her mansion on Berkeley Square. How very like Coffen to be late! He knew she wanted to leave Pilchard's rout early. If they arrived too late, he would want to stay until dawn. She had a dozen things she ought to be doing: notes to be written summoning the Friends of the Orphans to organize their annual charity ball, a duty call on Lady Jersey to arrange for tickets to Almack's, a note requesting Signor Fratelli to perform at a musical soiree, to say nothing of reading that dreadful book Reggie had written.

A frown never sat long on her pretty face, however. Beau Brummell, the rogue, had told her her beauty was a mirage. Like the shifting pattern of a flame or the constant movement of water, it was animation that riveted folks' attention and earned her the reputation of an Incomparable. Still, her mirror told her that her raven curls looked very well against her creamy complexion. Her eyes were undeniably large, and of an unusually deep green. If her nose was neither dramatically aquiline nor retroussé, it was a good straight nose with delicately carved nostrils.

She rose, showing off an elegant figure encased in a pomona-green evening gown. It was a daring innovation to abandon the empress style currently in vogue and wear a gown that showed off her trim waist. Luten, she thought, would like it. Her butler, peering in from the hallway, cast an appreciative eye at the figure. Black had long harbored a secret passion for his mistress.

Satisfied that the gown was a success, she began to think of the other dozen things she had rather be doing than twiddling her thumbs while waiting on her cousin, Coffen Pattle. There were plans to begin making for her coming marriage to Luten. Should she try a new coiffure? With her wedding approaching, matters of toilette loomed large in her mind. She rather liked the cherubim do the ladies were wearing this Season. The tousle of untrammeled curls rioting over the head was interesting.

"Oh what the deuce is keeping him!" she said impatiently, and flouncing back down on the sofa, she picked up her book, Byron's poem, *Childe Harold.*

Lady deCoventry had not always lived such a pampered life. As Corinne Clare, she had been born and raised on her papa's farm in Ireland, where her days were more likely to be spent picking berries or shelling peas than driving about in a fine carriage. All that had ended seven years before when Lord deCoventry had visited his farm that neighbored her papa's and chanced across Corinne, tearing through the meadow on her bay mare, with her black hair streaming over her shoulders. It was that old cliché, love at first sight for him. Corinne had never claimed undying passion for her aging husband, but he had been kind and generous during the four years of their marriage, and at his death, he had left her well provided for.

He had turned her out in the first fashion, polished her manners and her taste in literature, art, and music, presented her at Court, told her to call a duke and duchess "Your Grace," not "milord" or "milady," and even told her which knife or fork to use at the grander banquets. Done it all without once making her feel inferior.

These vague thoughts drifted through her mind as she waited for Coffen, with the open book on her lap. After a while she began reading and was soon engrossed. When she heard the door knocker, she shook herself back to the present.

"Good evening, sir," Black said.

"Is your mistress in?" a fluting voice inquired. Not the voice of Coffen, but of her friend and neighbor across the street, Sir Reginald Prance, Bart. She frowned; Prance had decided to go to the rout in his own rig. Black apparently nodded, for Reggie's voice continued, "No need to show me in. I am familiar with the route."

As he sauntered in, Sir Reginald's eyes did not see the manifold charms of Lady deCoventry or the new gown, the classical workmanship of Adam, the splendor of Persian carpets, nor the artworks decorating the walls—all items that would normally have interested this demanding dilettante. His attention was focused on a book. The wrong book!

He scowled. "Aha!" He had caught Corinne dead to rights, with her head sunk into a copy of *Childe Harold's Pilgrimage*.

He wished someone would round up all the thousands of copies of that appalling book and throw them into the Thames. They littered every saloon in London. He had come to hate the very sight of those leather-bound volumes. What folks *should* be reading, only they had no taste, was the *Round Table Rondeaux*, his own stirring stanzas in blank verse on the knights of the Round Table. He had spent months, on and off, studying up all the history of Arthur, *dux bellorum*, and giving himself a headache thinking up rhymes. Try rhyming *dux bellorum*! Or Sir Galahad for that matter, without sinking into farce.

Anyhow, his book, full of exciting historical stuff, sat gathering dust behind the counter since milord Byron had come pouncing on the scene to steal his thunder with his demmed Eastern poems, full of pirates and pashas and brigands.

Corinne tore her eyes from the book and glanced up. "Just having a peek to see what all the clamor is about, Reggie," she said.

"It has more to do with Byron than the poems," Reggie said, trying valiantly to subdue the edge of rant that tinged his tone. "Dashed fellow is the perfect embodiment of his hero. A jaded cynic and world traveler, his soul burdened with nameless crimes. Handsome—if you care for that rather vulgar, obvious type of good looks—and a baron to boot. The ladies are all running mad for him." What chance had a mere baronet whose sole travels were from Land's End to Tom O'Groats? Lady Caroline Lamb had made an utter ass of herself over Byron, dressing up like a page boy and hounding him through the streets of London. Prance had always had a secret *tendre* for the fey charms of Caro Lamb.

Looking at her caller, Corinne had to admit the disparity in the appearance of the two poets. Reg was an elegantly slender dandy with the lean, narrow face of a greyhound. He had allowed his dark hair, usually brushed forward in the Brutus do, to grow longer, perhaps in emulation of Byron. With the best will in the world, she could not call him handsome, but only elegant. Even the elegance was so meticulous as to border on the foppish. The amethyst in his cravat exactly matched his plum-colored jacket. The narrow stripes in his cream waistcoat echoed the shade.

"I see you're reading his book!" he said, his eyes narrowing suspiciously. "Bought it, did you?"

"I tried to get it at the circulating library, but the six copies are reserved for months ahead. It was a regular scramble at the book stalls—for both your books," she added hastily, when Reg's pink cheeks turned an alarming purple that matched his jacket. "This doesn't hold a candle to your book," she lied loyally. Even as she spoke, her eyes returned hypnotically to the page, and a smile drew her lips upward in appreciation.

"Lord Byron has corrupted the morals of every lady in England," Prance announced. His real chagrin was that this wholesale corruption could not be placed in his own dish. His publisher (and Byron's), John Murray, had thought his rondeaux "a little broad." Broad, good God! He had not even mentioned Lady Guinevere's carrying on with Sir Lancelot. If his reference to the camp followers trailing after the knights was broad, Byron's stuff was licentious. No other word for it. Prance knew, because he had devoured every line, his eyes growing greener as the reading progressed.

He could not even claim youth for the inferiority of his own rondeaux. To set the cap on his humiliation, he was an ancient twenty-seven, three years older than Byron. Of course, he hadn't got a limp to elicit pity and aid sales.

"Toss that trash aside and let us go," he said testily.

She closed the book, carefully marking her place. "I am

waiting for Coffen. He wanted me to visit someone with him before the rout."

"Who?" Prance asked at once. "Odd he did not invite me along."

"We didn't know you planned to come with us."

"I changed my mind. I told him so. Who is he visiting?"

The three were virtually inseparable. The fourth corner of the quartet was the Marquess of Luten, presently in the country arranging for the disposition of a small farm that had been bequeathed to him by the death of a cousin. Jointly they were known as the Berkeley Brigade, as they all lived within yards of each other on Berkeley Square. They were the unofficial leaders of the young ton. Luten, their captain, was a member of the Whig shadow cabinet in the House of Lords.

"I don't know. It has something to do with seeing some paintings," she said.

"What paintings? Whose? You know nothing about art. He should have spoken to me."

"He didn't say who."

"Can you not bear to put the book down and let us discuss it?" Lord, he sounded like a nagging wife. He was turning into a whiner on top of everything else. "Whoever it is will sell him some inferior work—fleece him alive. Pattle wouldn't know an oil painting from a Renaissance intaglio."

She hastily set the book aside and glanced up, to find Reg studying her. He had been practicing Byron's famous "underlook" in his mirror, and was trying it for the first time in company. The look drove the ladies into a perfect frenzy when Byron did it. It was achieved by keeping the head down and gazing up through long lashes. He lacked the length in lashes, but he fancied he could curl his lip as cynically as anyone.

"Have you got something in your eye, Reggie?" she asked.

He glared. "No. Get your pelisse. We'll call on Coffen. Byron's cantos will still be here when you get back," he added with heavy irony.

They were interrupted by the sound of scuffling in the hallway. The heavy, dragging step heralded the approach of Coffen Pattle. His usual toilette included mussed, mud-colored hair, a rumpled jacket, and quite possibly a stained cravat. Were it not for the ruddy complexion and blue eyes, they would scarcely have recognized him in the exquisite apparel before them. His hair had been coerced into order by a lavish application of oil. A white cravat of unusual size and intricacy lifted his chin an inch higher than usual, and his jacket was unwrinkled.

"Coffen, don't you look fine!" Corinne said.

He blushed. "Sorry I'm a tad late," he said, bowing and nodding. "Raven, my valet, had a spot of trouble with my cravat. Tarsome business, trying to turn out in style."

Prance pouted. She had not praised *his* toilette! But then elegance, like sweets, grown common lose their delight. "What is the occasion for this grand toilette?" he inquired.

"La Comtesse Chamaude," he announced in reverent tones, as if he were saying "His Majesty, the king."

Corinne gave a start of alarm. "What! How the devil did you meet that dasher?"

She knew Lady Chamaude was a French countess of a certain age, though she was remarkably preserved. The lady admitted to thirty, but as gossip claimed she had been a widow upon her arrival at Brighton twenty-odd years previously, this claim was treated with a large sprinkling of salt. She had been smuggled out of France during the revolution and had hung on to the fringes of Society ever since. Recently she had managed to inveigle her way a little inward, due to the good graces of Lord Yarrow, according to rumor. Lord Yarrow was married, but his wife was invalidish and did not interfere with her lord's pleasures.

"Why, one may meet her anywhere nowadays. I ran into her at the exhibition at Somerset House this morning. Henshaw dragged me along to look at some pictures. Chamaude is mad for pictures. Knows all about key-roscuro and composition—a regular connoisseur. She knew Henshaw a little and stopped us out of the blue. Said if I liked French art, she had something that might interest me."

"Since when have you acquired an interest in French art?" Prance asked.

"Since I met Chamaude."

"Odd you did not invite me along."

"Three's a crowd," Coffen replied, unfazed.

"So much for arithmetic."

"Eh?"

"You, Corinne, Chamaude—does that not make three?"

"I daresay it does, but I had mentioned when I was at the gallery that I was taking Corinne to a do tonight, and the comtesse said why didn't we stop in en route. So that's what we're doing. We'll meet you at Pilchard's."

"She'll try to sell you something," Prance said. "I had best go along to protect you."

Prance never neglected an opportunity to meet an interesting character, especially a slightly déclassé one. His own reputation was a sovereign preventive against scandal. He ushered Corinne and Coffen into the hallway. Black lovingly placed a mantle over her ladyship's shoulders, and they were off.

Chapter Two

The aromas of autumn were carried on a gentle breeze—the smells of leaves and earth and dying vegetation. Prance delayed their departure while he darted across the street to pick up a few copies of his *Rondeaux*. To encourage distribution, he had purchased a hundred copies at discount, which he was busily distributing gratis to anyone who would take one.

"It's rather late to call—nine o'clock," Corinne mentioned, as the carriage drove off.

"She said she would be at home till nine-thirty," Coffen replied.

"I wonder what lucky gent is calling at ten," Prance said musingly.

Coffen gave him a sharp look. "Eh? Whoever he is, he will be out in his luck. She said she would be going out at nine-thirty."

"That might be French for saying she does not wish to be disturbed after that hour."

"Just like a Frenchie. Why the deuce can't they say what they mean?"

The carriage lumbered along the streets of fashionable London, passing private chaises and landaus, some with a crested panel indicating a noble owner, as well as hired hackney cabs and a few gents on foot, before drawing to a stop in front of a modest brick house in Half Moon Street.

Before descending, Corinne said, "I hope we won't be *de trop* on this call, Reggie. Perhaps she understood an evening visit to be romantical in nature."

"Rubbish. She's just going to show me some pictures," Coffen said. "Dashed civil of her."

"Mark my words, she's peddling them," Prance averred.

"Daresay you might be right. She could sell me the Tower of London if she had a mind to. Killing eyes, Prance."

"She is much too old for you!" Corinne scolded. "Furthermore, buying a painting you do not want is an expensive way of furthering the acquaintance."

"True, but as she said, a picture is an investment, you see. And Chamaude has the goods. Her husband had a famous collection. They managed to smuggle some of them out of France."

Prance reached down and picked up a copy of his book. "Better take a couple," he said, picking up another. "She might have company. She is not the sort of lady to sit home alone during the Season, even before nine-thirty."

They were admitted by a butler with a French accent and the saturnine, dissipated face of an aging boulevardier. While waiting to be announced, Corinne glanced around the walls of the hallway. Above a bombé chest, a Watteau *fête champêtre* scene hung in a gilt frame. Dandified gentlemen were pushing ladies in broad-brimmed hats and floating gowns, seated on swings. Their toes disappeared into the branches of ethereal trees. Beneath the bonnets, eyes flirted at her across the century. The painting appealed to her highly developed sense of romance. Why couldn't life be like that nowadays?

"Charming," she said. "I wonder if our hostess would care to sell this one."

"Poisson," Coffen replied.

"Pray what have fish to do with anything?" Prance asked, sniffing the air. "Mutton, I would say."

"What she wants me to look at—a Poisson. Is that a Poisson?" He peered at the painting, looking for a signature. No one had ever accused him of knowing anything about art.

"Poussin?" Prance murmured. He and Corinne exchanged a look that spoke volumes of Pattle's ignorance of art. He glanced at the painting above the chest. "The Watteau appears to be genuine."

They soon found themselves in Lady Chamaude's saloon. It was not large, but its insignificant size was more than compensated for in elegance. Satin settees, a marble fireplace, tables littered with bibelots, a Persian carpet, and draperies of some material that emitted a golden sheen were the overall impression. Yet despite its charming decor, Corinne felt uncomfortable, as if she were in a prison. Was it the room's size that caused it? Soon her attention was diverted to Lady Chamaude.

It was hard to believe she was as old as arithmetic decreed. She was strategically placed with the light at her back, but even in the dull glow, one could see time had not got the better of her. Hair as black as jet was arranged in curls around a heart-shaped face. The darkness of her eyes was emphasized by delicately tinted skin, as flawless as a newly opened rose. No incipient sagging or wrinkling could be seen.

That pair of impertinent shoulders might have been carved by Canaletto from alabaster. A wine-colored gown showed them off to great advantage. At her throat she wore a set of diamonds. The diamonds were perhaps paste; they did not sparkle as real diamonds should. At her side, like a dog guarding a particularly tasty bone, sat the corpulent, bewhiskered Marquess of Yarrow. Corinne decided it was his jailerlike pose that caused that sense of confinement.

This gentleman was known to be quite an expert on art and ladies. He was one of the Prince Regent's rackety crew who gambled for high stakes, drank too much, and enjoyed great favor at the Tory-dominated court. He was also, if memory served, a member of the Horse Guards, and therefore no doubt a crony of the Duke of York, who was commander in chief of that mysterious institution. They were not guards, nor did they ride horses, but their administrative office was at that address. Corinne understood they were very influential in military matters.

"Lady deCoventry, gentlemen," Yarrow said genially, rising to pump their hands. The creak of whalebone revealed he was wearing a corset to control his girth. "Did you ever see such grand weather as this? Delightfully warm for September."

They all agreed it was superlative weather.

Lady Chamaude turned her brilliant orbs on them and said, "I don't believe I have the pleasure of your friends' acquaintance, Mr. Pattle." Her voice was husky, and tinged with an alluring French accent.

Coffen made the introductions. The loquacious Prance was bereft of words. He could only stare, employing the "underlook" in an effort to beguile the charmer.

It was Coffen who said, "A dandy dress, Comtesse, if you don't mind my saying so."

Lady Chamaude showed them to a seat and said, "Too grand for the evening I have planned, I fear. Lord Yarrow has been kind enough to help me in selecting an outfit in which to have my portrait taken. Actually, I shall be spending the night with a sick friend."

"Lady Chamaude says she has no use for a portrait, having no family to pass it on to," Yarrow said. "Rubbish, say I. It will be for posterity, like the *Mona Lisa*."

The lady gave a dismissing shrug of her marmoreal shoulders. "I never thought Mona Lisa, the lady, very attractive, though it is a stunning painting. I shall have my portrait taken to remember in my old age how I looked when I was younger. I do not say young, for I am long past that. My bloom has faded." Her voice held a wistful note, which was echoed in her dark eyes.

The words were designed to elicit pity and, of course, strenuous objection from the gentlemen. Corinne felt she ought to despise her, and was surprised to feel the stirring of pity. It was the way the comtesse spoke, with an air of genuine regret. There was a fragile air of vulnerability in her beauty, like a blossom whose petals have lost their firmness but have not yet begun to wither. How very fleeting were a lady's youth and beauty! Even she was no longer in the first flush of youth. Twenty-four—a quarter of a century on her next birthday, and what had she accomplished? She had no husband, no children. In her mind the image of Luten rose up to banish these gloomy thoughts.

"Why, you are still a young girl," Yarrow said in a kindly way. As he spoke, he clamped his sausagelike fingers on her white arm and squeezed. The comtesse stiffened, then smiled her thanks. "When you are half a century old like myself, then you may be allowed to speak of fading youth."

"Exquisite, charming," Prance breathed. He presented both Lady Chamaude and Lord Yarrow with a copy of the *Rondeaux*. "Just a few lines I scribbled off in my hours of idleness." Damme! He had inadvertently used the title of Byron's first youthful offering.

"But how charming!" the lady exclaimed. "You must autograph it for me. You English have so many clever poets. I have just been dipping into Lord Byron's poem."

Prance's jaw clenched in dismay. She rose from her chair abruptly, with an air of escape, and led him to a drop-leaf desk in the corner. Corinne observed Yarrow admiring Lady Chamaude's sylphlike figure. When he saw Corinne watching him, he gave a shake of his whiskers.

"Poor lady," he said. "She has had a rough time of it, in a foreign land. We ought to be a little kind to our French émigrés. Yvonne, that is her name, is quite like a daughter to my good lady and myself."

Corinne smiled benignly on this piece of fustian. Yarrow's sharp eyes held no hint of pity, but a definite gleam of lust.

Prance dipped his pen into the inkpot and began a flourishing inscription. He noticed Lady Chamaude used a violet color of ink. Charming! No discreet inscription occurred to him. He wanted to write *I love you*, in sulfur across the sky. The lady was exquisite! The boldest message he dared to inscribe was "To Lady Chamaude from an admirer, Sir Reginald Prance." He wrote a fine hand, if he did say so himself. Let Lord Byron match that *L* and *C*. Would she notice he had humbly not given his own "admirer" a capital?

Lady Chamaude read the inscription and rewarded him with a Giaconda smile, which he quickly imbued with a hint of invitation. Yarrow had set his copy aside unsigned.

She sent for wine, and when they were all served, she said, "I expect you want to see the Poussin, Mr. Pattle."

"Thankee, I do."

She rose again and led Pattle across the room. When

Corinne noticed that the picture occupied an ill-lit corner, she felt a spurt of alarm. The lady's reputation was not all one could wish in a purveyor of artworks, and that was certainly why Coffen had been invited here.

As if reading her mind, Lady Chamaude said, "We shall bring it to the light. Would you mind removing it, Mr. Pattle? It's rather heavy."

The painting, about two feet wide and eighteen inches high, had an embossed gilt frame. He had some little difficulty removing the picture from the wall and managed to bump a corner of the frame against a couple of tables while transporting it to the light. He noticed he had knocked a dent in the corner of the frame and very likely marred the tables as well. Pity. They all gathered around to study the picture.

Prance managed to wrench his eyes from the comtesse long enough to study the painting. Its patina, he observed, suggested the proper age, but that could easily be faked. The subject was an old man swathed in some sort of winding cloth, drinking from a goblet, while assorted people stood around looking morose. *The Death of Socrates,* of course.

Yarrow gazed at it and sighed in pleasure. *"The Death of Socrates,"* he announced in solemn tones. "From Poussin's more mature period, between 1640 and 1650, I should think."

"Yes, certainly," Prance agreed. "At that time he painted heroes facing a moral dilemma. You can see the traces of the French Royal Academy. Classical lines," he said vaguely.

Yarrow's eyebrows rose in approval. "I see you know something about art, Prance."

"Un petit peu," Prance replied.

What Corinne saw was an extremely tedious, old-fashioned picture. The colors, borrowed from the Venetians, had faded with age. The composition, borrowed from Rubens, was stilted by the dull classical elegance the French Royal Academy insisted on. The workmanship, however, was more than capable. As an investment it might be worthwhile. Yarrow was extremely knowledgeable about such things. He often acted on the Prince Regent's behalf at auctions and sales.

"What do you think, Coffen?" she asked, making no effort to conceal her own lack of interest.

"Now, that is what I call a picture!" he exclaimed. "Socrates! It would be the last picture ever painted of him. Mean to say, he's downing the hemlock even as the artist painted."

Yarrow's jaw fell open in astonishment. "It was not painted from life, Pattle!" he said.

"No, it couldn't be, come to think of it. But you could never tell to look at it. What are you asking for it, milady?"

"A thousand pounds."

"A bargain!" Yarrow exclaimed.

Coffen said, "Yes, by the living jingo, I'll—"

Corinne darted a warning look to Prance, who had fallen into a trance as he gazed at la comtesse. "He'll think about it," she inserted hastily.

"Don't dally too long, or it will be snapped up," Yarrow warned, gazing fondly at the picture. "There is a wine merchant coming to look at it tomorrow."

They finished their wine, and Yarrow said to Lady Chamaude, "I know you are going out as soon as you change, madam, so I shall not detain you. I think the deep red gown will do very well for the portrait, but you will want to consult with the artist first. It depends on what background he has in mind. If he chooses to use nature for the setting, then perhaps he will want something less formal than silk and diamonds." He lifted a bushy eyebrow at the other callers, who were obliged to rise as well.

"When will you let me know about the Poussin, Mr. Pattle?" Lady Chamaude inquired, not eagerly, but in a businesslike way.

"Tomorrow. I'll sleep on it. Not on the picture itself! I'll think about it, is what I meant."

The comtesse smiled sweetly. "Of course."

The four callers left together.

"A fine lady," Lord Yarrow said, as they walked toward their waiting carriages. "It is a boon to England that so much of the Chamaude collection is ending up here—and at such reasonable prices. I cannot tell you how many masterpieces I have managed to get hold of for Prinney. You must drop around to Carlton House tomorrow evening and have a look for yourself. I shall arrange it with Prinney for you to receive invitations. He is having a few connoisseurs in to see his latest acquisitions."

"I don't call myself a connoisseur," Pattle said, though he had no objection to others calling him one.

Prance, who assumed that "connoisseur" was directed at him, and was in any case determined to be included in any invitation to Carlton House, said, "We would be honored, Lord Yarrow."

Yarrow then turned a sharp eye on Lady deCoventry, who had said nothing. "I sense you are not smitten with the Poussin, milady."

"It is not in my style. That Watteau in Madam's hallway, however, is quite another matter."

"A charming thing. Lady Chamaude is particularly fond of it herself and has no immediate plans to dispose of it."

"It is odd she is selling so many pictures now, when she has been in England for over two decades."

"Nothing odd about it," Yarrow said, quick to leap to her defense. "She wants to buy a house in town. I spotted a small mansion on Grosvenor Square that is up for sale and suggested to her myself that she ought to put a bid on it. It is difficult for a lady in her position, with no one to advise her. That little box she is in at the moment is only rented, you must know. Pictures are all very nice, but they make poor walls and roofs."

"True," Coffen said, nodding. "And you think the Poosan a good investment, milord?"

"I do, certainly. With art, however, it is best to buy what you like, then you have the pleasure of looking at it, if it goes out of fashion. I am buying up some paintings by a fellow from Suffolk myself. A strange duck. Constable is completely out of fashion. You may pick him up for an old song, but the things will be worth something one day, or I don't know a thing about art."

No one was ready to dispute Yarrow's knowledge of art.

"I think what set Lady deCoventry off," Prance confided, "is the picture's being in that dark corner."

"You saw it by lamplight," Yarrow said. "I am sure Lady Chamaude will have no objection to your taking it out into the sunlight tomorrow if you want to see it by daylight. Any fool can see it is an original." He turned a fawning eye on Corinne. "And Lady deCoventry, it hardly needs saying, is no fool."

Yarrow's carriage was reached first. "Ah! I forgot to bring the book you so kindly gave me, Prance. I shall just run back in and pick it up."

"It happens I have another in my carriage—"

"But mine is autographed," Yarrow said, and returned to the house.

"It ain't, you know," Coffen said. "You didn't sign his, Prance. Should we wait till Yarrow comes out, and you can sign his copy?"

Prance scowled. "Don't be obtuse. He just wants an excuse to go back. He left it behind on purpose to be rid of us."

"You don't mean that old crock is carrying on with her!"

"Of course he is," Corinne said. "He takes a very proprietorial interest in la comtesse. I worry a little about that close alliance."

"I daresay she'd prefer a younger man," Coffen said hopefully.

"I am not talking about your romantic hopes." She turned to Prance. "Is it possible he's claiming the painting is authentic to fill her pockets? That is a new way of supporting a mistress."

Prance considered the matter a moment. "I shouldn't think so, if Yarrow is buying them for Prinney."

"Prinney is not buying the Poussin. Why not, I wonder, as Yarrow recommends it so highly?"

"We don't know she is his mistress," Prance said.

"It's common knowledge. Everyone says so."

"I am not everyman. I think for myself." They entered Corinne's carriage. "Let us drive around the block and see if he comes out."

They did this. As they rounded the corner back to Lady Chamaude's house at the close of their circuit, they passed Yarrow's crested carriage, going the other way.

"You was wrong," Coffen said. "There's hope for me yet."

Prance's sharp eyes were looking farther along the street, where a hired carriage had already drawn up at the house. A younger gentleman descended and ran up the stairs.

"Do we know that set of shoulders?" he asked.

Coffen peered into the distance. "Not by name, but I've seen him about here and there. One of those French émigrés, like Chamaude herself. A handsome rascal. No point sticking around. She don't love me, but I'll take the Poosan all the same. I've taken a fancy to it. Socrates—there was a fine fellow, but he could do with a good tailor."

The carriage continued rattling past the house. "All set for Pilchard's rout?" Prance asked. "The whole world will be there."

"I shan't stay long," Corinne said. "Perhaps one of you should take your own carriage."

"You'll want a good night's sleep to be bright-eyed and bushy-tailed for Luten's return tomorrow," Prance said. "Berkeley Square it is."

Corinne expected Prance would make some ironic comment about her missing Luten, but he sat silently brooding, which was unusual for him.

When they reached her house, Coffen got out of the carriage and went to his own house to call his carriage.

Prance said, "Can we talk for a minute, Corrie?"

"Of course. Come in and have a glass of wine. In fact, I am not at all sure I shall even bother going to the rout."

"Anxious to get back to *Childe Harold*?" he asked archly.

"No, anxious to discuss Chamaude, and that picture."

"That is what I want to talk about as well."

Chapter Three

"I daresay there will be no talking Coffen out of buying that ugly picture," Corinne said, as she handed Prance a glass of wine.

Prance stared at her with glazed eyes. "Picture?" he said. "Ah, the Poussin. That is not what I wished to discuss. It is a matter of much more import." He drew a deep sigh, gave a dramatic little shudder, and announced in a hushed voice, "You are looking at a man in love."

"Not with her, I hope!"

"Who else? The moment I gazed into her eyes, I knew. I felt our hearts touch—no, collide. It was no brushing of angels' wings, but a primordial thunder. And did you ever see such eyes? I gazed into them for close to half an hour, yet after all that time, I could not tell you what color they are. Is that not odd?"

"Not so odd when she stationed herself in shadows."

"Every curve and angle of her incomparable face is carved into the marrow of my bones, but those eyes! I have only a shimmering memory of darkness and depth. What mysteries are concealed in those bottomless pools?"

"Don't be absurd, Reggie! The lady is much too old for you. She's ancient!"

"Not ancient, ageless!"

"And she's too fast, too."

"I grant you she is probably a daughter of the game. It is her experience of the world that lends her that aura of . . . Ah, one hardly knows what to call it. Infinite woman! The gentleness of a dove, the vulnerability of a moth hovering toward the flame, the allure of a courtesan, and the passion of a Gypsy queen, all rolled into one exquisite she. I have wrestled with my conscience about pursuing her. Not for any feeling for that old slice Yarrow but because of Pattle. He fancies himself in love. She is worlds too experienced for him. He wouldn't know what to do with such a woman."

"That should be no problem. I wager she knows exactly what to do with him, or any other man. Fleece him! It won't do, Reggie."

He talked away every objection with a tolerant, forgiving, infuriating smile. "But I shall learn from her. Love should be broadening. I know she will break my heart. That is a foregone conclusion. Such women can never belong to one man—but I shall be a better man for it. What do a couple of thousand pounds matter? I was never greedy of filthy lucre. Loving her will be an education."

"You're raving like a lunatic. I think you've lost the use of your wits."

"Drunk on love! I shall follow where my heart takes me, though the devil lead the measure. I always feared, you know, that I would never experience a truly grand passion, of the sort that made Dante and Beatrice immortal. I have had dealings with countless ladies and other . . . er, females, but never before felt this trembling in the blood, this deep oneness, this touch, almost, of the infinite when I gazed into her eyes. Oddly, the French do not have a word for it, do they?"

"The English have. Folly."

"No, that does not begin to do my feelings justice. It is the divine Goethe to whom we must turn. *Sturm und Drang!* There is *Sturm und Drang* in my heart, stolen from her eyes. Say what you like, it is the Germans who take love seriously. For the French it is a game, and for the English, of course, it is a mystery."

"What the devil are you talking about?"

He looked at her as if she were a complete illiterate. "Geothe's *Goetz von Berlichingen*. Surely you are familiar with Scott's translation at least? I own I have only read it in English. *The Sorrows of Young Werther*. Like Werther, I shall gladly relinquish any hope of enduring happiness for a few weeks in the company of my beloved. And I promise I shan't commit suicide when it is over, like poor Werther. Suicide is seldom a viable alternative, if you will pardon the redundancy."

"You've barely met the woman, Prance. You can't be in love with her yet."

"I come to see love at first sight is the only love worth pursuing. Don't be selfish, my pet. You cracked my heart a little when you chose Luten. You cannot begrudge me a crumb of happiness."

"I begrudge having that woman make a fool of you."

"Surely a hopeless passion is an allowed infirmity in an old friend?"

"You'll get over it. It is Coffen we should be worried about."

"I do feel for him, but he hasn't my sensitivity, you know. His heart is a sturdy old muscle, only excited by food, and perhaps agitated a little by actresses. He is not cursed—or blessed—with my deep well of feeling."

"It's his pockets I'm talking about, not his heart."

"He can well afford a thousand pounds. Dear heart, let us not discuss trifles. What you must do is help me bring the comtesse into fashion—well, respectability at least. We can do it, if we all stick together. Society will not spurn her if she is seen about with the Berkeley Brigade."

"You expect me to make a friend of Yarrow's mistress? Luten would hit the roof if I did such a thing."

Prance gave her a sly look. "I shouldn't think so. He is a man, after all. Is that what concerns you, that he'll fall under her spell?"

"He has more sense—and better taste."

Prance rose up from the sofa like an outraged Methodist who has been offered strong drink. "No one has ever questioned my taste! Especially a lady who has no notion how to dress!" He regretted that indiscretion as soon as it left his lips, but it was true all the same. Corinne's toilette was always just a little too busy to please his austere taste.

He hastened on, before she could flare into a temper. "Very

well. If that is your final decision, that you refuse to help me in this utmost crisis of my life, then I must carry on on my own."

"I'm doing what I think best for you, Reggie. And I'm sure Luten will agree with me."

Prance gave her a mischievous look, said, "We shall see about that," then he bowed punctiliously and made a chilly departure, leaving Corinne alone, and more than a little concerned that Prance would draw Luten into the comtesse's dangerous orbit—and wondering what he meant about her style of dressing, too. Fop!

She had initially felt some pity for the comtesse, but as she considered the evening, she felt the pity was misplaced. The woman had caught Coffen in her web at a public art exhibition; she had smitten Prance in the space of ten minutes. Already she and her old friend Prance were at daggers drawn. What effect would this mischievous beauty have on Luten? He was not entirely impervious to beautiful women.

For three years Corinne had reigned supreme as the queen of the Berkeley Brigade. All the gentlemen were in love with her, to a greater or less degree. Coffen, her cousin, loved her like a sister. Sir Reginald never loved anyone as much as he loved himself, but when he felt the need to be in love, it was with her. But of course, it was Luten that worried her most. She must keep Luten away from that siren.

She made a careful toilette the next afternoon to greet her fiancé on his return from the country. As he entered her saloon, she viewed him as the comtesse would no doubt view him. He was tall and lean, with the broad shoulders of a sportsman. His crow-black hair grew in a dramatic widow's peak. Finely drawn eyebrows over cool gray eyes lent him an ascetic touch. It was his strong nose and square jaw that gave authority to his face, and his haughty smile that gave it a touch of arrogance. A blue jacket of Bath cloth clung to his shoulders like paper on a wall. His modest cravat was immaculate, his buckskins the same, and his Hessians as bright as mirrors. And on top of it all, he owned an abbey and was a marquess. Those last two, she felt, were the attributes that would excite the comtesse's interest.

All of this flashed through her mind in a second, then Luten smiled and held out his arms, and she rushed into them to be thoroughly kissed.

"Did you miss me?" he asked, in a husky voice unlike his usual bored drawl.

"Desperately." She held his hand tightly as she led him to the sofa. "How did everything go with the farm?"

"I hired a bailiff to take care of it. I'll probably sell it. It's a hundred miles from the abbey, too far away for me to conveniently keep an eye on it and not large enough for us to keep for our second son. And what's new here?"

Her heart swelled in pleasure at that casual "second son," which suggested a long and happy marriage.

"Prance has fallen into a wretched muddle," she said.

"The *Rondeaux* are not leaping off the shelf, I take it? The deadweight of all that poesy suggests it would require a derrick to hoist them. We must give him a hand."

"He can hardly give them away, but that is not what I mean." She outlined the situation, just mentioning the comtesse's age and lack of character.

"And on top of Prance fancying himself in love, Coffen is going to buy a horrid old picture from her—for a thousand pounds."

He patted her fingers indulgently. "It seems I returned just in time. Fear not, my dear, I shall handle Yvonne."

Corinne's heart leapt in her chest. She had not mentioned the comtesse's Christian name. So Luten already knew her. That he called her Yvonne suggested a certain intimacy. With such a woman, there was only one sort of intimacy that came to mind.

"Oh, you know her?" she said, staring at him in surprise that was already tinged with mistrust.

"I have her acquaintance," he replied.

Before Corinne could learn more, the door knocker sounded and within seconds Coffen and Sir Reggie came in.

"Saw your rig arrive," Coffen said. "Saw you dart over here.

Gave you two a few minutes alone, then came along to welcome you back."

"I tried in vain to restrain him," Reggie said, with an air of apology. "How did it go in Somerset, Luten?"

"I've put the farm up for sale or rent. The next-door neighbor is interested, but he wants it as a gift."

"If you manage to sell it," Coffen said, "I can put you on to some bargains in art. I'm buying a Poosan from Comtesse Chamaude. She's French."

"Yes, the 'Comtesse' gave me a hint," Luten replied. "I was just telling Corinne I know the lady."

Prance flew into a frenzy of excitement. "You know her? Who is she? Is she really a countess? You wouldn't know her age? And what, exactly, is her relationship with Yarrow?"

Corinne listened with both ears cocked, scrutinizing every word that left Luten's lips for clues to his past relationship with the woman.

"Yes, she is actually a countess. One of the émigrés who were chased out of France by Robespierre in the last century. The only other member of the family who made it was Chamaude's mama, who died a decade ago. The elder Lady Chamaude brought a load of jewels with her and was able to set up in some style. She eventually married a large landowner from Yorkshire."

"Odd we didn't hear of our comtesse sooner," Prance said.

"The old lady wouldn't sponsor her into Society. Pity, for she would certainly have made a brilliant match, when she was younger."

"What age would she be now?" Corinne asked. That "when she was younger" gave her hope.

"She must be forty if she's a day," Coffen said. "A bit long in the tooth for my taste, but a looker, all right."

"A little younger, I think," Luten said. "Late thirties. She married very young."

"What did the mama have against her?" Corinne asked, unhappy with Luten's quick objection to forty and expecting to hear something scandalous.

"Yvonne was an actress at the Comédie Française."

"An actress!" Coffen exclaimed. He had a great love of actresses. "By the living jingo, I didn't know that."

"The Comédie Française is not considered so déclassé as our theaters," Prance said. "That would hardly sink her chances."

"The story I heard is that Yvonne was from a rather common background, but being an actress, she managed a decent accent, and with her looks she would have fared well had not the old comtesse shut the door on her," Luten explained. "Didn't leave Yvonne anything in her will either."

"But Yvonne brought some valuable paintings with her, eh?" Coffen asked.

"Not with her. She landed at Brighton in a dinghy with only the clothes on her back. Yarrow was the one who ferried the family paintings ashore years later. Her husband had hidden them somewhere in France—in a church basement, I believe. Only Yvonne knew where, or no doubt the old comtesse would have got hold of them. Perhaps that is what they fought about. Or perhaps it was the by-blow Yvonne tried to palm off as her husband's child a year or so after his death. I have only Yvonne's side of the story. She was quite frank about her background and her affairs. Yarrow was running back and forth across the Channel in some diplomatic capacity during various lulls in the fighting. Yvonne caught his eye, and he did what he could to help her."

"Is she his mistress?" Reggie asked eagerly. "Was the by-blow his?"

"I believe the by-blow preceded Yarrow's acquaintance by a few years. Perhaps he only brought the pictures across to ingratiate Prinney, who ended up with most of them."

"She may be his mistress, but I can tell you one thing," Coffen said. They all looked at him. "She can't stand the sight of the old blighter. Winces when he latches on to her with those fat old sausage fingers of his. She looked like a baited animal when he touched her."

Corinne remembered how the comtesse had stiffened when

Yarrow put his hand on her arm. She hadn't noticed the woman's expression. Surely she had smiled, though?

Prance stared as if he had been shot in the heart. "Why did I not notice that?" he asked in a hollow voice. "But you know, I did sense some negative ambience in her saloon. I am sensitive that way. I thought it was just Corinne's reaction to another beautiful lady, but perhaps it was Yvonne's loathing of Yarrow. She must be rescued. Surely we all agree on that?" He looked about the room for support.

"Rescued, my foot!" Corinne scoffed. "I didn't notice her wincing. Yarrow was very kind to her."

Coffen screwed up his forehead and said, "I went to her house planning to fall in love with her, but I have no intention of falling afoul of Yarrow. He could ruin a fellow. All I want to know is that the Poosan I'm buying is the goods. She ain't the sort that would sell a fellow a forgery, is she?"

"Sell forgeries to the prince, and with Yarrow's approval?" Luten asked, his thin eyebrows lifting. "Your wits are gone begging, Pattle. Yarrow would never contrive at something so dangerous to his own welfare. And he would certainly know a forgery from the genuine thing. He's sharp as a needle about art."

"But would she try to palm a fake off on someone like me?"

"I wouldn't put it a pace past Yvonne, but she would not do it with Yarrow's knowledge or approval. If he was there, you need not fear."

Corinne heard that casual "Yvonne" with deep distrust. "She might have arranged to have Yarrow there to authenticate the original Poussin, then slip you a copy today when you go back," she said to Coffen.

Luten's thin lips parted in an anticipatory smile. "In that case, I had best go with you, to make sure she don't fleece you," he said.

It was exactly what Corinne had feared. The comtesse was a magnet, drawing men to her. To object would reveal her rampant jealousy to Luten, to say nothing of bringing Reggie's contumely down on her head. Luten would not want her to go with him. Reggie, on the other hand, would push for it to bring

Chamaude into fashion. She would go, if she had to tag along behind in her own carriage. She would not let that man-eating Frenchie get her talons into Luten.

Chapter Four

"We were to go for a drive this afternoon, Luten," Corinne reminded her beloved.

"Of course. We'll go now," Luten replied, with just a wisp of impatience. "I've sent for my carriage. What time do you plan to pick up the painting, Coffen?"

"I didn't set a time, but some wine merchant is to look at it today. I wouldn't want him to beat me to it."

"Then we shall go to Yvonne's first, and I'll return for our drive shortly, Corinne," Luten said. A certain something in her eyes caused him to add with unusual thoughtfulness, "If that is all right with you, my pet?"

"Why don't I go to Chamaude's with you and we can continue from there? I'll get my bonnet," she said, and darted out of the room before he could object.

She heard his objection perfectly well from the hallway, however. "You take her for a drive, Reg," Luten said.

"I? I know as much about art as you. More! I'll go to Chamaude's and make sure the painting is original. You go ahead for your drive with Corinne."

When she realized Luten was trying to get rid of her, she had no compunction about lingering at the mirror by the open doorway, ostensibly arranging her bonnet, but with her ears on the stretch and her heart pounding angrily in her chest.

"I don't want Corinne calling on Yvonne," Luten said.

"What harm can befall her when she is with us?" Reggie parried.

"Dammit, a woman like Yvonne is no fit friend for her. You shouldn't have taken her there yesterday."

"I did not take her," Reggie said. "It was Coffen."

"Didn't know at the time there was anything wrong with the comtesse," Coffen said.

Sir Reg saw that Corinne's jealousy was succeeding in forwarding the comtesse's entrée into Society where an appeal to humanity had failed. "We don't know there is anything wrong with her," he said. "I think if the Berkeley Brigade took her up, she'd be accepted anywhere."

"I suppose there's no getting out of it now. Ah, there you are," Luten said, smiling as Corinne came in with her bonnet tied and her pelisse over her arm. She sensed that the warmth of his return had already cooled noticeably.

"It shouldn't take long to buy a picture," she said, looking at him from eyes bright with suspicion. "We will be on our way for that drive in no time." She handed Luten her pelisse, and he helped her put it on.

His carriage had arrived when they went to the doorway. They had only to wait a moment while Prance darted home to pick up a few spare copies of the *Rondeaux*. The four entered the carriage, and they were off to Half Moon Street. While the roué butler went to inquire if Madame was "at home," Corinne pointed the Watteau *fête champêtre* painting out to Luten.

"Now, if it were that painting Coffen was buying, I would not object," she said. "Lovely, is it not?"

"Charming. I'll ask her what she wants for it."

"Oh, it is not for sale. I've already inquired."

The butler returned within seconds to admit them. The comtesse sat alone in her elegant little saloon, reading by the light of one lamp and looking extremely demure and pretty in a dark green gown cut up to her collarbone, where a pretty fall of Mechlin lace tumbled under her chin. She wore no brooch, no earrings, no jewelry but a plain golden band on her left hand. Her hair was casually arranged in a youthful tousle of curls rather like the cherubim do Corinne had been contemplating.

"Company! How nice," she said, rising with effortless grace from her chair to greet them. As she arose, any suggestion of demureness fell from her. The modest gown clung like the skin of a peach to ripe bosoms and wasp waist. "I have just been reading your beautiful poem, Sir Reginald. I shall treasure this copy you were kind enough to give me." She held it to her breast a moment, then set it aside reluctantly.

"My pleasure, Comtesse," he said in soft accents, while he gazed into her eyes, trying to discern the shade. Large and bright as they were, he could still not determine their color. They changed, like the Atlantic on a stormy day, now throwing off hints of green, now black. Charming! In his state of infatuation, he didn't notice how often the dark eyes flashed in Luten's direction, but Corinne saw, and her heart thudded angrily.

The comtesse turned to Luten. "Milord, it is a long time since I have had the pleasure of entertaining *you*," she said, with a smile not an inch short of flirtation. Her seductive accent managed to imbue that simple "you" with a world of meaning.

"Too long," he replied gallantly, and shook the hand she proffered. Corinne had the distinct impression that if she had not been present, he would have lifted the fingers to his lips and kissed them. It was that sort of lingering handshake. A spasm of alarm coursed through her as their eyes locked and held.

Corinne and Coffen were greeted less lavishly. The formalities accomplished, they got down to business at once. The Poussin sat on a brass easel by a window.

"Here is the painting you are interested in, Mr. Pattle. The wine merchant balked at the price," she said frankly. "So absurd. I am practically giving it away. But a man like that would know nothing of art." Coffen's breast puffed at the implied compliment.

Luten accompanied Coffen and the comtesse to the easel. He lifted his quizzing glass and studied the painting's surface for several minutes. "Do you mind?" he asked, and turned it over, but the back was covered with thin strips of aged wood and told him nothing.

"Prance?" he said, inviting Prance to add his expertise to the evaluation.

"Lovely," Prance said, with hardly a glance at it. "Delightful—but it has strong competition in this room," he added gallantly. He allowed his gaze to rest on the lady's sparkling eyes for a longish moment. He didn't think he was imagining the flash of interest in those orbs, the infinitesimal lifting of the eyebrows. Yarrow was no doubt useful to her, but if he judged rightly, she was interested in younger game.

"If you're all happy with it, then I'll take it," Coffen said, and drew out his check. "Wrap it up and I'll take it with me now."

Comtesse Chamaude accepted the check, and it disappeared into a pocket. She called the butler. "Mr. Prance will be taking the Poussin," she said. "Have it wrapped up carefully."

The butler removed the painting. She ordered wine, then led the gentlemen to the sofas and chairs.

"Dare we hope you will be at Carlton House for the Prince's *vernissage* this evening, milady?" Prance inquired.

A white hand fluttered over her bosom. "I could not bear to see my paintings hanging in their new home, though it is so much grander than the one they leave." She gave a Gallic shrug of her shoulders as she glanced around the little saloon. "They are like my children. I feel I have put my own children out for adoption. Silly of me," she said, with a sweep of her lashes in Luten's direction. "But we French, you know, are emotional."

Corinne's lips tensed in derision. Just what had Chamaude done with that by-blow Luten mentioned, if not put it out for adoption? There was no sign of it in the house. As to Carlton House, she would be there as fast as a dog could trot if she had been invited. She had not been so coquettish when Yarrow was present.

"Claret," Lady Chamaude said, when the wine arrived. "That is what you English gentlemen like, I think?" She cast another of those speaking glances at Luten and directed her next speech to him. "It is made with cabernet sauvignon grapes for vigor, and merlot for softness and suppleness." Her velvet voice fairly purred the last words. "I am coming to know, a leetle, what pleases English gentlemen."

"You always d—" Luten's eyes flickered uncertainly to Corinne, who was listening like a spy. "I'm sure you do, Yvonne," he said.

Corinne's anger simmered hotter. Did! "You always did!" That was what he was going to say.

Over the wine, the comtesse tried a few more lures on Luten. With his fiancée playing chaperon, nothing came of them.

Sir Reginald asked her if she knew of any paintings of King Arthur for sale, in an effort to hear more praise of his *Rondeaux*.

"Alas, no," she said, "but I shall make a few inquiries if you are interested, Sir Reginald." Then she recalled the *Rondeaux* and added, "But of course, you would be interested in that subject, on which you are such an expert."

"What of the Watteau in the hall?" Luten asked.

"I should dislike to part with it," she said with a sad sigh. "As I am trying to accumulate money to buy a house, however, I could not refuse if a truly . . . *interesting* offer were made." Her eyes smoldered into Luten's. A sudden silence descended on the room.

Corinne could take no more. She set aside her wine and said, "Shall we go now, Luten? You have not forgotten we are going for a drive?"

"My picture," Coffen said. "Ah, here it is now. Dandy." The butler appeared, carrying the painting, now wrapped in plain brown paper. "Then we're off?"

"Must you leave so soon?" the hostess asked with a pretty little moue. "You haven't finished your wine."

"We really must be off. Thank you so much," Corinne said.

Coffen emptied his glass, smacked his lips, and nodded to the butler to carry the painting out to the carriage.

"Well, what do you think of her?" Prance asked eagerly, as the carriage lurched away.

"I think she is a hussy!" Corinne said angrily. "She practically threw herself at you, Luten."

"We used to be friends, some years ago."

"The thing is," Coffen said, "she don't know you two are engaged. She likely took the notion Prance is your fellow, Corinne, as you came twice with him. Mean to say, there was no engagement notice in the journals."

"I shall tell her, the next time I visit," Sir Reginald said, happy to have discovered a reason for the comtesse's lack of interest in himself.

"You're not going back there, Reg!" Corinne exclaimed. "What on earth for? You can't possibly hope to bring a trollop like that into fashion."

"I'm going because she is obviously on the lookout for a new patron, goose."

"I can't believe men are so gullible." As Luten was wearing his stiff face, she decided to say no more on the subject.

"The comtesse appreciated my *Rondeaux*," Sir Reg said, smiling contentedly. "And by the by, Luten, I have not heard your verdict."

"Oh, admirable, Prance. I was highly impressed with your grasp of the subject. Shall we go on the strut on Bond Street and check out the bookshops?"

Corinne suspected this was suggested to avoid being alone with her. She hadn't seen him for over two weeks, and the minute he got home, he went pelting off to visit Chamaude, then to waste the afternoon walking on Bond Street with Reg and Coffen. It was really too bad of him. She had displayed quite enough jealousy for one day, however, and pretended to be happy.

"Yes, let's," she said, with well-feigned pleasure. "And tonight we are to go to Carlton House. Pity you were not invited, Luten, but we shan't stay long." She waited, hoping to hear an objection. Luten just nodded.

"Did any of you receive the invitation?" Coffen asked, looking at the others.

"Not I," Prance said.

"No, nor did I," Corinne said. "Do you think Yarrow forgot to tell Prinney?"

"They wouldn't come in the post," Luten said. "They'll be delivered by a royal footman. They've probably arrived by now."

"What will you do while we're gone, Luten?" Corinne asked in a seemingly casual way.

"What else but wait on pins and needles for your return, my beloved?"

Luten was not given to flowery speeches, except in derision. His facetious reply goaded her into ill humor.

"Why, I thought you might take the opportunity to renew your friendship with the comtesse," she said, smiling snidely.

"From the way you were staring at us, I thought you realized I had already done that."

Prance would normally have enjoyed this little altercation, but his mind was on other things. "We are on Piccadilly," he said. "Let us get out and stop at Hatchard's."

He was eager to look at the window of London's premier bookshop and see what was on display. He had a dreadful foreboding it would be *Childe Harold.*

Chapter Five

To facilitate the distribution of free copies of the *Rondeaux*, they descended from the carriage and strolled along Piccadilly. Each member of the Berkeley Brigade carried one book as they proceeded toward their inevitable destination, Hatchard's bookshop. As they approached the bow window, Prance drew a little ahead of the others.

When they reached him, he was standing like a statue, frozen in consternation, with his nose perilously close to being pressed against the windowpane. They were soon in possession of the cause. The entire window was filled with copies of *Childe Harold's Pilgrimage*. Corinne instinctively put a hand on his arm to comfort him in his distress. This was poorly done of the bookshop. If Prance's *Rondeaux* were not considered worth promoting, what of other authors? Were Scott and Rogers, Southey and Wordsworth and Coleridge, not worth a few inches? What of the ladies, Fanny Burney and Maria Edgeworth? She cast a beseeching eye on Luten.

She had come to learn that under his veneer of haughtiness and sophistication there beat the softest heart in London. He was one of the driving forces of the Whigs, not because he wanted to make a great name for himself, but because he genuinely believed that the underprivileged deserved a better lot in life. He revealed no lack of ease at enjoying to the fullest the perquisites and pleasures of his position, but at the bottom of his heart there must rest some feeling that he didn't really deserve them.

When he spoke of politics to her, it was the usual party line of ousting Mouldy and Company. It was only in odd moments when he was off his guard that he let slip little things about the conditions in the rookeries and prisons and almshouses. He had visited them all. He knew firsthand the trials of society's misfortunates. She often puzzled over this strange admixture of pride and genuine concern for others.

Luten would spare no pains to aid the distressed, and when the distressed party was one of his own brigade, he would move heaven and bend earth. And he would not make a public display of his kindness either. He seemed almost ashamed of it.

One glance at Prance's drooping shoulders and Luten determined on the spot that he would return later and speak to the proprietor. Whatever number of copies was required to make a success, he would buy them, and get Prance's work into that window. The tricky bit would be concealing the purchase from the others.

"This is only one shop," he said dismissingly to Prance.

"Too kind, my dear Luten, but we all know this is *the* shop. I mean to say, where is the glory in being sold in the stalls? You may find Mrs. Radcliffe's gothic novels there, along with chapbooks. There is nothing else for it. I must shoot off a toe and take up limping."

"That would hardly make the *Rondeaux* more interesting," Luten replied. "Not that they aren't plenty interesting enough," he added hastily, when Prance squinted at him.

"Did you really find them interesting?" Prance asked with pathetic eagerness.

"Certainly I did."

"They are fascinating," Corinne lied earnestly.

Coffen, with an equally kind heart but less finesse, stared from Luten to Corinne with a wrinkled brow.

"What did you think of my characterization of the *dux bellorum*? Both of you. The truth, now."

"Very interesting," Luten said, with an earnest frown, as if recalling various intriguing details.

"I tried to give him a broad interpretation," Prance said, his face assuming a professional air that threatened expansion of his favorite theme.

"I was just a little uncertain," Coffen said, for he didn't want to make a faux pas in his praise, "was it Arthur you meant by the *dux bellorum*? It might have been clearer if you had called him King Arthur."

"Bah! You are biased by the works of Geoffrey of Monmouth. Total fiction."

"Geoffrey Monmouth, you say? Can't say I ever heard of the fellow."

Luten said, "We don't know that the whole story isn't fiction. Surely it is myth, or legend."

Prance shook his head at their abysmal ignorance. "The Arthur you were expecting is the product of the French Middle Ages. Arthur is much older than that. My research goes back to Nennius, the *Historia Britonum*, a ninth-century compilation. According to Nennius, Arthur was, in fact, a mercenary. Nothing but a professional soldier."

"That don't add much to the romance," Coffen said.

"It adds considerably to the authenticity!" Prance snapped. "It is only the French, and of course, the Welsh, who transform Arthur into a man of miracles and marvels, slaying monsters and shooting the boar."

"I noticed all that sort of thing was missing from the *Rondeaux*," Coffen said. "It's all arguments between leaders before the battles, then the actual battles."

"Naturally I tried to include some parallels to our Peninsular War, to give the works a modern meaning. I saw the *dux bellorum* as a symbol for our Wellington."

"How clever!" Corinne said. She saw he was enjoying himself and decided to indulge him with a question. "I am halfway through the book, Reg, and I have not read anything of the Round Table yet," she said with a questioning look.

"That is more nonsense!" Prance cried, his ire rising at this familiar complaint. "There was no mention of a Round Table until Wace's *Roman de Brut*. A French author! Then Layamon, cribbing from Wace, came up with the actual carpenter and implied dimensions of the table. The table held more than sixteen hundred men. It's ridiculous. I did the arithmetic. Do you know what the diameter of such a table would be?"

"Nope," Coffen said, scratching his ear and glancing along the street in a way that implied he was ready to move on.

"One thousand and nineteen feet. That is the diameter, mind, not the circumference, and it allows only two feet apiece at a conference. This is scarcely room for a chair. Not that they had chairs at the time. At three feet each, and some of them must have been fat, the diameter would be over fifteen hundred feet. There isn't a room in all of England big enough to hold such a table."

"You might squeeze it into Westminster Abbey, or Saint Paul's," Coffen said, in an effort to be helpful. "I never thought poetry would take so much arithmetic."

Luten and Corinne exchanged a look. Her lips moved unsteadily.

Luten said, "Perhaps you are too literal, Reg. Poetic license, you know . . ."

"Need a license to write rhymes, do you?" Coffen asked. "Another dodge to squeeze money out of the taxpayer."

"I was just giving you a notion how unreliable later accounts are," Prance said, high on his dignity. "It was perfectly clear to *me* there never was such a thing as a Round Table."

"Now, there you're wrong. My mama has one at home," Coffen said.

Prance threw up his hands in defeat. "You are a disgrace to the mother who bore you, Pattle."

Coffen's blue eyes snapped. "I'll thank you to leave my mama out of this. And besides, she never bores me. She's dashed interesting. More interesting than your dashed *dux bellorum*."

Corinne darted in to forestall a nasty exchange. "If there was no Round Table, Reg, why did you call your poem the *Round Table Rondeaux*?"

"It is called a metaphor," he said icily. "I see you ignored the footnotes."

"I hate footnotes," Coffen muttered into his collar.

Prance ignored him. "There is no head to a Round Table. It was a meeting of equals, of which Arthur was one, and not a king. He was a *dux bellorum*. I expect they sat on the ground with a fire in the middle for roasting wild boar. No one mentioned a Round Table before Wace, and that I do know."

"Speaking of wild boar, ain't it time for fork work?" Coffen said, but no one paid him any heed.

"Well, this is very interesting, Reggie. I'm glad you explained about the metaphor," Corinne said. "I hope you aren't going to rob us of the legend of Guinevere and Lancelot." That, and her feelings for Reggie, were all that kept her plodding through the dreadful book.

"Why should I drag in that hussy? The real meaning of the work is the search for the Holy Grail. Guinevere was a mere distraction."

Coffen scowled. "Then why did you call it a romance of the Middle Ages, raising hopes—"

"You surely didn't think I had written a maudlin love story! I meant a romance in the true sense—chivalry, adventure, stirring deeds."

"Of course. That was obtuse of you, Coffen," Corinne said, with a warning look.

"But you found it interesting?" Prance asked, turning again to Luten and Corinne.

"Very interesting," they both agreed, and could not for the life of them come up with another complimentary adjective. "Scholarly," Luten finally said in desperation, as Prance was eagerly waiting for more praise.

"Exactly!" Prance smiled. "I did a deal of research, winnowing the wheat from the chaff."

"Superb research," Luten said. "But perhaps—"

"I knew there would be a *but*!"

"Never mind. It's nothing."

"No, let me hear your thoughts. I want your true opinion."

"Perhaps, for nonscholars, you know, a little chaff would have lightened the hard kernels of fact, since it was couched in the poetic idiom. Something to stir the emotions and imagination. Only if you are interested in a wide sale, of course, such as Byron is enjoying."

"We who are not so intellectually inclined as you, like a little circus along with our bread," Corinne ventured.

"Byron is certainly providing the circus," Prance snipped.

And Prance, in her opinion, had provided a great lump of unleavened bread.

"Here come a couple of likely recipients," Prance said, as he spotted two bucks walking toward them. Their closely fitting blue jackets, fawn trousers, and sprigged waistcoats proclaimed their status as gentlemen of fashion. Both wore curled beaver hats, York tan gloves, and Hessians.

The gentlemen were Robert Marchant and Peter Inwood, both MPs holding Tory seats in the House of Commons from rotten boroughs in the West, while endeavoring to win acclaim in Parliament. Marchant was a self-consequential sprig of a noble family, with no title of his own. He was tall and blond, with a voice in training for perorations to his fellow members in the House.

Inwood was shorter, darker, more handsome, less sure of himself, and more likable. The young men drew to a stop in front of Hatchard's and were presented to Lady deCoventry.

"Prance, are you sunk to handing out copies of your *Rondeaux* on street corners?" Marchant asked with a smirk.

"You'll have to buy a copy if you want one, Marchant," Luten replied, even as Prance's hand moved forward. "These copies are spoken for. If you hurry, you might get one before they're all taken."

"Both copies?" Marchant replied waggishly.

"Where could I get one?" Inwood asked, with apparent sincerity. "I've always been interested in King Arthur."

The solecism of mistaking the *dux bellorum* for King Arthur was noted, but forgiven. "You can have this one," Prance said, handing it over. "I have a spare copy in the carriage."

"I daresay you can spare me a copy as well," Marchant said, glancing at the copies each of them carried, and biting back a grin.

"Afraid not," Luten said.

Inwood opened the book and began leafing through it. It was enough encouragement for Prance, who immediately began to speak of *dux bellorum.*

Marchant turned aside in disdain and said to Luten, "Where are you folks off to on this fine day?"

"To call on the Countess de Lieven, who is eager to receive this copy of Prance's book," he lied. "And you?"

"Inwood and I have a very important meeting this afternoon. We have been assigned to a special project of the Ordnance Committee, under the secretary for war."

"Meeting before the House sits to prevent us Whigs keeping an eye on you, eh?" Luten said, only half joking.

"The world doesn't stop wagging because some of the members want a long summer vacation, milord," Marchant replied.

"Any news from the Peninsula? I've been out of town for a spell."

"Not what Grey and Grenville and you Whigs would like to hear. We're not pulling out of Spain and Portugal to let Bonaparte bestride the world like a colossus. We thank Lady Hertford for Prinney's support," he added with a lecherous laugh. "She is a staunch Tory, of course. The prince's carriage is at her door in Manchester Square every afternoon. He will hear what he ought to hear there, no fear."

"I asked if there were any *new* developments," Luten said dampingly. It was hardly news to him that Prinney was courting Lady Hertford.

"After our stunning triumphs, we feel confident of total victory. We've sent Wellington the reinforcements he needs to take care of it. He'll soon have the Frenchies rooted out."

"Thank God for Wellington. A fine tactitian."

"The opinion at the Horse Guards is that he depends too much on his thin red line, actually."

"Have the Horse Guards yet discovered that it works?"

"He overlooks more modern methods, was my meaning." Marchant so enjoyed being seen in public chatting to such an out and outer as Lord Luten that he soon slipped into indiscretion. "The rocket devised by Congreve, for instance." He lowered his voice and drew Luten a little aside. "This is not for the common ear, but we have sent rockets to Canada to fight the Yankees."

"They were not very accurate when Haidalr Ali used them against us in India in the last century," Luten said doubtfully.

"True, we suffered heavy losses at Mysore, but the development of the rocket has come along nicely since then. They're lighter now, cheaper. They've increased the range to over a mile and a half, nearly two miles. They'll revolutionize war, only Wellington is too blind to see it. He'll use the rockets if the Duke of York tells him to use them, however. York is the commander of the army. War is too important to leave to—"

"To soldiers?" Luten asked with a derisive smile.

"To an Irish upstart. If it weren't for Wellington's friendship with Castlereagh—but enough of that."

"Quite. Am I to understand we are sending rockets to the Peninsula?"

Marchant looked about for listening spies. "That is the idea," he allowed.

"I see. We shan't detain you. Lord Bathurst will not want to be kept waiting."

"Oh, as to that, the meeting ain't for an hour yet."

After being away for the summer, Luten was eager to discover what new tricks Mouldy and Company, as the Whigs termed the Tories, were up to.

"About these rockets," he said. "Congreve will be the supplier?"

"He is one of the suppliers who sent in a bid."

"Who are the others?"

Marchant hesitated a moment before replying. "Only one other. Gresham, from the Gresham Armaments Works in Colchester."

"Which one—"

Marchant stiffened up. "I'm not at liberty to say, milord. Actually it hasn't been decided yet. That's why we're meeting this afternoon, to discuss it. Come along, Inwood. We must get busy on those notes for Lord Bathurst." He glanced around to see if passersby were harkening to this important name.

"Thank you very much, Prance," Inwood said. "I look forward to this." He lifted the book, then bowed to them all and left with Marchant.

Luten was preoccupied as they continued their walk. Not, as Corinne suspected, with thoughts of the comtesse, but with the question of who would get the rocket contract. Logic decreed that it should go to Congreve, who had developed the device and was more familiar with it. But as the Tories were hastening the business along before the House resumed after the summer recess, there was a possibility of chicanery. The shares of Gresham could be bought for an old song today. If they got the lucrative contract, they would soar. He would pay a call on Grey or Grenville, the leading lights of the Whig party.

When he drew out his watch, Corinne knew he was eager to leave. And as she was eager to be alone with him, she made no objection when he suggested they go home.

Chapter Six

When Coffen received his gilt-edged card to Carlton House, he was thrown into a pelter. He had never been there before. What did a fellow wear to say good day to the Prince Regent? How, precisely, did he word his greeting? What did he say if His Majesty wished to discuss art? Of course, the whole world and his brother knew Prinney was a lecher and a clown, so he would not be allowed to show the glee he was feeling when he casually mentioned the evening to his friends, but still there was some éclat in being invited to the prince's own house to meet him.

When in doubt, Coffen appealed to the omniscience of Corinne, who had been to Carlton House any number of times with deCoventry when he was alive. Coffen was jabbering incoherently when he called on her a moment later. She was in no good humor herself, after being summarily dumped on the doorstep by Luten with the excuse that he was going to Westminster. Black, her inestimable butler, had reported that Luten left his premises again within ten minutes. The suspicion in her mind was that he was even now ensconced in the Comtesse Chamaude's cozy saloon, renewing past intimacies.

She poured Coffen and herself a large glass of sherry and tried to calm him down.

"It is not a coronation after all, Coffen, but an informal evening to look at some pictures. As to what you say, you admire them."

"What if I don't like 'em?"

"You admire them, whether you like them or not. To do otherwise would cast aspersions on the prince's taste. You accept one glass of wine—or maraschino, if that is the abomination he is serving—and sip it slowly. Carlton House is not the place to get foxed, or you'll end up at the card table, where you will be fleeced by experts."

"I expect the monkey suit must come out of the cedar press? Mean to say, Almack's insists on it."

"Very likely, though Yarrow called it an informal do. Brummell has allowed Prinney to switch to pantaloons, so perhaps—"

Coffen's eyes grew big as saucers. "You never mean Beau Brummell will be there?" This was nearly as frightening as meeting the prince.

"He may not. There are rumors of a coolness developing between them."

"If Brummell is there, I'm done for," Coffen said, gulping down the sherry. "Mean to say—I can praise a dashed picture as well as the next commoner, but if I have to look stylish, the jig is up."

"I'll handle Beau, if he is there."

Brummell was susceptible to flattery. A mention that Coffen was eager for his opinion of the Poussin would go down well. Praise whatever cravat the Beau was sporting that evening, and the thing was done.

"What is Prance wearing?" she asked. This arbiter elegantiarum would surely know the correct dress.

"I'll ask him. Let us go in your rig with a lozenge on the door tonight. Mean to say, Carlton House." He took one last, loving look at the gilt-edge card that was already dog-eared from handling and trundled out the door.

Corinne sat on alone, looking through the window across the street for the return of Luten's carriage. She had not invited him for dinner, not thinking it necessary. After his absence, she assumed they would share an intimate dinner on his first evening home. This meant dining at his house, as Mrs. Ballard would sit with them at hers. At six-thirty she went abovestairs, where Mrs. Ballard, her companion-cum-dresser, assisted her into an elegant Italian crepe gown of Olympian blue and dressed her hair *en corbeille*.

When she returned below, Black, her dark-visaged butler, said in his insinuating way, "His lordship's carriage arrived home ten minutes ago, milady. I take the privilege of mentioning it since you've been keeping an eye out."

"Thank you, Black," she said, and bit back the eager question. "Did he send a message?"

Corinne always felt she ought to depress Black's pretentions, but as he had been with her for as long as she had been in London and had helped her out of more than one scrape, she hardly knew how to go about it.

"His lordship wasn't in the carriage," he added, peering to see the effect of this marvelous news.

"Indeed?"

"What it was about, I believe, is that picture Mr. Pattle bought. The coachman darted it across to Mr. Pattle's place. I'll keep an eye out and let you know as soon as his lordship returns—and in what rig," he added with a piercing eye.

As this was precisely what Corinne wanted to know, she said only, "Thank you, Black," in a falling voice, and went to join Mrs. Ballard for a glass of wine before dinner.

Black, of course, knew all about Pattle's purchase of the Poussin. It was not a case of a servant being invisible, and thus privy to all the family's secrets. Black's avocation was eavesdropping. He had the ears of a dog. Hearing conversation through an open doorway was obviously no challenge to a man who could hear a carriage a block away and could usually tell whose rig it was by the sound of the wheels and the trot of the team.

How could he respond to his beloved's unspoken needs if he didn't know all her doings and the doings of her friends? He had seen her strained face when Lord Luten dropped her at the door that afternoon. It was not the way Lord Blackwell would have treated her after a longish absence! Lord Blackwell, the butler's fantasy alter ego, would have swept her into his arms and not let go for a week.

In Prance's dressing room, knee breeches and silk stockings, commonly known as a monkey suit, had been agreed upon, but an argument ensued over the all-important arrangement of the cravat. Coffen felt such an evening called for the extravagance of the Oriental and was summarily overruled. When he was as fashionable as Prance's valet could make him, they sat down to one of André's gourmet dinners and a selection of vintage wines. Prance ate even less than usual. While he tenderly dissected a carrot, he ranted on about the comtesse and inevitably about *dux bellorum.*

" *'Incipit Vita Nova,'* Pattle," he said, gazing at the floral centerpiece as he lifted his wineglass. The small conservatory behind his house had been an inspiration. Fresh flowers without the tedium of buying them or having them sent from his estate. That little bouquet of Provence roses, still blooming in September, reminded him of Yvonne. French, and the petals with that same delicate texture and hue as her cheeks.

"Eh? You know I don't parlay the bongjaw."

"Latin, actually. An old Italian rubric. I feel a new life beginning. Ah, how clearly I see the folly of the old. I refer, of course, to the *Rondeaux*. How could I have been so supremely blind? You are all too kind to say the obvious: the *Rondeaux* are not poetry at all. They reek of lamp oil, dull evenings poring over dusty tomes."

"They ain't that bad."

"Out of the mouths of babes! Are you sure you have read them?"

"Of course I am. I read part of them all the way through. Page thirty-nine, if you want the exact page."

"*Pas nécessaire.* Dante should have been my inspiration—as I had not yet met *her.*"

Coffen lifted a piece of mutton from the ragout and peered at it warily. "I always thought Dante was a him."

"The comtesse, I mean." He lifted a carrot to his lips and set it down again, untasted. "Dante and Goethe. The latter to teach me that woman is the energy of poetry; Dante to guide my quill in the choice of phrases. I hear an echo of eternity in every line of Dante's *Vision.*"

"Is there any mustard?"

"One does not put mustard on André's ragout! It is seasoned with wine and herbs."

"Is that what ails it?" The footman handed him the mustard pot. "Thankee kindly."

Prance stared at the flowers and murmured, " 'Love with delight discourses in my mind.' There is a phrase for you. 'A light between truth and intellect.' "

"More like darkness between lies and flirting, if you're talking about the comtesse. The woman's a flirt, Prance. Shocking the way she was trying to steal Luten from Corinne. And she's older than thirty, too. That's why she keeps her saloon so dim."

"She's thirty-three or four, perhaps."

"Eh? Nudging forty is what I meant."

"What has age to do with anything?"

"It has for women. An old woman like that wouldn't do your reputation any good, I can tell you. I spotted crow's-feet at the corner of her eyes this afternoon when the light from the window struck her."

"I spotted black diamonds in her eyes. But we were speaking of my poetic failure. 'Worldly renown is naught but a breath of wind.' How did I have the effrontery to write a poem when I had not yet lived? I have lived a sham life, Pattle, harkening to every wind of fashion, thinking of the impression I was making, forsaking the true meaning of life."

"Money, you mean, or food?"

Prance winced. "Love, dear boy. 'The love that moves the sun and other stars.' The sort of eternal love inspired by those marvelous *Sturm und Drang* eyes!"

"You're making a dashed fool of yourself, Reg. Tarsome fellow. We've all heard enough of them stern danged eyes. Too much."

Prance sniffed and finally got a small piece of carrot into his mouth. With no ladies to keep waiting, the gentlemen soon left off gourmandizing and decided against the taking of port. They went to call on Corinne immediately after dinner.

"I thought Luten would be here, urging you not to attend the *vernissage*," Prance said, looking all around the saloon.

She tidied her skirt with an air of unconcern. "No, he just returned," she said.

"Did he bring my picture?" Coffen asked. "I left it in his rig when you two went dashing off this afternoon."

"Black says he sent the picture home in his carriage earlier. It was taken to your place. Did the servants not bring it to you?"

"They might have tried. I've been at Prance's, getting cleaned up and fed."

Prance studied Corinne's strained face and suspected there was trouble between the lovebirds. "Where has Luten been all this time?" he asked.

"I don't know, Reg. He just dropped me off and left. He said he had some things to do at Westminster after his long absence from town. I haven't heard from him—but he returned in his hunting carriage," she said, with dilating nostrils.

"The devil you say!"

"Don't mean a thing," Coffen said, and was ignored.

It was well known that what Luten hunted in that particular unmarked carriage was women in whose company he did not wish to be recognized. As far as Corinne was concerned, it was confirmation that he had been with the comtesse.

"We all know what it means. I'm sorry, Reg," she added. "I know you fancy yourself in love with the comtesse."

"A double villainy!" Prance cried. He felt a strong jolt of some emotion composed of anger, pain, jealousy, sympathy for Corinne, and even joy. The drama of it appealed to the rogue in him. Betrayal, heartbreak, jealousy—and infinite possibilities for future scenes of high melodrama.

"Daresay there's some simple explanation," Coffen said. "Shall we be off?"

Chapter Seven

The carriage drove at a good clip to Pall Mall and soon entered the Corinthian Portico of Carlton House, the prince's London residence contrived by Henry Holland, James Wyatt, and John Nash. Inside, they dismounted and the groom removed their carriage. They were met at the door by the butler, flanked by a bevy of footmen in dark blue livery trimmed with gold lace, and led into the finest marble entrance hall in all of London. A plethora of porphyry columns soared ceilingward like trees in a forest. Etruscan griffins glowered from cornices.

As they advanced, they caught a glimpse of marvelous rooms with magnificent cascades of crystal chandeliers, silver walls, and pier glasses throwing back another forest of columns. They were led down a circular double staircase, past bronze statues and assorted artworks to an apartment below.

For this informal gathering they were directed to a room vaguely Corinthian in architecture, but overlaid with so much finery and such a surfeit of magnificence that its original character was lost in a blur of crimson and gilt. There were Gothic windows, spandreled ceilings with gold moldings. The room was overly hot and brighter than the outdoors at noonday.

"One would think a gentleman of his fading looks would want a darker room," Prance murmured.

Corinne smiled demurely. "Like the comtesse, you mean?"

"Cat! Save your ill temper for Luten."

Of the three dozen people present, mostly gentlemen, half stood sipping wine and chatting while the other half strolled about, examining the new acquisitions on the walls. Coffen was relieved to see Beau Brummell was not present. Conning the throng, Corinne recognized Countess de Lieven, the wife of the Russian ambassador. The prince's current favorite, the comely Lady Hertford, was magnificent in a magenta gown. The gentlemen were his card-playing friends and a clutch of Tory ministers, there to curry favor. It promised to be a very dull do. There was not a single handsome gentleman present of whom she could speak to Luten later.

Lord Yarrow was with the prince, helping him praise the paintings. When Yarrow spotted Lady deCoventry's party, he drew the prince's attention to them and beckoned them forward to be presented.

Coffen, who had never been close enough to touch the prince before, though he had occasionally glimpsed him in passing, gazed in awe at the corpulent figure stuffed into the blue satin jacket weighed down with ribbons and medals. His brown hair was elegantly barbered, but the luxuriance of his brown whiskers owed more to art than nature. The sagging royal neck might nestle in a fold of cravat, the gray eyes might water, but when the prince opened his mouth, all imperfections were forgiven.

He was called the First Gentleman of Europe, and his reputation rode more on his graceful manners than his pudgy shoulders. "Lady deCoventry," he said with a bow, and inquired politely for her brother-in-law, Lord deCoventry, and a few other relatives. Then he turned his charm on Coffen. "We are always pleased to meet a fellow admirer of the arts, Mr. Coffen," he allowed with a gracious inclination of the head.

Coffen bowed and murmured, "Your Majesty."

Prance stood, waiting to be recognized as the author of the *Rondeaux*. He had sent Prinney a copy.

The prince just nodded to Prance and continued speaking to Coffen. "Yarrow tells me you have bought a Poussin. I am a secret admirer myself, but for me to be buying paintings by French artists at this time would be maladroit. I most reluctantly limited myself to the Dutch masters, for the nonce. You must come and tell me what you think of my latest acquisitions."

Coffen went in a daze of glory to stare at a series of paintings. The royal hands, well shaped and well manicured, gestured as they pointed out details of chiaroscuro and color, of composition and what he called "integrity of rendition." In the case of Rembrandt, this seems to refer to the face of an ugly old woman, which was really all that could be made out in the painting. Some of the other pictures were so finely rendered that you could see on the table a drop of water that had fallen off some flowers. Dandy flowers they were, in all shapes and colors, but wilting a bit.

"Very well done, that," he said, pointing at the droplet, when the prince asked for his opinion.

"Veritable trompe l'oeil, though not so crass as a fly on the nose, what?"

Coffen bit back the instinctive "Eh?" that rose up in his throat. He bowed again and said, "Not a bit crass, Your Majesty."

His Majesty's eyes turned occasionally to include Prance and Corinne. When the paintings had all been praised and the prince turned to Prance, Prance sensed his moment had come, and he was as nervous as a deb at her presentation.

"Sir Reginald, your *Rondeaux* have a place of honor in my library," he said. "I enjoyed your poems immensely. So you are the new poet I have been hearing so much about." His rheumy eyes gleamed with approval as they made a tour of Prance's toilette.

"I have the honor, Your Majesty," Prance replied, feeling it was a pompous speech. His voice sounded all hollow and grave.

The manicured fingers reached out and patted Prance on the shoulder. "A singular achievement," he said with a smile of unmatched condescension. "The *Round Table Rondeaux* are delightful. A tale of King Arthur in verse. What an ingenious notion."

The phrase *dux bellorum* died aborning. If the Prince of Wales called the *dux* King Arthur, then King Arthur he was.

"Thank you, Your Majesty," he whispered.

"Excellent work. We must not let these ancient English myths die out. They are the very cornerstone of our traditions. They must be reinterpreted for each generation. If you write another book, Sir Reginald, you may dedicate it to us," he said.

Of course, angels did not really sing. Lightning did not flash, and thunder did not roll, but that was how Reggie perceived the world. He bowed gravely and said, "It would be an undeserved honor, Your Majesty."

"What is your next subject?" the prince inquired. Prance's mind went blank. He stared, with still that ringing in his ears. "Will it also be a medieval tale?"

Unable to speak, Prance just bowed again and mumbled, "Your Majesty."

"We look forward to your next composition," the prince repeated. The rheumy royal eyes turned to Prance's cravat. "Very elegant, Sir Reginald. I have not seen that arrangement before. What is it called?"

Prance had slaved over the arrangement. He had planned to call it the Prancer, but at that moment, his only wish was to honor his prince. "The Carlton, sir, if you permit?"

"We are honored." Prince George gave him a roguish smile, laughed, bowed, and allowed Yarrow to lead him away.

While Prance enjoyed his moment of triumph, Corinne scanned the room for some agreeable company. Finding none, she glanced to the doorway, where she saw a dark head standing a little above the throng of bald pates, grizzled heads, and feathered turbans. Luten! And looking, as usual, as if he had just stepped out of a bandbox. Now, what on earth was he doing here? And why had he not told her he was coming? The comtesse! She looked all around but saw no sign of her. She noticed that Luten was also looking about, probably for herself. She took a deep breath to steady her nerves and went forth to meet him.

"Luten," she said, not acknowledging his bow with a curtsy. "What are you doing here?"

His slender eyebrows arched in a quizzing way. "Need you ask? Whither thou goest, my pet. Ah, I have just caught Prinney's eye. I had best go and make my bows. These princelings take a pet so easily. Don't go away. I shall be right back."

She watched as he went forward to do the pretty with Prince George. The contrast between the two gentlemen was remarkable. The prince so fat and common-looking in his garish outfit; Luten so leanly noble in a sedate jacket of dark green. The First Gentleman of Europe's smile was somewhat strained. The meeting was brief.

When Luten came back, Corinne returned to her question. "How did you wangle an invitation?"

"I dropped in to speak to Yarrow while I was at the House this afternoon and dropped a few broad hints. The invitation was waiting for me when I got home."

She was gratified to hear that Luten had really been at the House and had been at pains to join her in the evening's outing. She was still curious to discover why he had called for his hunting carriage, but disliked to quiz him, especially at the prince's party.

Coffen spotted him and came hastening forward, his brow crumpled with curiosity. "Told you not to worry," he said to Corinne, who gave him a sharp poke in the ribs.

They discovered Prance across the room, staring like a moonling at the prince's back, and joined him.

"We can have a glass of wine now. It'll buck us up," Coffen said, and stopped a passing footman to snare four glasses. He sipped the red liquid, frowned, and sipped again. "What kind of wine is this?" he demanded.

"It's not wine. It's maraschino," Corinne told him. "A cherry liqueur."

"Dandy stuff," Coffen said, and emptied the glass.

"We are to dedicate our next book to him," Prance announced in a hushed voice.

"Are we indeed? I wager Byron was not invited to do that," Luten said.

Prance looked around the room, fearing he might espy his nemesis, but he was soon assured of his absence. Other guests came forward to chat, and after a deal of lively bantering, during which Prance stood mute and Coffen downed two more glasses of maraschino, an extremely meager repast of anchovy sandwiches, crackers, and cheese was served. The prince was on another diet. Soon the prince led his claque to the card parlor, and the guests were free to leave.

"We are to dedicate our next book to the Prince Regent," Prance said again, still in that unreal voice that sounded like an echo.

"I am very happy for us, but perhaps now that you're outside, you can drop that persona and become you again, Prance," Luten said. "The royal we is not contagious."

"A fine gentleman, the prince. I did not hear *him* spouting of *Childe Harold.* What we poets must do is keep alive the English myths, and never mind the pashas and *banditos*. Now, what should w— I write about next? My patron is eager to know. It should be something to reflect on him, don't you think?"

"Have you considered Punch and Judy?" Luten suggested. "A fine old English tradition, and Princess Caroline is well suited to her role."

"It is not a joke, Luten. I shall be writing for the prince—and for posterity."

"Famous! I shouldn't be at all surprised to see the *Rondeaux* in Hatchard's window tomorrow." Over Prance's shoulder, he winked at Corinne, who felt a sudden warmth invade her.

"That would be asking too much," Prance said modestly. But he'd drop around and have a look all the same. "Shall we tackle a rout? No, I believe I shall go home and give some thought to my next oeuvre."

"I could do with another glass of that masherino," Coffen said, looking about for a footman.

"Let us all go home," Corinne said. "You have had enough to drink, Coffen, and we have all had enough of crowns and crownets for one night. We came in my carriage," she added, looking to Luten.

"Prance and Coffen can take it home. It is time we lovebirds had some privacy."

The warmth and tenderness in his eyes went a long way toward dissipating her fears. But she would still find out why he had come home in his hunting carriage.

Chapter Eight

Lord Luten did not receive his usual familiar greeting from Black as the butler admitted them.

"Wine, your ladyship?" Black inquired, pointedly ignoring Luten.

"We don't want to be disturbed," Luten said, and handed Corinne's mantle to the butler.

"Why am I in Black's black book?" he asked, as they took up a seat on the sofa before the grate.

She gave Luten a quizzing smile. "Perhaps he suspects you of some foul deed. You know how closely he monitors all our comings and goings."

"You should keep better discipline among your servants."

"He has my best interests at heart. How can I chastise him when his nosiness practically saved my life last spring? So what have you been doing all afternoon, Luten?" she asked, handing him a glass of wine.

"I called on Grey to let him know I'm back. The Tories are sending rockets to Spain. That is a secret, by-the-by. Grey has appointed Henry Brougham to handle it, in my absence. Brougham and I are to work together. He's a clever fellow, a Scot. Matriculated Edinburgh University at thirteen. He's published scientific papers and is a lawyer and writer besides—and he's only a few years older than myself. Makes one feel a bit of a loafer. He's also a fine orator. I see him as Fox's successor as leader of the party.

"He suspects, as I do, that the Tories are up to some chicanery with the tenders, giving the contract before the House resumes for autumn." He lifted his glass in a silent toast and they drank.

"The exigencies of war cannot wait until the House resumes," she pointed out.

"The exigencies of war make a credible excuse, at any rate."

To discover more of his doings, especially regarding the hunting carriage, she said, "Coffen was wondering if you had sent his Poussin home." It was not precisely a lie, merely a prevarication.

"I sent it hours ago! Did he not receive it?"

"If you sent it, then I assume it's there. He dined with Reggie."

"Did you not dine with them?" he asked, surprised.

A flush of remembered annoyance warmed her cheeks. "No, I had thought you and I would dine together, since we haven't seen each other for nearly three weeks."

He gave a charmingly rueful smile. "I had been looking forward to it. I was detained. This rocket business . . . Sorry, love. We'll make it up tomorrow."

"Sure it was not this Comtesse Chamaude business?" she asked, softening the question with an arch smile.

Luten either misunderstood or chose to misunderstand. "I shouldn't be surprised if it's all part and parcel of the same thing. Yarrow is on the Ordnance Committee that will assign the contract."

"What can that have to do with her?"

"Perhaps nothing."

"Did you call on her?" she asked, her heart beating faster. She knew Luten disliked being questioned about his doings, but as his fiancée, she felt it her right.

"Why do you ask that?"

"Why do you not answer?"

"No, I didn't call on her. I was busy following a portly country gentleman in an ill-cut jacket, answering Brougham's description of Gresham. Gresham is the other contender for the rocket contract. It was Brougham who put me on to him. He mentioned that Gresham is in town, putting up at Reddish's Hotel, ostensibly having his portrait taken, but actually trying to sell the Ordnance Committee on his rocket. We thought it a good idea to see who he calls on. He didn't call on Yarrow, but then Yarrow is too cunning to meet the man publicly if there is any trickery afoot between them. Gresham did call on Yvonne." He cocked his head aside and lifted his eyebrows over his intelligent gray eyes. "Interesting, *n'est-ce pas?* I had sent for my hunting carriage and risked driving past her place on Half Moon Street a few times. Gresham was there for an hour."

With her fears regarding the hunting carriage allayed, Corinne turned her attention to Gresham's suspicious behavior. "Perhaps Gresham met Yarrow there," she said.

"No, Yarrow didn't show up. He was at the House all afternoon, but it's an odd coincidence, Gresham's visiting Yarrow's mistress."

"Perhaps she is trying to influence Yarrow to choose her friend, Gresham's, rocket," Corinne suggested.

"Yarrow is the likelier culprit. He's the one who would be engineering any chicanery. But enough of politics. You now know why I was driving my hunting carriage." A teasing smile creased his face, for he was flattered at her jealousy.

"Black did mention it. Knowing its function, I wondered."

"Surely you didn't suspect me of carrying on with a light-skirt, when we are planning our wedding!"

"Why, no, Luten, to tell the truth, I suspected a light-skirt of trying to get her claws into you. She made no secret of her intentions. Are you not flattered at my concern?"

"Vastly flattered, but one does not hanker after ale when he has champagne at hand."

He set aside his glass and drew her into his arms to convince her he was marble-constant in his devotion. As his arms crushed her against him and his lips seized hers in a fevered embrace, she was left in no doubt.

Their lovemaking was interrupted by a commotion at the front door. "Dash it, this is more important than snuggling!" Coffen scolded.

"The estimable Black is barring the door," Luten said, as the scuffling grew louder. "We'd best find out what ails Coffen.

Too much maraschino, I fancy. How he could guzzle down that disgusting syrup!" He rose and opened the door. "What is it, Coffen?" he asked irritably.

Coffen barged in, his finery all askew, his hair hanging in oily strands over his forehead, and his blue eyes bulging. "I was burgled while we was at Carlton House!" he announced.

Corinne jumped up from the sofa. "Good gracious! What was taken?"

"That dandy brass jug from the hall table, the one I put my hat on; my silver candlesticks that I had in the saloon—I don't know what all."

"How did they get in?" she asked. "Your servants were there."

"Playing cards in the kitchen. Three sheets to the wind, the lot of them. They got into the wine cellar. My butler left the door on the latch for me in case I forgot my key—which I did."

"Let us go over and see what else is missing," Luten said.

"We'll search for clues," Coffen added. He placed a strong reliance on the efficacy of clues.

They all darted across the street. Prance, who had been pacing his saloon to aid conjuring up a theme for his next oeuvre, noticed the movement and joined them.

"What is up?" he demanded.

"Coffen's been burgled," Corinne told him.

"The Poussin?"

"By the living jingo, that's it!" Coffen cried.

His penitent butler, Jacob, stood in the hall listening, with his head hanging in shame and a strong aroma not of wine but of ale emanating from him. He looked like a scapegallows and was, in fact, a poacher from Coffen's country estate who had been lured from decimating Pattle's game by the offer of employment in London. He was a dark-haired man with round shoulders and a shifty eye.

"The picture is in your study," he said. Then as he remembered that guests were present, he added, "Sir." They could all see the man was foxed.

"Let us have a look," Prance said, and darted down to Coffen's study.

He returned with the picture, still in its wrapping. He undid the wrapping, and they all examined it, front and back.

"This is the original, all right," he said, setting it on a chair.

Coffen examined it. "It is. There are the nicks I put in the frame when I hit it against her table."

"What all is missing?" Luten asked.

They examined the familiar rooms. The permanent state of disarray made an inventory difficult, but this was not entirely the servants' fault. The silver epergne that should have been on the dining-room table sat on the floor in the saloon, where Coffen had been flipping cards into it. A clutter of cards were scattered around it. Journals were tossed about on the sofa. Used wineglasses were on every dusty table.

Corinne went to check the silverware. The cupboard in the butler's pantry was not locked as it should have been, but the silver was all there. A few paintings of some value still hung on the dining room walls.

Coffen ran upstairs and returned to tell them his jewelry was intact.

Prance, who had been checking the saloon, said, "They made off with that ugly Capodimonte statuette of Columbine that used to sit on your mantel. You say the brass vase and silver candlesticks are missing. We are looking, then, for some thieves with eclectic and abominable taste. Are you sure it wasn't your own servants?"

"Nay, they're all drunk as Danes. I quizzed them. They're in no shape to keep a secret. When they steal, it's usually money from my desk drawer."

Prance shook his head. "Kind of you to keep a supply there for them."

"Only a few pounds. Saves them stealing my stuff."

"It sounds like some passersby who perhaps saw the door ajar and risked slipping in," Corinne said. "With Jacob in the kitchen . . . You really must speak to your servants, Coffen."

"I will, as soon as they're sober," he replied, though they all knew how vain the effort would be.

Prance tossed up his hands. "For God's sake, put this Poussin away. And lock the door when we leave."

Coffen handed the painting to Jacob, who looked at it a moment, then slid it behind the chair, handy to any thief who opened the front door.

"Thankee for coming, folks," Coffen said, shamefacedly. "Can I give you a glass of wine for your trouble?"

"I could do with a posset," Prance said, then with a memory of Coffen's kitchen, he shook his head. "Never mind. My André will prepare me one." He looked with some interest at Luten. "Well, Luten, we are all on nettles to discover why you called out your hunting carriage this afternoon. Beating my time with la comtesse, hmmm?"

Luten directed a mock scowl at Corinne. How else did Prance know what carriage he had been driving? Prance's butler was not a spy. They went into the untidy saloon, removed assorted debris from the sofas, and sat down. Coffen gave them a glass of wine, and Luten outlined what he had learned of the comtesse and Gresham and Yarrow.

"The comtesse is a schemer," Coffen said. "I'll take my Poosan to an art dealer tomorrow and make sure it ain't a fake."

"That's not a bad idea," Luten agreed.

Prance did not object to this slur on his beloved's character. He liked his friends to have a few interesting faults. "If it is still in your possession by tomorrow," he added. "What else have we planned for the day?"

"Corinne and I plan to go on the strut on Bond Street," Luten said. Corinne looked at him in surprise. He had not mentioned it to her.

"May we join you?" Prance asked. "Or is this a *pas de deux*?"

"Pas du tout," Luten replied. "Let us all go. Pattle can bring his Poussin along, and we'll stop at Mercier's to have the painting authenticated."

They finished their wine and left, waiting outside until they heard Coffen slide the bolt.

"Very odd, that burglary," Prance said musingly. "I mean to say, a prigger entering the house when there were lights on and only making off with a few tawdry bits and pieces. Highly unlikely."

"Coffen is much too careless," Corinne said. "I wager Jacob left the door wide open."

"At least they didn't get the Poussin, or I should have to suspect the comtesse said a careless word to someone."

"Or had it stolen herself," Corinne added.

Prance shook his head. "Luten has given an account of his afternoon, my pet. There is no further need for you to be jealous of Yvonne."

"Good night, Prance," she said coolly, and taking Luten's arm, they returned to her house, while Prance darted across the street, smiling to himself. What was Yvonne up to, the sly piece?

"Why did you invite him and Coffen to join us tomorrow, Luten?" she asked. "I am beginning to get the notion you don't want to be alone with me."

"You wrong me. Every way you wrong me, my sweet idiot. I just want to see Reg's face when he sees the *Rondeaux* in Hatchard's window."

"Luten, you didn't! How did you arrange it?"

"You'll have to help me get rid of the hundred copies I bought—while you suspected me of dangling after Yvonne."

She colored up prettily. She was not only embarrassed for mistrusting him, but proud of Luten for his generous gesture.

"How do you plan to be rid of them? He has already given a copy to everyone we know and fifty-odd people we scarcely know."

"I count on your help. Dry matter burns well," he said. "But use an upstairs fireplace, in case he drops in during the conflagration. The covers are slow burners, and the leather smells like burning flesh."

Black held the door open as they came up the steps. "I trust Mr. Pattle lost nothing of great value, your ladyship?" he asked.

This, of course, was officious in the extreme, but she replied, "No, nothing of great value."

Black lifted his heavy eyebrows and said waggishly, "Did

you figure out what was in the bag the fellow carried out of the house?"

"What do you mean? Black!" she exclaimed. "Did you see the burglar?"

"I didn't know he was a burglar," he said, half-proud of being able to identify the man, but unhappy that he had not apprehended him. "I mean to say, he knocked and went in without waiting for Jacob to admit him. I figured he was a friend, though I did wonder when he left with that bag, along with the picture."

"Left with the picture?" Luten asked. "He didn't steal the picture."

"No, milord, he brought it with him, didn't he?"

"What picture?"

"I didn't see it. 'Twas all wrapped up in brown paper. It was the same size as the one you had delivered this afternoon. I figured there'd been a mix-up at the comtesse's house and he was exchanging it."

"No," Corinne said, "he took silver candlesticks, a brass vase, and a little statuette."

"That's what would have been in the bag he carried out." Black nodded, satisfied.

"Why the devil didn't you go after him?" Luten demanded.

"He was a gentleman, wasn't he? Wearing a dandy jacket and cravat, though I did think it odd he came on foot and carrying that big parcel."

"The picture—this has something to do with Chamaude," Corinne said.

"I'd swear that picture Coffen has is the same one we saw in her saloon," Luten said. "What did the man look like, Black?"

"Tall and well built. A good-looking fellow, from what I could see. Youngish, stylish."

"Harry!" Luten exclaimed. This matched the description of Corinne's in-law, Lord Gaviston, who had been known to pocket a trinket or two in his time.

"Nay, it weren't Lord Harry. This lad who came tonight has never visited any of youse before or I'd know him," Black said.

"We'd best tell Coffen," Corinne said.

"Allow me to fetch him, milady," Black said with a gracious smile. "You must be fagged."

"No, we'll go back and have another look at that Poussin," Luten said. He grabbed Corinne's hand, and they darted across the street.

Coffen answered the door himself, holding a poker in his hand. "Oh, it's you," he said. "I feared it might be the burglar back for another go at my stuff."

"Where is that picture, Pattle?" Luten asked.

The picture was retrieved from behind the chair and taken into the saloon to be examined, while Luten told Coffen what Black had seen.

"This is my picture, right enough," Coffen said, fingering the nick in the frame.

Corinne said, "Why would the fellow have carried along a big, bulky parcel when he was doing a spot of burgling?"

A triumphant smile quirked Luten's lips. "Because he wasn't doing a spot of burgling," he said.

"He got away with my brass jug and silver candlesticks," Coffen reminded him.

"Window dressing. What he came for was to exchange the pictures."

"Then he's a fool, for he didn't do it. I still have my original."

"Who is to say you had it before his call? You hadn't opened the parcel."

"That don't make any sense, stealing a copy and leaving an original."

"It does if Yvonne originally gave you the copy and feared you would know the difference."

"Why would she think I know the difference now, if she didn't think it a few hours ago? She knew you and Prance would see it. You know about art, if I don't."

"He's right," Corinne said.

"So am I," Luten insisted. "She planned to palm off the forgery, but something changed her mind." After a frowning pause, he added, "Or someone."

"Yarrow?" Corinne said. "He found out what she was up to and made her exchange the pictures? And who would she use for the job but her other suitor, the tall, handsome Frenchman we saw calling on her the first evening we were there. You weren't there, Luten," she added. "You know who I mean, Coffen."

"I do. Not his name, nor where he lives, but I'd recognize his phiz if I saw him again, the scoundrel."

"Chamaude is using Yarrow to authenticate her paintings, then selling copies," Corinne said. "You ought to warn Yarrow, Luten."

Luten cocked his head and pointed a shapely finger at the Poussin. "He already knows, to judge by this evening's work. But to be sure, we'll take this to Mercier's tomorrow for authentication. Come, let us go. Lock the door behind us, Coffen."

"I will, and I'll take my Poosan to bed with me. Dashed Frenchies."

Corinne could not fail to notice Luten's cheerful mood as he accompanied her home.

"Presuming you are right," she said, "though in fact we don't know that the burglar was carrying a painting at all, it might have been something else entirely, or the footman who wrapped it up may have made a mistake and wrapped the wrong one. But if you are right and Yarrow made her exchange the paintings, how did he find out what Chamaude was up to?"

"I have no idea. It seems we have stumbled into another imbroglio." He cast a playful smile at her. "Do you think it will leave us time to plan our wedding?"

Corinne felt a shiver of apprehension up her spine. She trusted Luten, but she could not trust Chamaude. "We could get a special license and do it up in a hurry, before the comtesse decides to substitute a different bride," she suggested, and listened eagerly for his reply.

He smiled insouciantly. "Oh, I think I would notice the difference, after a day or two."

"Luten!"

He was about to kiss away her little fit of pique when Black opened the door. "Tomorrow morning. Ten-thirtyish," Luten said. Then to Black's deep chagrin, he kissed the countess.

Chapter Nine

Luten called on Corinne at ten the next morning. She had breakfasted and was having a second cup of coffee with Mrs. Ballard, bringing her companion up-to-date on such aspects of the Chamaude affair as would not dismay a simple village vicar's widow. Any mention of the comtesse's attempting to steal Luten away was avoided. It was of the Poussin that they spoke.

"Good morning, ladies," Luten said, when Black showed him into the morning parlor. It was a small room, but cheerful with sunlight splashing through the east-facing window and onto the table.

He thought his fiancée looked particularly delightful in a green worsted walking suit with a fichu of Mechlin lace at the collar. It did not occur to him that it was similar to the outfit in which Yvonne had looked so delectable the day before. Mrs. Ballard, as usual, wore mouse-gray to match the gray hair beneath her widow's cap.

"You're early. It's only ten o'clock," Corinne said. "Sit down and have some coffee, Luten. Coffen won't be ready a minute before ten-thirty."

"I thought we'd go on ahead in my rig and meet them downtown. I left word with Prance, as there was no answer at Pattle's. Jacob is sleeping it off, I expect."

"Very likely. I shall just get my bonnet, then."

Luten exchanged a few pleasantries with Mrs. Ballard before joining Corinne. One was always expected to inquire for her health, though she had never been sick a day in her life so far as he knew. Perhaps it was just that she was difficult to talk to.

A night's sleep had repaired Black's humor.

"I'll keep me daylights open for mischief whilst youse are gone," he said, in quite a civil manner, as he held the door for them.

"If the Frenchman comes back, follow him," Luten said.

"Not likely he'll show his phiz hereabouts, is it?"

"No, not likely," Luten agreed, and left, topped—again—by a butler.

It was a beautiful, balmy autumn day. The sky was that deep azure blue of a tropical clime, with not a cloud to be seen. The sun was already warm. By noon, it would be hot.

"A lovely day for a wedding," Luten said, looking about.

"We should have taken the curricle, to enjoy that sun."

"The closed carriage gives more privacy. That seems a short commodity, between Black and Ballard and Prance and Pattle."

"And Brougham," she added, suppressing the name Yvonne as she settled into the luxury of deep blue velvet squabs and silver appointments.

"And Brougham. He has dibs on my company for this afternoon, which is why I hoped we could steal a few moments together this morning. I asked my driver to take us to Hyde Park. It should be fairly private at this hour."

"What we really ought to do is go to Southcote Abbey for a week, just the two of us. Well, the three of us. I could not go without Mrs. Ballard, but the abbey is big enough for us to lose her." She looked hopefully to Luten.

"A tempting notion," he said, but his diffident tone suggested the temptation would be overcome.

She waited a moment, then said, "But? What prevents it?"

"This Yarrow and the rocket business. If we can prove corruption, it will go a long way toward unseating Mouldy and Company. My thought was that while I work on this, you could make the wedding arrangements. Nothing lavish, I expect, as this is not your first—that is—"

"As I am a widow," she said bluntly.

"Well, yes. That was my meaning," he admitted, with a sheepish smile. "But if you wish a big wedding, I have no objection. Saint George's, Hanover Square, perhaps?"

"Certainly not," she said, rather sharply. She could not say exactly why she was annoyed, although his refusing to go to the abbey had something to do with it. It was unlike the suave Luten to bring up that she had already been married when they were discussing their wedding, but it was only the simple truth after all. No, what annoyed her was his putting politics first and fobbing her off with making the wedding arrangements, so that she would not object to his absence from the courtship.

"You don't have to snap my head off. Shall we choose a date?"

"You already know the date I wished was September the fourteenth, my parents' anniversary. As that is only a few days away, the only way we could marry on the fourteenth is if we got a special license."

He frowned his dissatisfaction. "That doesn't give us much time."

"Quite enough for a small wedding, befitting a widow."

"You will want to acquire a trousseau fit for a bride."

"And more importantly, you will be at the party's beck and call," she snipped.

Luten looked at her in a sober, penetrating way. He reached across to her banquette and seized her two hands in his. "It is important, my dear," he said gently. "You know this is the work I've chosen. I have been given undeserved wealth and considerable power. If I don't use it to better England, then I am merely a parasite, a cipher. This is the Whigs' chance to knock the Tories down and begin the reforms we've planned. Don't make it difficult for me. You have always approved of what I do."

"I know," she said, feeling the full weight of his charge. It was selfish and foolish of her. And in the bottom of her heart, she knew it wasn't really his work that bothered her at all. It was that beautiful, predatory French comtesse, lurking in the background, waiting to pounce. "It's all right, Luten, but I don't want to go ahead and plan our wedding alone. When this rocket business is straightened out, we'll plan it together."

"Along with Prance, of course," he added, smiling his relief. "One trembles to think what extravaganza he'll want to mount. He spoke of a Venetian masque party for our engagement."

"I haven't heard anything about the masque since he fell in love with the comtesse."

"He can usually entertain two follies simultaneously."

"Yes, but he has the *Rondeaux* in his dish as well, to say nothing of *our* being invited to dedicate *our* next oeuvre to the prince."

The moment's uneasiness passed, and they were soon back on a familiar footing. When the carriage was passing through a private stretch of road, they stole a kiss.

At ten-thirty the carriage turned in to Piccadilly. "There is Reggie's rig," Corinne said. "Coffen is with him. Let us get out and meet them. I want to see Reggie's face when he sees Hatchard's window."

Prance and Pattle dismounted, each carrying a copy of the *Rondeaux*. Prance had outfitted himself as a poet for the nonce. He was letting his hair grow long enough to dangle over his brow in artistic abandon. It was clear at a glance that he had been curling it in papers. It was usually bone-straight, but today a curl wantoned in the breeze. In lieu of a cravat, he wore a Belcher kerchief of saffron yellow at his throat.

"Ah, there you are! I had the deuce of a time getting Pattle out of bed and the oil washed out of his hair." They exchanged greetings, then Prance said, "Shall we take a stroll down Piccadilly?"

"Glutton for punishment," Coffen muttered. "Knows perfectly well what'll be in the window. That *Harold Child* of Byron's."

Prance managed to hold his pace to Coffen's as they advanced. He had no intention of gazing into the window. Just a quick glance from the corner of his eye to ascertain the favoritism being show to Byron. A glance was enough. The image of the *Rondeaux* was indelibly etched in his memory. He recognized the slender red morocco-bound volume, with the gilt trim. He first thought it was just one copy. He glanced again and saw a windowful of the familiar shape and color. He could no longer feign indifference. He stopped and stared, then turned around and looked at the others in disbelief. A beatific smile illuminated his lean face.

"This is the prince's doing!" he exclaimed. "Oh, how excellent a thing it is to have a royal patron!" A customer came out, clutching a copy of the *Rondeaux*. A squint into the shop showed him half a dozen customers, some of them leafing through his book.

"About time!" Corinne said, exchanging a smile with Luten.

"Something fishy here," Coffen murmured, and was ignored.

"Shall we go inside?" Luten suggested. "You might want to autograph a few copies, Prance."

The dream continued inside. The clerk whispered to a young lady who was buying the book that the author was in the shop.

"Would he autograph a copy for me?" the lady asked eagerly. She did not fail to observe that the dashing Lord Luten was of the party and hoped to scrape his acquaintance.

"I'm sure he would. He is most agreeable," the clerk said. Prance had been in the shop a few times buttering up the clerks and rearranging the few copies of his works for maximum visibility on the shelf.

The lady bought a copy and went mincing forward, with many a bashful smile at Lord Luten, who praised her excellent taste. Others noticed the hubbub and soon discovered its cause.

"The author of the *Round Table Rondeaux* is autographing copies of his book."

"The *Round Table Rondeaux*? What the devil is that? I never heard of it."

"Oh, it is famous. See, there he is, with Lord Luten."

Prance had the pleasure, never to be surpassed in his lifetime, though the prince's approval ran it a close race, of being besieged for no fewer than five autographs. And the books were not gifts; they had been paid for. Flushed with success, he finally allowed himself to be led from the store, glowing like a

Derby winner. To put the cap on his excitement, he encountered Robert Marchant outside the shop and could retaliate for yesterday's slights.

Prance accosted Marchant. "You notice who is in the window today, Marchant?" he asked, trying to appear debonair, and only succeeding in sounding like a boasting schoolboy.

Marchant glanced sideways and said, "Oh, it is your verses, Prance. Congratulations." He raised his hand, which held a copy of the familiar morocco-bound volume. "I picked up a copy last night. Inwood recommended it highly. Haven't had a chance to dip into it yet. You heard about poor Inwood?"

Prance noticed then that Marchant was wearing a black band on his curled beaver and a black ribbon around his sleeve. Luten, Corinne, and Coffen nudged closer.

"What about him?" Prance asked. He assumed the crape had been donned for some ancient relative and didn't associate it with Inwood's misfortune.

"Dead. He was killed last night."

"Good God!" Prance gasped, his face blanching. "I was talking to him right on this spot not twenty-four hours ago. What happened to him? A duel, a tumble off his mount?" he asked, choosing the two misadventures most likely to snuff out a healthy young life so quickly.

"He was shot to death last night outside his own house. He had rooms on Craven Street, just around the corner from Whitehall Street. His wallet and watch were taken."

"By Jove, I've been attacked by highwaymen myself," Coffen declared. "You mind, Corinne. You was with me last spring, only they didn't kill us."

Marchant shook his head. "It just goes to show you the city isn't safe to live in. The highwaymen aren't satisfied with terrorizing travelers. They are moving into town—either that or the footpads have turned to murder. I mean to raise the issue in the House. Townsend must do something—put more officers on the street and hang the bloody scoundrels."

The others listened while Marchant and Prance discussed the murder. Nothing was known of Inwood's attacker or attackers, as he had not survived to tell the tale. His body had been found early in the morning by a dairyman bringing his milk to town. The authorities thought the body had been dead for several hours. Common sense suggested that death had occurred when he was returning from his night's revels. Marchant mentioned that Inwood had planned to attend the newly constructed Drury Lane Theatre with some of his friends.

"I wanted to go with him, but I was invited out to dinner. The timing of poor Inwood's death, of course," he continued, assuming his sonorous speech-making voice, "could not be worse. We were to vote on the contract for the rockets today. Now there will very likely be a tie. The chairman will cast the deciding vote. He does not vote unless there is a tie. The Commission has an uneven number of members so that a tie could not occur if we were all present. Well, I had best be off."

He took a few steps, then turned around and said, "Perhaps you'd autograph this copy for me, Prance? I was hoping to meet you."

"If you want to step into Hatchard's . . ."

"I'm in a bit of a rush. Why don't you take it, and I'll send my footman around to Berkeley Square for it later."

"Very well." Prance accepted the book with an air of condescension befitting the holder of Hatchard's bow window.

As Marchant left, Luten drew Corinne aside. "I know you're not going to like this, but I—"

"You're going to discuss Inwood's death with Brougham. I understand. Do you suspect it has to do with the rocket contract?"

"As Yarrow is the chairman who has the deciding vote, I fear so."

"Really? Surely you don't think Yarrow had him killed!"

"I shouldn't think so."

"Then who?"

"Someone who has invested heavily in Gresham stock and wants to make sure Gresham gets the contract. You know who I mean." She assumed he was referring to Chamaude. "My hope is to delay the vote. You can cadge a drive home with Prance?"

"Of course. Hurry, Luten."

Coffen borrowed Reg's rig to take his Poussin to Mercier's gallery for authentication. Corinne continued walking with Prance, who had no notion of leaving the environs of Hatchard's in the near future.

As Luten was driven to Whitehall, he thought about the ramifications of Inwood's death. If Chamaude was selling off her pictures to invest in Gresham's company, and she learned Inwood was voting for Congreve, then she might have her colleague, the tall Frenchman, get rid of Inwood, knowing Yarrow would cast the deciding vote for Gresham. What he did not know for certain was which bid Inwood favored. He felt Chamaude's aim was to make enough money to be free of that old slice Yarrow once and for all, now that he had served his purpose, and to set herself up in style in that house on Grosvenor Square that Yarrow had mentioned. Amazing what a pretty woman could accomplish if she had no scruples and kept her wits about her. But he still didn't know why she had suddenly decided to switch Pattle's Poussin last night.

Brougham had not yet arrived at Whitehall. Luten left a note telling what had happened to Inwood and what he suspected, along with directions that Brougham was to receive the note the minute he arrived. He then drove to Brougham's house, where he discovered that Brougham had left for work ten minutes before.

His next stop was Half Moon Street. The comtesse would have no reason to suspect he knew of Inwood's death. He wouldn't mention it or the rocket contract, but he would try to cozen his way into her confidence. The lady was open for a dalliance, if he was any judge of the fair sex. He would use the excuse of putting an offer on the Watteau. It would be a fine balancing act to keep the comtesse interested, without Corinne hitting the roof. She was already suspicious. To further complicate matters, he wasn't driving his hunting carriage today. If he took Chamaude out, it would be in his own rig, which half of London would recognize. No, he'd have to send John Groom off to exchange it for the unmarked carriage and hire an anonymous team from Newman's Stable.

Prance eventually accompanied Corinne home in a hired hackney. He had conceived the brilliant idea of inviting the comtesse out for a drive and walking her past Hatchard's.

Coffen dropped in at Corinne's house an hour later. "Reg will be mad as a gumboil that I didn't get his rig back to Hatchard's in time. He hates taking hired hackneys."

"He didn't mind today."

"Aye, he's merry as a grig about seeing his book in the window. I wonder what ails Hatchard. The book is a clinker, ain't it?"

"I fear so, but you didn't hear it here."

"Well, my Poosan ain't. Mercier tells me it's the genuine article," he said with satisfaction. "You'll have to help me decide where to hang it."

"Oh, in your bedchamber, surely, where you can see it every morning and evening." And where she would never have to see it again.

"Not sure I want a suicide picture staring me in the face before I've had my morning tea. I'll think about it." He helped himself to a glass of wine. "Seems we ought to be doing something about poor Inwood," he said.

"Luten was wondering if he was going to vote for Congreve's rocket."

"Very likely." He had thoughtlessly carried a copy of the *Rondeaux* into the house with him. He opened it, furrowed up his brow, and rubbed his ear.

"Here's an odd thing," he said, and showed Corinne the flyleaf of the book.

She read, "To Lady Chamaude from an admirer, Sir Reginald Prance." She sat staring at it a moment in confusion.

"That's the book Prance gave Chamaude," Coffen said.

"Yes, I realize that. But where did you get it?"

"Reg gave it to me before I went to Mercier's. It's the copy Marchant gave him to sign. Marchant didn't buy a copy at all. She gave it to him—the comtesse. Poor Reg. We'll not tell him about this, eh? Bruise his feelings."

"But this means Marchant called on Chamaude. Where else could he have got this?"

"Aye, I mind he *said* he *bought* a copy last night, and he went out for dinner. He must have gone to Chamaude's and taken it home with him. They're friends, or cohorts. Clear as a pikestaff she's influencing him to vote for Gresham. We ought to tell Luten."

"You had best drive to Whitehall, Coffen. It would look odd for a lady to go. Take the book, and tell him where you got it. He'll understand what it means."

"Yes, by Jove. And mind you don't tell Reg."

Reggie's sensitive feelings were the least of Corinne's worries. But the cloud had one silver lining at least. It would prove to Luten that the comtesse was a cunning, low conniver.

Mrs. Ballard came downstairs, and they began to discuss wedding plans. The dame was concerned that she would lose her post after the marriage and was reassured that her mistress would still require a dresser.

Chapter Ten

Luten was kept waiting longer to see Lady Chamaude than he expected. The boulevardier-butler showed him into a small parlor, poured him a glass of wine, and withdrew. The desk in the corner suggested Yvonne used this room as her study. While awaiting his summons to enter the saloon, Luten made a quick examination of the papers on the desk, a few bills and one half-written letter. It was from Manchester—Gresham? No, a female called Sylvie. The subject appeared to be gowns, but it was interesting that Yvonne had connections in Manchester, where Gresham's armaments plant was situated.

The paintings on the wall were also of some interest to him. One was a watercolor of the Louvre; another was of a young girl done in the style of Greuze, the French genre painter from the last century. In this picture, Greuze (if the artist was Greuze) had restrained his love of melodrama. The girl was not mourning the loss of her sparrow or canary but smiling.

Something in that smile held an echo of the young Yvonne he had known a dozen years ago. Was this a portrait of her? The face was fuller, the eyes less large and lustrous and more innocent, but it was possible. The loss of weight might have given the eyes more prominence, and the trials of her life since then explained the loss of innocence. Greuze was still painting at the turn of the century, when Yvonne would have been this age.

He had not been working in England, however, and Yvonne claimed never to have returned to France. Had she returned, and if so, did it have any significance? Had she been, and was she still, working for France? Perhaps hoping to recover

Chamaude's estate by doing a spot of work for Napoleon in England? It would explain why she tolerated Yarrow as her lover, when it was clear she despised the man. Yarrow knew all the secrets of the Horse Guards—and he was Chairman of the Ordnance Committee. Luten thought of his message to Brougham and hoped Brougham had managed to get the awarding of the rocket contract delayed.

His mind flew to the rockets and a spasm of alarm shook him. Was Gresham supplying some inferior sort of weapon, one that would not do its job? He examined the picture for a signature; if it was not a Greuze, all this conjecture was futile. The signature was stuck off in the bottom right corner, most of it covered by the frame. The letters were indecipherable. And to quiz her about the picture would only alert her of his suspicions, for she knew that he knew something of art.

The door opened without warning, and the butler was back. As Luten was bent over, studying the picture, he said, "Is this a portrait of Lady Chamaude?"

The butler's dissipated face revealed nothing but disdain as he tossed his narrow shoulders in a Gallic shrug. "Madame will receive you now in the saloon, melord."

When Luten was led in, he had the distinct impression that Yvonne had been crying. With his suspicions on the boil, he even wondered if she had rubbed her eyes into redness to engage his sympathy. She wore a draped robe of sky-blue, which would have looked more at home in the boudoir. It clung to the outline of her extremely curvaceous body. She had certainly kept her figure! The violet smudges beneath her eyes suggested a sleepless night. Her coiffure was tousled, attractively so, as if she had run her fingers through her curls in a fit of abandon. An English lady would not have received any gentleman but her lover in such a beguiling state of disarray.

"How kind of you to come, Luten," she said, offering both her dainty white hands. He noticed that the wedding ring formerly on her left hand had been replaced by a sapphire. She did not rise to greet him but lay stretched out on a sofa, propped up with pillows. He had to bend over to take her hands. She obviously expected him to kiss them. He dutifully raised her right hand to his lips in the familiar gesture. How soft and smooth it was. A hand that had never done any manual work. The musky scent of French perfume hovered about her.

"You must ignore my dishabille," she said, in her alluring accent. "I fear I have suffered a disappointment today."

"I am sorry to hear it, Yvonne," he said, drawing a chair up beside her. "Is there anything I can do to help?"

"Ah no, it is for me to deal with. The petite house I had hoped to purchase—it has been sold, and after I parted with so many of my old friends to gather the monies to buy it," she said with a moue. "I mean the paintings from the Chamaude collection," she explained, when Luten frowned at that vague "friends."

"That is a pity, but there will be other houses on the market."

"*Bien entendu*, but this one was suitable for me, as to price, *vous savez*. My pockets are not deep. *Peut-être* I shall have to sell my Watteau after all." Her dark, glittering eyes gazed into his. He noticed that she was sprinkling her conversation with French phrases in a way she used to do years ago, when she was looking about for a rich patron. Her accent was more pronounced than it had been yesterday, too. Very seductive, that trace of French accent. Prance had a theory that gentlemen always preferred foreign women for their mistresses and English ladies for their wives. They liked the mystery of the unknown but mistrusted it for such a serious business as raising a family.

"What price did you have in mind for the Watteau?"

"Twenty-five hundred. It is a very fine picture."

Luten nodded, interested. He had been thinking about the Poussin, which had been mysteriously exchanged the night before. If Yvonne was trying to sell him the Watteau, then presumably she would sell him the original. He felt it would give him some leverage against her if he could catch her out in selling a forged picture that she knew to be forged. He must, therefore, let her believe the painting was to go to someone less knowledgeable about art than himself.

"I have an old school friend who inherited a big house in Somerset," he said. "He mentioned his wife wants to buy some furnishings and pictures and so on to brighten it up. Deverel could well afford the Watteau, but unfortunately he is no connoisseur. It would seem a shame to send it off to the provinces to languish unappreciated."

She lowered her eyes and played with the silk of her gown, so that he could not read her expression. "You have lost interest in it yourself, Luten?" she asked.

To dilute her suspicion, he said, "Not at all. I have just had word from my bailiff at Southgate Abbey that the roof needs replacement. It cuts into my disposable income. I don't like to leave myself short. Might Yarrow know someone who would buy it, or buy it himself?" he suggested, to conceal his interest in the matter.

Her face tensed at the mention of her patron's name. "I would prefer not to be further indebted to Lord Yarrow," she said.

Luten had to force the hopeful smile that peered at her. "Indeed?" he said. "That is good news to the bachelors of London."

She smiled at him from the corner of her dark, liquid eyes. There was seduction in that look, and something else that he found upsetting. It looked like sadness, and he felt an unwelcome stirring of pity. He reminded himself that she was a professional actress.

"I am long past the age where I excite the interest of young gentlemen," she said, rather archly.

"It is ungentlemanly to disagree with a lady, but I fear I must be ungentlemanly in this matter."

She reached out and patted his hand with her soft, warm fingers. "You were always so sweet, Luten," she said, in a fond, nostalgic way.

"I could still be sweet, if you would allow. . . . Come, let us go out for a drive in the country. It will help you be rid of these blue devils."

She sat up, excitement flashing. "Dare we?" she asked.

"You are thinking of Yarrow?"

"He would dislike it very much, I fear. He was extremely jealous to hear you had called the other day. I did not tell him, *naturellement*. I believed he heard of it at the prince's little soirée."

How cleverly she had pitched them in league against Yarrow, devising secrets to bind them together. "Then it is fortunate I sent for my unmarked carriage, *n'est-ce pas?* Your butler—is he to be trusted?"

"I chose my own servants. They are faithful to me. We shall drive in the country, *non*? I prefer not to be seen in town. I daresay you feel the same?" she asked, with a teasing laugh.

Luten managed to reply with an air of nonchalance he was far from feeling. If Corinne ever found out about this! "Oh, I am still single."

This business of the rockets was too important to let his own interests stand in the way. Corinne would understand. If Chamaude was influencing Yarrow to supply inferior weapons, perhaps perfectly useless ones, it could cost the lives of countless English soldiers.

"Allow me a moment to make my toilette. I shall return *tout de suite*," she said.

She rose and glided from the room in a silken rustle, leaving behind a miasma of musk. The few moments until she returned showed Luten what a perilous course he was running, but he must just count on Corinne's common sense. And besides, he thought, she might never hear of it. He would tell her after it was all over. His hunting carriage drew up to the door just as Yvonne returned, wearing a hooded mantle that would cover her face in the carriage. She was obviously no tyro at this sort of thing. She had slipped out on Yarrow before.

Before calling on the comtesse, Prance visited his little conservatory to select a bouquet. Provence roses, of course, would be the basis, but they must be set off with interesting greenery and presented in a vase. He had a surfeit of interesting vases; the only difficulty was to choose the most suitable. He settled on a tall, elegant vase of Murano crystal that sparkled like her eyes. With his clasp knife, he removed every thorn by hand from the rose stocks. When one of them pierced his finger, he squeezed a few droplets of blood and deposited them on a rose petal. It seemed symbolic, but of what, he was not quite sure. A promise that he would gladly spill his blood for her, perhaps? A few drops anyway.

He rearranged his poetic toilette, exchanging the saffron kerchief for one of a pale indigo, which was a more romantic shade. When all was ready, he carried the vase to his carriage and directed his coachman to drive carefully, to avoid damaging the roses and spilling the water.

The worst Prance expected was that Yarrow would be visiting Yvonne, in which case his own conversation would sparkle so brightly that she would realize she was wasting her time on that aging crock. It was also possible that the comtesse would not be at home, in which case he would wait until she arrived, or leave the posies and return if she was to be gone for hours. What never crossed his mind was that he would actually see Luten lead Yvonne from the doorway, she concealed under a dark hood, he peering up and down the street in a furtive manner before hustling her into his hunting carriage

The enormity of it quite took his breath away. Luten betraying not only his fiancée but his best friend as well. Prance had thought Corinne ridiculously jealous, but he now realized that she knew Luten better than any of them. Her feminine instinct had caught the whiff of lust in the air between Luten and Yvonne. For lust was obviously all it was in Luten's case, of course. He was taking pains to make sure Corinne didn't discover his stunt, which meant he still wanted to marry her.

As much as Prance thrived on drama, this was more than he had bargained for. What was the gentlemanly thing to do in this circumstance? Corinne must be shielded from the awful truth, of course. That was paramount. But Luten must also be brought to his senses—and he must pay the price for this treachery.

He wondered just how far the affair had gone. Were they even now on their way to a romantic tryst in some country inn, away from London's prying eyes? It was clearly his duty to follow them. He must do it at a discreet distance to avoid being seen and recognized. Hiring a hackney cab would help, but it would never keep up with Luten's team. As the rig turned the corner, he noticed that the hunting carriage was not drawn by Luten's blood nags but by a hired team. He was certainly taking no chances of being recognized!

Prance followed along behind as the carriage turned west on Curzon Street, then north on Park Lane. There was enough traffic that keeping his presence unknown was no problem, though the fast pace was hard on the roses. He expected the carriage would continue out of town via Edgeware Road and was surprised when it turned east again on Upper Grosvenor Street and continued on to Grosvenor Square, right into the heart of polite London, where everyone would recognize him. What consummate folly!

When the carriage drew to a stop, Prance remained at the corner. In a rare fit of good luck, an empty hackney cab passed by, and he hailed it. His coachman was ordered to take his own carriage to the mews. Prance withdrew into the shadows of the corner as the hackney drove past Luten's carriage. He saw Luten assist Yvonne from the carriage. They were going into the house! No, they stopped and just stood, looking and pointing out various features.

Prance studied the house to make sure he could recognize it again. Smallish, brown brick, white columns and pediment, two windows on either side of the doorway. He glanced at the landscaping, and his eyes beheld the To Be Sold sign. His heart fluttered painfully, like a wounded doe's. Luten was buying her a house! He was setting Yvonne up as his mistress on the very eve of his marriage to Corinne! Prance's aspirations had never extended to buying Yvonne a house. Luten must be extremely serious about the woman. And of course, he had the cash on hand, or would have as soon as he sold that little property his cousin had left him. The unfairness of it! This was really doing it too brown. He would not get away with this!

The hackney circled the block, while Prance wrestled with his conscience over telling Corinne. She, he felt, was the only chance of bringing Luten to his senses. He might drop Yvonne if Corinne threatened to break their engagement. Or he, Prance, might tell Yvonne that Luten was engaged. She obviously didn't know, or she would not have been throwing her hankie at Luten right in front of his fiancée during that visit. But would a mere engagement be enough to stop Yvonne? A battle between Aphrodite and . . . well, another Aphrodite. Or was the judgment of Paris a fitter metaphor?

When he passed the house again, Luten and Yvonne were returning to the carriage. Had he not bought the house, then? Were they just looking for a suitable love nest? The hackney cab was heading in the wrong direction to follow them. Prance had the driver circle back and continue after the hunting carriage. It now proceeded north on Edgeware Road, as he expected, and on out of town via the Maida Vale Road to St. John's Wood, where it drew into a half-timbered inn.

Prance had seen enough. He asked the hackney driver to take him to Berkeley Square, where he ordered his butler to draw the curtains and tell any callers that he was not well. He required solitude and silence to work out this monumental moral dilemma, and perhaps a glass of brandy and a little browsing through Dante to dull the sharp edge of pain occasioned by this monstrous betrayal.

No more to gaze into those *Sturm und Drang* eyes for a glimpse of paradise. The view now would be tainted with a brimstone tinge of hell. The fire in his veins had turned to ice. Would he ever see the stars again? "Without hope, we live in desire," he read, and realized again the genius of Dante Alighieri, for his desire was not only alive but enhanced by Yvonne's carrying on. Say what you like, where women were concerned availability was the strongest aphrodisiac. If she accepted one lover while under Yarrow's patronage, would she not accept another? Rather fun, actually, to have an affair with Luten's mistress. The rogue in him enjoyed a cynical little smile. He would not have to feel guilty, when Luten was being such a wretch.

Between the brandy and the quantity and quality of the mischief all around him, he soon felt well enough to call on Coffen. He had to share all this with someone or he would burst, and of course, he could not whisper a word to poor

Corinne. Though if Coffen or some kind friend did not let the whole thing out, he would be greatly surprised. No matter, that was not his responsibility.

Chapter Eleven

Luten had a busy afternoon. After spending an hour in flirtation with Yvonne, hinting that he was interested in a liaison, he had to smuggle her home, then dart off to visit Brougham, where he learned that the Ordnance Committee had given the rocket contract to Gresham. Due to Inwood's death, Yarrow had cast the deciding vote. Brougham had demanded a meeting with Lord Liverpool, the prime minister, who assured him that every aspect of the contract had been looked into, by the Tories, of course, and Gresham's rocket, while a little more expensive, was the superior weapon.

"Your first love was science, Brougham. Which do you think the superior weapon?" Luten asked.

"My instinct tells me Congreve's, but that is only because the Tories have chosen Gresham's." A trace of a burr clung to Brougham's speech. "I mean to delve into the matter as soon as I get a moment free. Pity I hadn't done it sooner, but they kept the whole business quiet."

"You're an old hand at manipulating the press. If we leaked word that the contract was given to the wrong company, we might raise a public hue and cry."

Brougham explained, "It would take time, and I've no proof as yet that Gresham's design is inferior. I was with Liverpool for an hour. He said the Duke of York had personally come out in favor of Gresham. The royal nod pretty well settles it."

"We are all aware of York's character, or lack of it," Luten replied. "The Parliamentary Enquiry found him guilty of allowing his mistress to sell army commissions and promotions, and sacked him a few years ago. It's a scandal that Prinney reappointed him to his position. He'd sell his title for money. I wonder what Yarrow promised him in return for recommending Gresham."

"Yarrow is close as inkle weavers with Prinney. That kind of talk will land you in the Tower, Luten, unless you can find something to substantiate it."

"Then I'll damned well find something."

"It had best be ironclad."

"This book proves Chamaude was entertaining Marchant," Luten said, holding out the copy of the *Rondeaux* Coffen had given him. "And Marchant was on the Selection Committee. Inwood's murder is highly suspicious, to say the least."

"Yes, I do have an inkling that he favored Congreve. That is the way the rumors fly."

"I'll search his office. He may have left some notes that indicate—"

Brougham shook his head. "Too late. It has already been cleared out. I went to have a look. Turner, the new MP from Yorkshire, was already installed. He was not forthcoming as to what happened to Inwood's papers."

"Turner was moving in the very day of Inwood's death? That reeks of chicanery."

"Perhaps not. Space is at a premium."

"I feel in my bones Chamaude exerted her influence on Yarrow to vote for Gresham. She's getting a cut from Gresham."

"But if Yarrow is not getting anything—well, he's not the first gentleman to have his head turned by a pretty lady. He'll look a fool but not a traitor. What you ought to do, however, is unmask this comtesse. We can't have her exerting a malign influence on a member of the Horse Guards. You said she might have been in France since her arrival?"

"And possibly arranging the odd murder as well, but it is only a suspicion that she was back in France. That painting in her study that I mentioned—I wish we could get a look at the signature on it. I ought to have offered to buy it."

"It wouldn't prove anything. She has only to say she wasn't the model. It didn't look that much like her, you said."

"True, and I didn't want to alert her that I'm on to her. I have every intention of unmasking the comtesse. And I suggest that you get a team of engineers up to Colchester to go over Gresham's rocket with a fine-tooth comb, to make sure it works."

"Aye, and I'll make sure I wipe my nose next time I sneeze as well. I didn't come down in the last rain, Luten."

"Sorry, Henry," Luten said with a charming smile as he rose to take his leave. "I keep forgetting you're the wise man of the party. You're such a young wise man."

"There's naught to do in Scotland but sit and think and grow wise," Brougham replied with a laugh, pleased with the compliment.

"And eat oatmeal."

Like Prance, Luten required solitude and silence to ponder the matter at hand. Unlike Prance, he did not seek it at home but in the privacy of his office at Whitehall. If he could get Yvonne arrested for selling forged paintings, that would at least put her out of commission for the nonce, hopefully until this war was over. She had asked him to write to his friend in Somerset and inquire whether he was interested in the Watteau. To speed matters up, he had told her that the gentleman had asked him to scout some pictures for him and the answer was a foregone conclusion.

He assumed that she would send the picture off to whoever made her copies for her, secure in her mind that the buyer was well removed from London and knew little of art. To discover who the forger might be, Luten had set a footman to watch her house and follow her if she left, or if she sent a servant out on an errand. Winkle was to report to him at once if he discovered anything of interest. Winkle was a good lad who had done this sort of work for him before. He would dress himself up as a dandy and drive a gig to the corner of Half Moon Street and busy Piccadilly, with a view of Chamaude's house. There he would remove the bolt from a wheel of the gig, which could quickly be replaced to allow him to follow anyone leaving her house. Meanwhile, he would watch the comings and goings while ostensibly awaiting the arrival of the wheeler.

In a little over an hour, Winkle came tapping at his door, big with news. He looked so elegant in his blue jacket and curled beaver that no one would ever suspect his humble origins, until he opened his mouth.

"Boisvert!" he exclaimed triumphantly.

"What about him?"

"A footman went to visit Boisvert. He was carrying a big parcel wrapped in brown paper. Looked the right size for the picture you mentioned."

"Who's Boisvert?"

"A French artist. He has what he calls an ay-tell-eeay in Shepherd's Market," he said, struggling over the French word. "A ratty little place between Curzon and Piccadilly. Not far from Half Moon Street. The fellow didn't even take a carriage. He went on shank's mare."

"Shepherd's Market. I know the place."

"The footman took the parcel in and come out whistling ten minutes later. Went back to Half Moon Street empty-handed."

"You're sure he didn't see you?"

"Nay, he never looked behind him. I got the wheel back on the gig and followed him at a distance, drove past as he was going into Boisvert's, then drove the rig around the corner and walked back. Met up with a race-track tout that was selling tips on the races, so as to look natural, walking two by two."

"Good work, Winkle. Did anyone else call on the lady?"

"A handsome-looking gent went in earlier and was still there when I left. Tall, dark."

"The mysterious Frenchman!"

"He looked like it, though I didn't hear him speak at all."

"You've done good work, Winkle. You can go home and await further instructions. Have a few ales on me," he said, and handed Winkle a golden coin.

"Do I keep on me fancy duds?"

"Yes, best be ready for another assignment, but don't go back to your old post or she'll suspect you."

Luten was feeling the weight of conscience where his fiancée was concerned and decided there was no reason he couldn't take Corinne with him to visit Boisvert. In fact, he would ask Boisvert to do a portrait of her. That would please her and get himself into the atelier. He assumed Boisvert was capable of painting a decent picture if he was the artist who was doing the forgeries for Yvonne. While Boisvert discussed costume and setting and so on with Corinne, Luten planned to ferret around the studio to see what he could discover.

At Berkeley Square, Corinne was becoming impatient at being virtually abandoned by her fiancé at this romantic period of her life. She had thought they would get down to serious wedding plans when Luten returned from the country, and instead of that, they had hardly seen each other. She had seen Reggie dart over to visit Coffen. When the knocker sounded, she thought it was them calling on her. She was surprised and delighted to see Luten shown in.

After a somewhat perfunctory embrace, for Black was watching like a hen guarding its chick, she said, "You had a call from Coffen?"

"Yes, with Chamaude's copy of the *Rondeaux* that mysteriously ended up in Marchant's hands. It was very helpful. I fear Gresham got the contract, however. Yarrow cast the deciding vote."

"At her instigation, I warrant!"

"Very likely. But enough of that. We have more pleasant things to discuss. I would like to give myself a wedding present."

She looked a question. "I am reluctant to ask what," she said.

"A portrait of you, as you look now, all brightly radiant and happy." He gazed at her, smiling softly, until an answering smile stole across her lips.

"Lawrence?" she asked, naming the foremost portrait artist. "Let us have one done of you, too. A pair for the family gallery."

"Lawrence, certainly, for our formal portraits for the gallery at Southcote, but I would like something more informal for my own sole enjoyment. Brougham mentioned to me this morning a fellow who does good work. Has a little atelier in Shepherd's Market."

"Shepherd's Market? Can he be any good, working out of that squalid place?"

"Perhaps he can come here to do the actual job. I thought we might drop around there this afternoon and have a look at his work. If we don't like it, we need not hire him."

Corinne was flattered that he wanted her likeness and agreed to go at once.

Prance, watching the comings and goings from Coffen's window, said, "The deceiver! There he goes off with Corinne, and she smiling, unaware of his treachery. Friendship is full of dregs, Coffen."

"So's wine. What of it?"

"I always admired Luten, but as the poet says, 'Friendship is constant in all other things, Save in the office and affairs of love.' "

"More Dante?"

"No, fool, Shakespeare."

"I never thought I'd hear you call Shakespeare a fool."

"Nor will you, though I hate all mankind. I am become a misanthrope."

Coffen gave him a wary look. "Miss who?"

"Misunderstood."

"You mean Miss Underwood, Prance. Your mind's going on you."

"So it is. There is no point sighing over the problem like Tom o' Bedlam. To work!"

"You're right. Thing to do, charge Luten with it. Can't tell Corinne. It would break her heart. She's my cousin—I'll be the one to tackle Luten, but you must come with me. You're the one saw him with the comtesse."

"With my own eyes. This is a dark day in the annals of friendship. You must deliver an ultimatum, Pattle. He never sees Yvonne again, or we tell Corinne."

"He'll have to see her once to pay her off. Diamond bracelet, I fancy. After all, he's only been out with her once."

"That we know of," Prance added with a questioning look. Then he shook his head. "What a ready tongue suspicion has."

"And your tongue don't need any help. Let us go have a look at this house they was looking at. It'll give us a notion how highly he regards the comtesse."

"It is smallish, but a good address."

While they waited for the carriage, Prance said, "I discovered an odd thing today at Hatchard's, Pattle." Coffen rolled up his eyes, fearing another lecture on the *dux bellorum*. "Someone has bought one hundred copies of my *Rondeaux*. I was chatting to a clerk, and he said several boxes were delivered somewhere, but he didn't know who the purchaser was. Odd, is it not? Now, who could this rabid fan be?"

"Dashed odd," Coffen said, truly mystified, for Luten had not told Coffen of his stunt. "Might have something to do with Oxford or Cambridge. A bookstore there buying them up to make lads study them."

Prance preened. "Oh Lord! I hope not!" he said, but he was secretly thrilled to death. "It happens I did send a copy to my old tutor at Cambridge, Sir Vance Dean. He thanked me most graciously and said he looked forward to reading it. I always take that for a sign the recipient has, in fact, read the work and can think of nothing complimentary to say, but perhaps I am too cynical. Cambridge does give a course on medieval literature. The fate of dull literary outpourings, forcing the youth to read them under pain of withholding a degree. It was Cambridge that gave me such an unutterable dread of poor Milton, who is actually very good in his own dry way."

"No, really, Prance, you're going too far, comparing yourself to Milton. You ain't *that* bad. I could understand quite a bit of your poem."

"I am flattered, Pattle. I do feel that, despite the *Rondeaux*' glaring faults, the poems were at least lucid to the meanest intelligence."

"Very likely," Coffen said, frowning. He reamed out his ear with his finger and said, "Did I just hear you say faults? And dull—a while back you said dull. Have you been reading the thing yourself, then?"

"Strangely, the answer is yes. I took the *Rondeaux* to bed last night and fell sound asleep at the end of Rondeau Seven, and there are, you recall, an even hundred rondeaux."

"Then you have another couple of weeks easy sleep to look forward to."

"The point I was endeavoring to make is that the *Rondeaux* lacked esprit. Next I had planned to write an epic poem on the French Revolution, featuring a young noble lady."

"With them dashed stern eyes, I suppose?"

"No, paradisiacal eyes."

"If you're going to use that kind of language, you'll have another clinker on your hands."

"No, no, I shall couch it in metaphors."

"I pity the poor lads at Cambridge. You haven't learned a dashed thing from your failure, Reg. And for God's sake, leave off them little notes at the bottom of the page that are so hard to read."

"One can hardly call a poem a failure when Cambridge has put it on the curriculum as required reading! I must write dear Sir Vance a note and thank him. This is his doing. This does not mean I plan to disregard your advice, Pattle. You have a point. I shall couch the French poem in a manner more pleasing to the common man. They like to feel their literature, rather than think it. Smells, sounds, sights, the haptic sense of touch, and of course, it must virtually wallow in emotion!"

"That's the ticket," Coffen said, nodding his approbation. "I do like a good wallow."

"Yes, you are everyman. I shall use you as my sounding board. Now tell me what you think of this."

Coffen looked around like a baited animal. "Ah, there's the carriage!" he exclaimed, and darted to the door before Pattle could bethump him with any more discussion of poetry.

They drove to Grosvenor Square, just as the To Be Sold sign was being removed.

"We're too late!" Coffen said in a voice of doom. "He's already bought it for her. Didn't waste any time, did he?"

"Let us speak to the follow removing the sign. He's no common laborer. Those kersey small clothes and crimson waistcoat bespeak a man of business. The estate agent, likely."

He dismounted and went forward, lifting his curled beaver and smiling. He was back within two minutes.

"Well, was it Luten that bought it?" Coffen demanded.

"No, it was a company, but the fellow hinted that it was bought for a lady."

"What company—and what lady?"

"An aunt lady. Need I say more? A gentleman always claims his *chère amie* is a close relative when his aim is to make her respectable. The company is one of those anonymous outfits MPs use to hide their business dealings. Luten has a couple of them to my knowledge. The agent hinted it is owned by a melord."

"Luten, the bounder!"

Prance sat, dejected. He felt his enthusiasm for the French poem seeping away. In fact, he felt as jaded as Lord Byron and wondered if he shouldn't turn his hand to a cynical love poem on the fallibility of ladies in general, and French courtesans in particular.

"We shall beard the lion in his den," he said.

"I don't know about that, but I'll dashed well have a word with Luten," Coffen said, and gave the draw cord an angry jerk.

Chapter Twelve

"I shall certainly not want to come here to have my portrait done," Corinne said, peering from the carriage window out to a mean, narrow alley. Dust eddies rose from under the wheels as they lumbered over the uncobbled ground. Clapboard buildings, once a jaunty red but now faded to brick color, leaned against each other for support like drunken derelicts. Journals and discarded playbills weathered to papier-mâché by time and the elements clung like barnacles to the base of the buildings. "Why does Boisvert not remove to a better part of town, if he is successful?"

"Perhaps he will, when his fame spreads as a result of doing your picture," Luten replied.

She peered at him from the side of her eyes. "I always suspect you are up to something when you pour on the butter at this rate, Luten. And why, pray, do I have the honor of driving in your hunting carriage?"

"We are traveling incognito. You were always curious about this rig. Now that we are about to wed, I plan to be rid of it. I thought you might like to see what it's like. No concealed mattress, you see. No mirrors installed on the ceiling. Really a very boring carriage."

"I didn't ask you to be rid of it! It might come in useful after we are married."

"That is very lenient of you, my dear."

"For spying on villains, I mean, not its former use!" She stopped, blinked twice, and said, "What do you mean, we are traveling incognito?"

"It means, hopefully, we shall not be recognized."

"I know that! But why?"

"I don't want Boisvert boasting to all his sitters that he is painting Lady deCoventry. After he removes his studio to some more polite address and becomes respectable, but for the meanwhile . . ."

Corinne snorted genteelly. "What a whisker. When did you ever care about such things?"

"When I became an engaged man. I am turning over a new leaf, Mrs. Grundy."

The carriage drew to a stop at the end of the alley, in front of a door bearing a shingle sign: Atelier, M. Boisvert. Through the window they caught a glimpse of the signs of Boisvert's profession. Canvases stacked against walls, a worktable holding oils and pigments, soiled rags and bottles of brushes, a few easels with canvases propped on them. The shop was empty of clients. Only one head was visible through the window.

Luten tapped on the door and stepped into a modest room that reeked of turpentine and linseed oil, and beneath the sharp smell, the heavier aroma of boiled cabbage and gammon. Obviously Boisvert lived on the premises.

He was a stocky, muscular man in his mid-thirties with blue eyes and crinkly hair the tawny golden orange color of a cocker spaniel. He wore the customary artist's smock, liberally spotted with pigments of all hues. Were it not for his outfit, he would never have been taken for an artist. He lacked the dreamy quality. His sharp, ruddy face suggested a farmer. He did not look French either, despite his name, but when he spoke, his voice held the trace of an accent. His blue eyes were open wide in surprise at the elegance of his clients.

"Can I help you, sir, ma'am?" he asked, bowing to them both.

Luten proferred his hand. "Mr. Lucas, and my wife. We are visiting London for a few days. I would like to have my bride's portrait taken before we return to Devonshire." His drawling accent had turned to a clipped, provincial curtness.

As Corinne smiled and performed an abbreviated curtsy, she made a mental note not to remove her gloves. While Luten chatted to Boisvert, she had a moment to consider this visit.

Luten would not care a fig about having her portrait taken by an unstylish artist in an out-of-the-way place. In fact, he would delight in it. A small part of the Berkeley Brigade's reputation was based on being outrageous. So why had Luten driven his hunting carriage? He wasn't here because he wanted her portrait. He thought Boisvert was involved in the business of Coffen's Poussin!

"I am very busy at the moment," Boisvert said, wrinkling up his brow. "You see the many works in progress." His sweeping arm indicated three easels with canvases propped on them. "I regret— How long are you in town?"

"A week," Luten replied. "Money is no object," he added, with an ingratiating smile that sat ill on his haughty face. "You come highly recommended."

"That is very kind. Who did you say recommended me?"

"Who was that lady we met at the party the other night, dear?" Luten asked Corinne.

"Oh la," she said, tossing up her hands. "There were so many people there I never met before. The lady in the green gown with the funny red hair, was it not?"

Luten didn't volunteer a name. "We had the devil of a time finding your place," he said, strolling in and peering all about.

"I plan to move soon. You must forgive . . ." Again Boisvert swept his arm about vaguely.

"It was only a head-and-shoulders picture we wanted," Luten said. "That wouldn't take long, would it? We would really appreciate it. There is no decent artist near Tiverton."

"Lord knows when we shall get to London again," Corinne added, with a beseeching smile at the artist.

It was not often that Boisvert had such a pretty model. His usual customers were merchants with heavy jowls and lined faces, and often their matronly wives.

"Perhaps I could squeeze you in," he said.

Luten clapped his shoulder. "There's a good fellow," he said in that hearty, country voice. He turned to Corinne. "You set up the details with Boisvert, dear. I'll just take a peek about at what work he is doing. You don't mind, Boisvert? Can't buy a pig in a poke, eh? Oh, this is dandy! Look at this church, dear. Didn't we see it yesterday?"

Corinne sensed that Luten was looking for something, presumably the copy of the Poussin, and after glancing at the painting of a church, she made an effort to distract Boisvert. But why would Luten think the copy was here? Surely Chamaude would have it.

"Do you always paint here, Mr. Boisvert?" she asked, looking about doubtfully. "Or could you come to—to our hotel? The Clarendon," she suggested, and immediately wondered if a country couple would put up at such a stylish hotel.

"I prefer to work here, where I have all my equipment handy, and the light is good. I have had the window enlarged. I have a selection of curtains I use for a backdrop." He led her to a corner, where various rich stuffs were hung on rods. She thumbed through them, holding each up to her face, looking for his opinion.

"Do you think this green one might do? My eyes are green," she added, fluttering her long lashes.

"It is a little dark. I thought something lighter, to contrast with your black hair."

"This one?" she suggested, fingering a yellow velvet.

"I was thinking of red, if you don't think it too gaudy. And a white gown to recall your recent marriage. The red curtain would cast rose highlights on the white. With perhaps some jewelry . . ." His eyes, bright with anticipation, darted over his model. He wanted to do more than a head-and-shoulders portrait. That figure deserved immortalizing.

"My diamonds!" she exclaimed, clapping her hands. "Mr. Lucas gave them to me as a wedding gift," she said, and went on with a few other artless remarks.

While she entertained Boisvert, Luten quickly glanced at the works on the easels. They were all partially finished portraits, two of aging merchants, one of a severe lady with a scowl that would challenge da Vinci's genius to make her look anything but an antidote. The Watteau was not there.

He peered over his shoulder to see that Boisvert was enjoying his flirtation with Corinne, then turned to the other side of the room, where canvases were stacked against the wall, two or three deep. Behind a stretched canvas primed for paint, he saw the edge of a painting protruding. He lifted the canvas in front; peering behind it, he found himself staring at the Watteau. It was still in its frame. He had brought a grease pencil for the purpose of marking it. He leaned over and drew a small black dot in the upper right corner, put the stretched canvas back in place, and turned around to join the others.

"All set, dear?" he asked. "You know we were to visit my aunt for tea." He turned aside to Boisvert. "Rich as a nabob, and no children. Must do the pretty."

"Mr. Boisvert has agreed to come to the hotel to do my picture," she said. "Is that not kind of him, Mr. Lucas? We thought tomorrow afternoon, around three. You have that business meeting, you recall. My dresser will be with us," she added with a shy smile to appease her groom's proprietorial instincts.

"Three it is. The Clarendon. What suite are we in, dear?"

"The Primrose suite," she said without blinking.

The gentlemen settled on a fee, then Luten took Corinne's elbow and they went out to the waiting carriage.

Before they had gone two paces, she turned on Luten. "Don't think you have conned me, Luten. You didn't want a portrait of me."

"I do!"

"But not by Boisvert. I know that charade had to do with Coffen's Poussin. Why do you think Boisvert has it?"

"It has to be somewhere. I felt you were not eager for me to visit Yvonne again."

"Was the Poussin there?"

"No."

Corinne felt a little guilty. Was her jealousy preventing Luten from proving Chamaude a thief? She still disliked his calling on Chamaude, however.

She gave a little sniff and said in an injured tone, "Well, you didn't want an informal picture of me for your own sole enjoyment, as you claimed."

"Beauty should be shared—to a point."

"Rubbish. You just wanted an excuse to prowl about Boisvert's atelier. I assume he is the fellow making Chamaude's copies for her. How did you find out?"

"I had Winkle watch her house," he said. "She sent a footman there with a picture this morning. It was the Watteau. I saw it hidden behind another canvas in the studio."

"The painting you told her you were interested in! She said it wasn't for sale when I admired it. Or actually I believe it was Yarrow who said it."

"She probably felt she could wring a higher price out of me. I marked it so I could identify the original if she tries to palm off a copy on me."

"You plan to buy it, then?" she asked, stiffening. How should he buy it without calling on Chamaude again?

"I'll wait and see if she contacts me. It will take Boisvert a few days to make the copy and age it to make it look older than brand-new."

"I doubt she'd try to sell you a forgery." Luten could not reveal how he had overcome this difficulty without admitting he had called on Chamaude, so he said nothing. "So why is she having a copy made?" she asked.

"To keep for herself, perhaps, as she is so fond of it."

"Let me know if she contacts you. Another point occurs to me. Why didn't you tell me I was to be Mrs. Lucas, from Tiverton?"

"I only thought of it after we were in the shop. I was sure you could carry it off—as you did, admirably."

"I'm not wearing a wedding ring—or even an engagement ring," she added. It rankled a little that Luten was in no rush to put a ring on her finger. "If I hadn't thought to leave my gloves on, it would have given away the charade."

"I'll send to the abbey for the family engagement ring. It was this inheritance in Somerset that put it out of my mind."

Corinne considered this a moment, not quite pleased at his forgetting to do it sooner. "What are we to do about Boisvert's visit to the Clarendon? Are we actually to hire a suite there as Mr. and Mrs. Lucas? He'll smell a rat if we aren't there when he calls."

"I'll drop him a line canceling the sitting. Tell him we were called back to Devonshire in a great hurry. Although actually I wouldn't mind another visit to just check and see that he is making a copy of the Watteau. He might just be cleaning it."

"I think we can assume he's going to make a copy," she said, always ready to suspect the worst of Chamaude, "but I doubt she'll try to palm it off on you. When both you and I expressed interest in it, she realized it has a broad appeal and plans to put it up for sale."

A glinting smile peeped out. "You're probably right. It would be fun to visit the Clarendon incognito as a married couple, though."

"We would be recognized in a minute. So you will let Boisvert know we have changed our minds?"

"I'll leave word for him at the hotel. That will ensure that the studio is empty tomorrow at three. A good chance to slip in and investigate. The back door will probably yield to my passe-partout. As he claimed to be busy, I assume he plans to get to work on the Watteau at once."

"We'll keep our ears on the stretch to discover who buys it. Boisvert seems like such a nice little man," she said, rather sadly. "Of course, he might be perfectly innocent. Chamaude need not tell him why she wants her pictures copied. He is obviously not sharing the profits. His studio is bleak."

"I expect he knows what's afoot. He mentioned moving up to better quarters."

They fell silent for a moment, then Luten said, "Have you seen Pattle and Prance? I wonder what they have on for this evening."

"I haven't see them since this morning. I saw Prance call on Coffen. Lady Birrell is having a small rout. Half the town has gone partridge hunting, of course, but whoever is in town will be there."

"We'll call on them after dinner. I hope you are free for dinner? I've asked my chef to prepare a special *dîner à deux*."

"About time!"

"I've been ignoring you. I'm sorry, darling, but—"

"I know. I don't mind, so long as you let me know what is going on, Mr. Lucas."

"Dinner at eight, Mrs. Lucas. I shall call for you."

"I expect I can find my own way across the street."

He didn't argue, but just repeated, "I shall call for you."

From Coffen's saloon window, Prance and Coffen watched the arrival of Luten and Corinne. They walked hand in hand, laughing in the sunlight. As soon as Luten went home, they called on him. He was tired and worried and in no good humor when he entered his house. He disliked deceiving Corinne, but to tell her the whole would surely throw her into a pelter and precipitate an argument. That Irish temper of hers would lead her to it. He decided a long soak in a warm tub, a shave, and a fresh toilette would do him the world of good. They would have a lovely dinner together and enjoy the party after. If Yvonne sold him the forged Watteau, he'd tell Corinne. The worst would be over then. He wouldn't have to visit Yvonne again.

"If anyone except Lady deCoventry calls, I am out. I don't want to be disturbed," he told his butler, and went upstairs.

Two minutes later, the butler delivered the message to the callers.

"Tell him it is us, Simon," Prance said. "Use your head, man. We'll go up. No need to bring his lordship downstairs."

"His lordship does not wish to be disturbed. He gave specific instructions."

"Well!" Prance snorted. "If that is the way he treats his friends!" He marched stiff-backed from the doorway. "You see how it is, Pattle? He is ashamed to see us. And well he might be. It is clearly your duty to tell Corinne all."

"Nothing of the sort. I'll speak to Luten before I do. Bound to be some explanation."

"We know the explanation. It is not fit for that darling girl's ears."

It came to him on the spot that if Luten was stealing Chamaude from him, he would steal Corinne from Luten. All was fair in love and war, and this present situation was obviously both. He culled a bouquet of flowers from his conservatory, which pretty well decimated the blooms there, and sent it across the street with a suggestive note.

"From a true friend, your faithful servant, Sir Reginald." He underlined the *true* and *faithful*. That would give her something to think about!

Corinne's head was too full of Luten and Chamaude to read any significance between the lines. She sent a note back to Prance. "Thank you, my friend. The flowers are beautiful. Shall we see you at Lady Birrell's this evening? Save me a dance. Love, Corinne."

"At least we know where he's taking her. Birrell's," Prance said to Coffen. He had darted to Pattle's place when he received her reply.

"We'll tackle Luten after the party."

"Yes, let poor Corinne enjoy her last evening with a joyful heart, for tomorrow . . ."

"Dash it, you sound as if she's dying."

Prance drew a deep sigh. "One can die of a broken heart, Pattle. At times, one wishes one could leave this vale of tears."

But as he enjoyed life too much to even consider suicide, he decided that he could take some petty revenge on Luten at the rout party. Drop a few veiled threats that he knew all and watch Luten squirm. Now, what should he wear?

Chapter Thirteen

"He is pulling out all the stops," Prance said over his shoulder to Coffen, as they stood by Coffen's saloon window, watching Luten accompany Corinne across the street to dinner. "Calling for her—he's never done that before. And carrying a bouquet of flowers. Strange how a guilty conscience brings out the best in men's behavior toward their victims. Many a wife owes her diamonds to her husband's mistress."

"If flowers are a sign of guilt, then you're guilty as well. You sent Corinne a bouquet."

"She is not my fiancée. I wager he sent Simon out for those flowers."

"Why wouldn't he? Simon has perfect taste."

"Simon has good taste, Pattle. *I* have perfect taste."

Coffen glanced at Prance's new coiffure and just shook his head. "Keep your jealousy on the chain, lad. You're making a fool of yourself." As Luten's front door closed, Coffen left the window. "I wonder what he's feeding her," he said.

"Compliments, evasions, outright lies, and presumably a sprinkling of kisses to help it all go down are the usual menu in such cases as this."

"Luten ain't like that. You haven't got a case to stand on. A bunch of flowers? Rubbish."

"It's not just the flowers. It is his nature to be sly. He is not a successful politician for no reason."

"I haven't seen any success. The Whigs have been in opposition forever. Anyhow, I meant what is he feeding her for food."

"Of course you did, plebeian."

Coffen sniffed the air. "I believe I catch the whiff of mutton. Time for fork work. Let us go and peck a little."

Prance went on dragging feet to Coffen's dining room, where his slatternly servants had thrown a handful of cutlery on a much-used tablecloth, stuck a few Michaelmas daisies in a glass jug, and called that a table setting. One thing Pattle did insist on, however, was decent wine, and plenty of it. The red burgundy was not what Prance would have served with a raised pigeon pie, or with ham either, but it was mellow on the palate.

"An excellent wine, Pattle," he said, raising his glass in a toast. "I must get the vintner from you. The last burgundy I bought bites like green gooseberries. The bully of the vineyard, I call it."

He toyed with a potato, mashed to anonymity, forming it into a pyramid with his fork, placed a brussels sprout on top, and surrounded the mound with a moat of carrots, while Coffen watched irritably.

"Waste of good food," Coffen said. "It ain't Corinne you're worried about, or Luten's nasty stunt either. It's the fail—the lack of success with your *Rondeaux*, but now that I've gnawed my way a bit deeper into them, I'm coming to think they ain't so bad after all." This was an outright lie but in a good cause.

"I have been bitten by cannibal critics before. It's not my artistic failure that bothers me."

"Then it's that dashed Frenchie. She's no good. Steal the ring from the pope's finger as quick as she'd trot, but if you're so mad for her, why don't you call on her? How can you hope to win her if she never sees you? She don't know you're pining your heart out. Ladies like that in a fellow."

Prance considered this advice and found it good, as Coffen's advice, being based on common sense, often was.

"Yes, why not?" he replied. "Though if Luten has just bought her a house—well, there is no way I can match that."

"You could match him—outdo him—outdo a whole roomful of gossips when it comes to talking. Talk your way into her heart. Turn her up sweet. She'll be on you like a hound on a fox."

"I do have rather a gift for words," Prance allowed. "I'll take her a little something as well, of course. That opal ring surrounded with ruby chips my aunt Ethel gave me."

"I don't know as I'd take her jewelry on the first call."

"With a lady like the comtesse, one takes a token, Pattle. Trust me."

"You make her sound like a dashed light-skirt."

"When one has reached her level of prominence, the more usual word is *courtesan*."

"Means the same thing, don't it?" Coffen asked, spooning in a forkful of the mashed potatoes.

"No, it means about five thousand pounds more per annum."

"Then forget her. You can't afford her."

"That is the very dilemma on whose horns I sit, most uncomfortably. I know she is bad for me. It is a part of her allure, that siren call to my fallen nature. Men have ever hankered after that sort of woman. Bad to the bone. Like Byron. Did you hear what Caro said of him? 'Mad, bad, and dangerous to know.' It might serve as an epitaph for la comtesse."

"Not till she's dead, I hope."

"Such women ofttimes die young."

"She's escaped that anyhow. Nudging forty."

"You will not dissuade me by these paltry objections, Pattle. It is you who has planted the seed of the idea in my head, and I shall call on her tonight, as I assume Luten is taking Corinne to Birrell's. I shall go from Half Moon Street to the rout and shower Luten with barbs."

"Tarsome fellow," Pattle said, and helped himself to another glass of burgundy, then offered the bottle to Prance.

"I shall have another as balm for my emotional bruises."

"To give you courage for your call on Chamaude, you mean."

"That, too."

Across the street, Luten's dinner party progressed more harmoniously. Corinne had often dined with him but seldom tête-à-tête. He had been at pains to arrange a romantic atmosphere with candlelight, wine, and a dinner prepared by his French chef. It was served in the more intimate morning parlor. Two at table in his long dining room designed to seat three dozen would feel like survivors adrift on the Atlantic.

Candlelight flickered on her raven hair and cast shadows on the delicate contours of her face. As the dinner progressed, she felt the worries she had been carrying around since Luten's return melt away, to be replaced by a golden glow of love. She opened like a flower in the sun, forgiving all his little transgressions as they discussed their wedding and honeymoon.

"I thought we might go to Ireland to visit my family," she said. "Since France and so much of Europe are out of the question just now, with Bonaparte on the loose, you know."

"I look forward to meeting your family. We could be married there, if you like. Your sister, Kate, could be part of the wedding party."

"I would love it, but we have so many friends here. Prance, you know, will want to be active in all the arrangements."

"Active? He'll insist on directing the whole show. We may count ourselves fortunate if he and Pattle don't stow away on our honeymoon. We could go to Ireland for our wedding trip."

Corinne smiled fondly. "I have been wanting Kate to meet them. I tell her all about our escapades."

Corinne harbored a secret hope that Coffen would fall in love with Kate, marry her, and bring her to England, before she turned into an old maid.

"Then we must invite Kate to visit us in England, for I do not want that pair on our treacle moon. By the by, did you discover what they are doing tonight?"

"I told Prance where we were going. He sent me a bouquet of flowers from that little greenhouse of his, and I sent him a thank-you note."

"Beating my time, is he?" Luten joked.

"He has given up flirting with me, since I am now engaged. He calls himself my true friend and faithful servant. Is that not charming?"

"He's a good fellow, beneath all the rodomontade. Oh, speaking of rodomontade, the boxes of *Rondeaux* have arrived.

I plan to ship half of them over to your place under cover of darkness tonight. You'll help me dispose of them?"

"Of course. Pity about the *Rondeaux*, he spent so much time on them."

"He should have taken another month and translated them into English. Contemporary English, I mean. All those medieval words—to say nothing of the footnotes."

"And no King Arthur, no Round Table."

"Worse, no Guinevere."

At half past nine, Luten called for his carriage and directed his coachman to deliver them to Lady Birrell's. As soon as Prance saw them leave, he put his aunt Ethel's opal and ruby ring in his pocket and proceeded to Half Moon Street. The Provence roses were still in the rig but too passé to give her. Coffen was to meet him at Birrell's.

Prance was admitted to la comtesse's saloon without being kept waiting. In a high state of agitation, he failed to notice the Watteau was missing from the entrance hall. His heart thrilled to see her looking exactly as he remembered, with those liquid, brooding eyes. She wore black, a low-cut gown to display her impertinent shoulders and the incipient swell of white breasts. No jewelry tonight. How wise of her. Perfection has no need of garnishing. She reclined on a chaise longue in a dim corner with a glass of brandy on the table before her, looking very French, and very seductive. Her pale face seemed to float in a dark sea, like a Rembrandt painting, except that the face was lovely.

She gave him a demure smile with just a Gallic hint of wickedness lurking in it. How did she do it? Was it the gentle lifting of the eyebrows that imbued her welcome with invitation? For a moment he stood silently gazing and feeling barbaric for not cropping out into poetry or song.

"Sir Reginald, how kind of you to call," she said in her charming accent and a voice like Devonshire cream, all rich and soft. She offered him a languid hand.

"How kind of you to receive me, milady," he replied, with an exquisite bow. As he bent over her, he thought he saw a trace of tears on those porcelain cheeks. Her shoulders drooped. The words of Suckling's (dreadful name!) poem flashed through his mind. "Why so pale and wan, fond lover? Prithee, why so pale?" Was it Luten she yearned for? "I came to call this afternoon and just missed you by inches," he said, looking about for a seat.

"Ah *oui,* I was out. A friend took pity on me and took me for a drive in the country. I trust Mr. Pattle is happy with his Poussin?"

Prance did not wish to discuss the Poussin. He said nothing about Pattle's mysterious caller the night before. "Delighted! The only dissatisfaction in it is that it reminds one of your financial difficulties."

Her dark eyes moved lingeringly over her caller. A very large diamond in his cravat, a jacket by the vastly expensive tailor Weston, of Bond Street. Everything about him smelled of money. And the "Sir," she had discovered, indicated a baronet, not just a knight.

"You are too kind to worry about me," she said. "I am surprised a handsome young bachelor like you is not out at some do or other."

"There is nowhere I would rather be than here, no one with whom I would rather be than you, Yvonne. May I call you so?"

She neither agreed nor objected verbally, but when she fluttered her long lashes at him and patted the edge of the chaise longue, he took it for permission. He went forward and lowered himself gracefully to the floor, not at her feet, but nearer her head. She put out her hand to him, and he raised it to his lips. He felt he was approaching the portals of paradise as his lips caressed her velvet fingers, perfumed with attar of roses. The third finger looked about the right size for the opal and ruby ring. He noticed the wedding ring had been abandoned.

Then she destroyed the mood by saying, "Where is your friend Luten tonight?" That was gauche of her!

"Out with his fiancée, Lady deCoventry," Prance said, trying to conceal his irritation. There was considerable satisfaction in his tone.

Let us see how she reacted to that stunning news. She obviously wasn't aware that Luten was engaged. He felt the white hand he was holding stiffen, heard a quiet little gasp. Then her dainty fingers tightened convulsively on his.

"Of course. Foolish of me to ask," she said in a nearly normal voice. That would be the actress in her. He peered up to judge her expression. She leaned toward him, gazed into his eyes, and said in a voice of satin seduction, "Lovers should be together at night, *n'est-ce pas?*" Then without further ado, she tilted back her head, closed her eyes, and offered him her lips.

The wayward animal in him gave a leap. He seized her lips in a frenzy of rapturous disbelief. For a long moment their lips clung without any other part of their bodies touching. A poignant moment, and the best part of the embrace in Prance's view. When she opened her lips to him, he drew her into his arms and squeezed gently. The openmouthed kiss was not the disgusting suction of a giant leech attacking him but a gentle, sensuous mating of liquid tongues. He tasted the echo of fine brandy on hers. It was a sublime kiss, the sort of kiss to instigate wars and legends. Helen of Troy and Paris might have kissed like this.

When she stopped kissing him, she lifted a silver hand bell by the chaise longue and gave it a tinkle. The boulevardier-butler appeared at the door. "We do not wish to be disturbed, Lalonde," she said, without ever removing her eyes from Prance. The butler directed a knowing look at Prance, bowed, and closed the door as he left.

"Now, where were we?" she asked with a coquettish smile. Her white fingers moved with languid grace to unbutton his waistcoat. There was no effect of rushing it, but before you could say Jack Robinson, she had it off, and her own gown as well, while Prance removed his trousers. He could not quite keep pace with her. He had to leave his shirt, unbuttoned, on his back as he proceeded to the carnal core of the business. Twice. The woman was a genius in the *ars amatoria*. Her fingers slithered like tiny, willful snakes over every part of his quivering body. Her tongue licked at him like liquid flame, igniting him to unsuspected, nay, unimagined, heights of delightful depravity. He felt a deep and profound pity for every man who was not he.

When she was through with him, Prance was as limp as a dishrag. He had not imagined himself capable of such impassioned surrender to all sense of decorum. The grunts and groans did not sound like him—or her. More like a couple of wildcats. He thought of the little ring in his pocket and knew it was not enough reward for the beneficence he had just received. Her weight in diamonds was more like it!

"You had best go now, Reggie," she said, in that soft French voice. Not Reggie, but more like Rezhie, with the accent on the last syllable. He had never thought Reginald suited him, but pronounced in that foreign way, it sounded exotic, like the name of one of Byron's amorous pashas.

"When may I return?" he asked.

"Whenever you wish to see me again," she said. "Just send me a little note first, in case . . . Oh, I plan to be rid of Yarrow. He has deceived me, Rezhie," she said, and gave an agonized little hiccup of a sob. When she resumed speech, her voice had a tremolo. "You have no idea! Most men are wicked deceivers. Of course, I don't mean *you*!"

He felt this was a slur on Luten, and his heart swelled in triumph. "I am not most men," he said, knowing it sounded pompous and foolish. But then a little folly was forgivable between lovers.

"Ah no, you are sweet," she assured him.

Sweet? He felt the compliment was grossly inadequate. He was eager to be off. Much as he loved Yvonne, his baser nature craved to see Luten and fling in his face where he had been and what he had been doing.

"I shall be free tomorrow afternoon," she said, looking an invitation at him.

"What time may I come?"

"After three, I think. This suits you?"

"*Pas du tout.* So many empty hours will seem an eternity, but I must do your bidding. At three I shall be here, begging an audience."

She smiled and stroked his cheek with her wanton fingers. How he burned at her touch! "You are too absurd," she cooed.

Reg hated to dress without his valet to assist him. Especially he disliked having to scramble into his clothes in front of the goddess, who did not bother to resume her gown but just drew a throw over her nakedness. Even in this dim light, the mirror told him his shirt and cravat were a disgrace. His face looked ravaged by exertion, though his tousled hair looked rather dashing. He would have to go home and make a fresh toilette before going to Birrell's.

"Do you think me horrid?" she asked, drawing her bottom lip between her white teeth and looking like an adorable child who has been caught with her fingers full of sugarplums. "To give myself to you so easily . . ."

"I think you are a sorceress," he said. Also a mind reader, for it had occurred to him that it had been a pretty easy capitulation. More of an attack than a giving way to persuasion actually.

"It is just that one gets so lonesome, and you—I felt a certain something—a frisson of recognition the moment I saw you. Was it only two days ago?"

"I felt the same," he said, and glanced at the clock. Eleven o'clock already? *"A demain."* He reached down to place a chaste kiss on her damask cheek. Her cheek was cool. How was it possible? His whole body was aflame from remembered passion.

He noticed, on his way out, that the Watteau in the hall had been replaced by an inferior landscape. This suggested that Yvonne was in dire need of funds. How much could he afford to give her? If he didn't throw one of his extravagant parties for Luten and Corinne's engagement, he could give her a thousand pounds. And there was that diamond necklace his mama had left him that was not entailed. The irony of commerce intruding on this moment of infatuation was not lost on him. It would find its way into the poem on the French Revolution.

It was well after eleven when he finally reached Birrell's rout. He gazed across the room and saw Luten smiling down at Corinne, and she smiling back at him, besotted. She had been redecorating herself. What had she done to her hair? And why did she wear a pearl comb in it when she was wearing her diamonds? Yvonne could teach her something about dressing. Not that Luten seemed to notice anything amiss in her toilette.

He would soon wipe that smile from Luten's phiz! He straightened his shoulders and went forth to do battle, in the name of love.

Chapter Fourteen

Prance went swanning across the busy ballroom, bowing to friends and acquaintances. "Charming, Lady Honoria," he said to the youngest daughter of the Duke of Cheam, who looked particularly ugly that evening in a puce gown that ill became both her sluggish complexion and her years. She had apparently not heard his decree that only ladies over seventy with snow-white hair ought to be allowed to wear that overpowering shade of red. He continued on to Luten and Corinne, where he made a graceful bow.

"Corinne, the belle of the ball, as usual. Lovely party."

As the party was far from a squeeze, and in fact very few of their friends were present, Corinne realized his euphoria had some other cause than the company.

"You are in high feather this evening, Prance," she said. "Do I smell a romance between you and Lady Honoria?"

Prance rolled his eyes ceilingward. "Please! I thought you knew my standards better than that. No, I prefer *older* ladies this season. Autumn is the time for a more *mature* lady. Someone who knows all the ways of love."

"Who is she?" Luten inquired. "Not Lord Halley's wife, I trust? He called out young Franklin last week."

"It is bound to happen when a gentleman is so unwise as to go falling in love with his wife," Prance said airily. He shot a keen glance at Luten and added, "But then I need not warn you of that, eh, Luten?"

"The warning comes too late for me, I fear."

Prance gave him a deprecatory smile, then glanced sadly at Corinne and shook his head. "No, it is not Halley's charming lady. Blondes have no appeal to me at the moment. It is a widow, so I need not fear her *mari* will challenge me, though I am not sure about her other lovers." He trusted that French word would alert Luten as to the lady's identity.

If Luten understood the hint, he gave no indication of it. It was Corinne, with her sharp feminine intuition and her interest in the comtesse, who leapt on the truth.

"Reggie! You are not seeing Chamaude!"

He pokered up. "Have you something against the lady?" he asked.

"Oh, you don't know what we discovered this afternoon. Tell him, Luten."

Luten was too suave to glower, but he shot Prance an icy stare from his cold gray eyes. "Perhaps this had best be discussed in private," he suggested.

"The library," Prance said. "It's bound to be empty. No one reads in this house."

Excitement caused unaccustomed flags of red to bloom on his sallow cheeks as he led the others to the library. Coffen spotted the group and went hastening after them, catching them up just as they reached the sofa.

"How'd it go with Chamaude, Prance?" he asked, in no soft voice.

"Your advice was sound, Pattle. It went—" He kissed two fingers to his lips. "Exquisitely. Perfection!"

"So it *is* Chamaude!" Corinne said.

"Indeed she is my new mistress. You may congratulate me that she chose me over other contenders." A smirk decorated his lips as he looked at Luten. Luten stood impassive, not revealing by so much as a blink that he wanted to knock Prance to the floor and kick him. "Of course, I have the advantage of being a bachelor, not entangled with any other lady at the moment."

The "bachelor" might be a dig at Yarrow, but that telling "not entangled with any other lady" suggested to Corinne that Yarrow was not who he meant. The sly way he was looking at Luten, too, sent shivers up her spine. What did Prance know?

"You wasn't there long," Coffen said. "Hardly seems long

enough to be talking her up as your mistress. Liked the opal ring, did she?"

"I didn't give it to her. It proved an unworthy reward for her—" he gave a leering smirk "—shall we say, generosity? As to time, it is not quantity but quality that counts in a special relationship of this sort. You are well experienced in that line, Luten. Would you not agree it is quality that matters?"

Luten said, "It has been my experience that it takes time to develop quality in relationships between men and women. Eh, Corinne?" he added with a smile. "It took us three years."

"Seven, if you count the time Corinne was married to deCoventry," Coffen said. "Not that I mean you was carrying on behind—heh heh. You've known her for seven years is all I mean."

"The comtesse and I moved more swiftly," Prance said. "Especially the comtesse. Those *Sturm und Drang* eyes fulfilled every promise."

"In just over an hour?" Coffen asked.

"It will astonish you that love can develop so quickly, Pattle. I wonder if it really surprises Luten. Was Yvonne always so impetuous, Luten?"

"I believe she had that reputation. Ladies' natures are like leopards' spots. They do not change. And now if you have finished hinting to my fiancée that Yvonne was once my mistress, which she was not, we have more important matters to discuss."

Prance adopted a moue. "I see the fact that I have fallen in love for the first time is not considered worth discussing."

"You can't love her, Reg. She's a criminal," Corinne said. "That is what we wanted to discuss with you. Luten expressed interest in the Watteau hanging in her hall. Well, she had her footman trot it straight off to Boisvert to be copied."

"She'd never try to sell Luten a forgery."

"I know, we have been talking about that. We think she plans to sell Luten the original and sell someone else the copy, probably someone from out of town, who will never know the difference and never hear that Luten has the same painting."

"Perhaps she just wants the copy for herself," Prance said at once. "No harm in that."

Corinne looked at Luten. "Perhaps that's it," she said.

As Luten had not confessed he had seen the comtesse and invented a country friend, he could only shrug, as if accepting this notion.

"About my Poosan," Coffen said, scratching his ear. "I wonder if she sent me the copy by mistake, then had her friend make the switch. Still, I don't see why she wouldn't have told me. Who's this Boisvert anyhow?"

"An artist in Shepherd's Market," Corinne said. "Luten and I went there this afternoon." She told them of the plan to search the shop while Boisvert was at the Clarendon Hotel the next afternoon.

Coffen said, "I wonder if he made any more copies of my Poosan for Chamaude to peddle. A hundred years from now when it's worth something, I might have a spot of trouble proving I have the real one."

"Will you really care, a hundred years from now?" Prance inquired.

"No, but my son might. Or my grandson. Or would it be my great-grandson?" He began counting off the generations on his fingers. "Great-grandson, I think."

Prance was still stinging from the short shrift his fabulous announcement had been given. To retaliate, he said to Luten, "Oh, by the way, Luten, did Pattle tell you the house on Grosvenor Square has been sold? The one Yvonne was thinking of buying. I drove by this afternoon and saw . . . er, a couple looking at it. Then later Pattle and I returned, and it was sold—to a melord, the agent said. He was just removing the sign."

Corinne had been reassured when Luten announced categorically that Yvonne had never been his mistress. Her suspicions came galloping back at the sly way Reggie was looking at Luten. The clenching of Luten's jaws told her the gibe had hit home, too.

Luten looked daggers at Prance. "That suggests Yarrow,

does it not?" he said. "You have stiff competition for the lady's affections, Prance. Take care or she'll beggar you."

"Oh, she is finished with Yarrow. She told me so this evening. He has deceived her, she said." Then he added with another of those piercing looks, "No doubt that is why she is on the *qui vive* for a new patron. But I believe she has become disenchanted with unfaithful melords and has decided to put herself under my protection instead."

"Why did you decide to call on her this evening?" Luten asked, reining in his temper.

"It was my idea," Coffen said. "Mean to say, he was pining away for her. Fast sinking into one of his dashed declines. Seemed worth a try, before he had his door knocker muffled and straw laid in the street."

"Well worth it!" Prance said. "I shall never be able to thank you, Pattle. And now that we have discovered the reason Yvonne is having the Watteau copied, shall we return to the ballroom? You and I have not had a dance, Corinne."

He sensed Luten's irritation with this. Before leading her away, he murmured softly to Luten, "Don't worry, I shan't reveal your nasty little secrets."

Luten went on nettles to the ballroom, where he watched Corinne like a hawk while she performed the cotillion, trying to judge by her expression what Prance was saying to her. Coffen, who was not much of a dancer, accompanied him during his vigil.

"Hope I didn't do wrong by sending Prance off to call on the comtesse," he said in a rather apologetic way.

"She'll eat him alive. I think you and Prance and I had best have a talk this evening. I haven't told you the whole of what is involved."

"I haven't told you everything either. Prance saw you and Chamaude at that house on Grosvenor Square this afternoon. Have to tell you, Luten, if you're setting her up as your mistress, I don't mean to let you marry Corinne. Ain't right. I'm her cousin. Someone has to look out for her interests. Besides, Prance would never let you get away with it. He's straining at the leash to tell her everything."

"I know it," Luten said. He didn't think Prance had told her yet, however. At just that moment, she looked across the room and smiled at him. His heart swelled, then clenched in fear that he was going to lose her—and over a French whore who had been too forthcoming and obvious for him ten years ago. With another decade of experience and maturity under his belt, he despised her. "I didn't buy her the demmed house! I suspect it was Yarrow."

"Said she's through with him. She'd hardly ditch him if he'd just bought her a house. Of course, she could be lying a blue streak. Talking don't butter no parsnips. Thing to do, keep an eye on Half Moon Street. See if Yarrow is still calling on her. But about Chamaude . . ." He leveled a piercing blue eye on his friend. "You did drive out with her this afternoon in your hunting rig. To a country inn."

Luten gave a jump of alarm. "Did you tell Corinne?"

Coffen snorted. "Is the pope Protestant?"

"You mean Catholic."

"Nothing of the sort. I mean no, I didn't tell her."

"Thank God for that." He took a deep breath to settle his nerves. "I see you spent your afternoon spying on me!"

"Not me, just Prance. Mind I don't say I wouldn't have spied if I'd caught you dead to rights smuggling her into your rig."

"I could hardly drive her to Hyde Park."

"Why'd you have to drive with her at all? Asking for trouble."

"Because I didn't want to be at her mercy in that brothel on Half Moon Street."

"So you put yourself at her mercy at a country inn instead? Don't see much difference myself."

"Yarrow was not likely to find us together at a country inn. We had tea, Pattle, and nothing else except talk. I wonder if Prance has thrown a spanner in the works by telling her I'm engaged."

Coffen's blue eyes narrowed to slits. "Why shouldn't he?"

"Because Yvonne will be more revealing if she thinks I'm interested in offering her a carte blanche."

"Don't see why she can't reveal whatever it is you want to know to Prance as well as you."

"Prance is besotted. This calls for a clear mind."

"What are you trying to find out anyhow?"

"How she was involved in the contract to Gresham for the rockets."

"You think she sweet-talked Yarrow into voting for Gresham, then dumped him?"

"I shouldn't be at all surprised. And there's damn-all Yarrow can do about it."

Coffen thought it all over for a moment, then said, "Don't see why he'd go buying her a house if that's the way the land lays. You figure she's holding him to ransom?"

"Yarrow is too cunning for that. He wouldn't have written anything incriminating. The house was probably sold to some melord who wants a house on Grosvenor Square."

"We ought to look into it."

"I am."

"Don't see why you've left the rest of us out of all your doings, Luten. We always worked together before. Because of Corinne, is it?"

"I was afraid you might inadvertently let something slip—or Prance would make hay of it. Corinne wouldn't understand."

"She'd never sit still for your making up to Chamaude, if that's what you mean. Nor would I. If I was a lady, I mean. Ain't there any other way you could go about it?"

"If I could think of any other way, I wouldn't be seeing Yvonne."

"Been throwing herself at *you* as well, has she?"

"She has let me know she's available."

"A dangerous thing in a woman. Well, I'll not tell Corinne what you're up to, but you'd best get it all settled dashed soon, for Corinne has her eye out for trouble where Chamaude is concerned. She was looking sharp as a fox when Reg was dropping all them hints."

"I know it."

At the end of the set, Corinne was still smiling at her fiancé.

"Shall we all retire to the refreshment parlor for wine—or

whatever Lady Birrell is serving?" Prance suggested, clamping his hand on Corinne's elbow. "With this company, I shouldn't be surprised if it's orgeat and punch."

"You go ahead, Reg," Coffen said, and lifted his hand from Corinne's elbow. "I'll stand up and jig it with Corinne."

As he led her off, he gave a wink over his shoulder at Luten, as if to say, "Have no fear. I am a perfect oyster. She'll get nothing out of me."

Luten led Prance back to the library, where he had a conversation similar to that he had just had with Coffen.

"Do I have your word as a gentleman that you're not interested in becoming Yvonne's patron?" Prance asked, when all had been revealed.

"I am offended that you ask, Prance, but you have."

"I am glad you said that, my dear Luten—about being offended, I mean. Otherwise I would have had difficulty believing you. I think you are undertaking a perilous course. Yvonne will have her way with you if you continue seeing her."

"The last I heard, it takes two to make love."

"Not when Yvonne is one of the partners. She has the stamina and lust of two," Prance said, with a dreamy look in his eyes. "And so had I. We made love twice. I amazed myself that I was up to it." He sighed. "At long last, lust."

"I am not interested in the details of your conquests. She also has the wits of two. Take care she doesn't fleece you."

"I shouldn't think it likely," he said with a little disillusioned sigh. "She has lost some of her attraction since I know you are not interested in her."

"There is not much point in my seeing her again since you've told her I'm engaged. She'll suspect I'm up to something. If this forged Watteau business works out, I'll have something to hold over her head to get at the truth of the Gresham business."

"That was naughty of me to tell her," Prance said. "I apologize for my pettiness earlier this evening, Luten, but when I thought you were double-dealing with Corinne, my chivalrous instincts were abominably riled. We are all so fond of her, you know. She's like a . . . er, sister to me." He smiled provocatively.

Luten felt again the urge to box his ears but decided it was wiser to let the tentative peace continue. Prance in a pique was a dangerous animal.

Chapter Fifteen

"So it's official, then," Coffen said to Luten the next morning. "Your secretary says it was Yarrow who bought the house on Grosvenor Square. Looks like Chamaude is lying about being through with him."

Coffen, determined not to be left out of the case entirely, had dropped in to learn Luten's plans for the day. They sat in the morning parlor, where a shaft of sunlight from the eastern window set the oak walls aglow. Delicious aromas of gammon and eggs and toast wafted from the covered dishes on the warming board to set Coffen's mouth watering. His breakfast had consisted of toast (which had fallen in the grate and was served with ashes), some plum preserves that had begun to turn to liqueur, and the last cup of coffee in the pot, served without cream. His cook liked to drink coffee well creamed and sugared while he cooked.

In Luten's breakfast parlor, silverware and glass twinkled, and the dishes shone. It was a sad commentary on the laxity prevailing in his own household, where the only thing that shone was the seat of his servants' trousers.

"My secretary spoke to the estate agent. The story he tells is that the house is for Lady Yarrow's widowed sister," Luten replied, and dipped his fork into one of a pair of fried eggs. A trickle of yolk just on the verge of hardening oozed out from the white. Coffen could nearly taste it.

"Yarrow would hardly tell the agent it was for his mistress."

"I don't believe it was. Lady Yarrow helped him pick it out and went with him to examine it. He'd hardly let her do that if he meant to set Yvonne up there." He lifted a triangle of golden toast and bit into it.

"I thought his wife was an invalid."

"Invalidish, but not bedridden. More a case of not wanting to bother much with Society. She goes out occasionally, even with her husband." He set the toast back down on his plate. Melted butter was soaked into it.

"You sure it's the same house Chamaude wanted to buy?"

"She took me to show it to me. She was astonished to see the sold sign on it. She had no idea it was Yarrow who had bought it." He lifted his knife and spread some strawberry jam on another triangle of toast.

"I wonder why he did, if it ain't for jam—Chamaude."

"Can I offer you some breakfast, Pattle? I thought you had already eaten. Remiss of me."

Coffen was up from the table and at the sideboard so fast he nearly upset his chair. "Thankee, don't mind if I do. I only pecked a nibble of charred bread."

He returned to his place with a well-laden plate and tucked into his gammon and eggs.

"We were discussing why Yarrow had bought the house, if not for Chamaude," Luten said. "Spite, perhaps, when Yvonne cooled on him."

"It sounds like him. A spiteful fellow, from what I hear. These are grand eggs, Luten. My compliments to your chef. Chamaude took on her match when she tangled with him—Yarrow, I mean."

"He was necessary earlier on to authenticate her paintings," Luten explained. "Selling some of them to Prinney established her as a provider of genuine goods."

"When you're at Boisvert's place this afternoon, take a peek around and see if he's got any more of my Poosans, will you?" He poured himself a cup of coffee and added a liberal helping of cream and sugar.

"I shouldn't think it likely, but I'll look. What are you and Prance up to today?"

"Prance is meeting Chamaude at three, he tells me."

"Excellent. That will take care of her while Corinne and I search the studio."

"I could go along with you. Mean to say, not much chance of getting caught with Boisvert and Chamaude both busy."

Luten would have preferred being alone with Corinne, but he was indebted to Coffen and felt obliged to let him tag along. "Very well," he said, and passed the strawberry preserves.

"Thankee, don't mind if I do. Did you do anything about watching Half Moon Street?"

"Winkle is there."

"It might look suspicious, him losing that wheel two days in a row."

"He took Limpy and hired a rig from Newman's Stable."

"Ah, that nag you got from Astley's Circus that knows how to fake a limp. I wondered when you bought it what you wanted it for. I thought you was playing a joke on someone."

"One never knows when a lame nag will come in handy. I ride Limpy occasionally when I am forced to take visiting relatives to Rotten Row. It shortens the outing amazingly. Limpy also makes a good excuse to dally about when I want someone watched."

"What time are we leaving this afternoon? Two-thirtyish?"

"Thereabouts."

"What are you doing this morning?" Coffen asked, and lifted a succulent piece of bacon into his waiting mouth. Delicious!

"Driving with Corinne. She wants to see the house on Grosvenor Square."

"Why?"

"I don't know. Feminine curiosity, perhaps. I'm curious myself to see who moves in. We'll just drive by."

"I'll stop in and see what Prance is up to. Try to talk him out of giving Chamaude his mama's diamond necklace. Feel bad about siccing him on to her. Never really thought she'd give him the time of day. Or night."

"Twice," Luten said, a smile quirking his lips.

Coffen shook his head. "Didn't think she'd settle for anything less than a baron. Mean to say, Yarrow's a marquess. It would be the sausage fingers that put her off. Of course, she's not as young and pretty as she used to be."

He noticed that Luten had set down his empty cup and put aside his serviette. "Are you waiting for me to finish? Don't mind me, Luten. You just go ahead with whatever you have to. I'll have another bite of that bacon."

"Make yourself at home. I have a few things to do before I call on Corinne."

He left, and Coffen settled in for his third breakfast.

Luten and Corinne were soon off. She was in good humor with him that morning. He was spending more time with her. And as Chamaude had become Prance's mistress, she had no fears of rivalry for Luten's affections. She did have some qualms for Reggie's welfare. He was prone to wild enthusiasms that were usually short-lived. His great romance would soon peter out, but in the interim, they must make sure he didn't squander his entire patrimony on the hussy.

"Coffen is coming with us this afternoon," Luten told her, as the carriage wended its way northward toward Grosvenor Square, through streets that were uniformly beautiful, with white-pillared brick houses rising impressively behind iron fences. Servants bustled about, polishing brass door knockers and windows. A few nannies pushed their charges in carriages, taking advantage of the fine weather. "I hope you don't mind?"

She had looked forward to being alone with Luten, but somehow, one never minded Coffen. "Prance, too?"

"He is seeing the comtesse at three."

"I wish you will caution him about spending a fortune on her."

"I have warned him. A word from you—his faithful friend—might be more effective."

"I'll have a word with him after we have all completed our afternoon business. He and Coffen were to attend Drury Lane with us this evening. I wonder if Prance will beg off."

"As long as he doesn't invite Yvonne to join us—"

She looked at him in alarm, fast turning to consternation. "Surely he wouldn't!"

"One never knows, with Prance. He enjoys to shock Society

from time to time, and she is not a complete social pariah. She does attend a respectable ball now and then. But no, I doubt he'd go so far as to bring her along when you are present. There's the house," he said, pointing it out. There was no sign of life, just the smallish brown brick house with curtainless windows, looking insignificant beside its grander neighbors.

"Shall we drive to Bond Street?" he suggested, knowing she liked to stroll along that busy thoroughfare, looking at the shop windows.

"Yes, let's. I have asked Black to begin burning the *Rondeaux*," she said, smiling at Luten's kindness in buying a hundred copies.

"Simon is handling the conflagration for me. He started the minute he arose this morning and had got through a dozen before I left."

"They burn slowly, don't they? Mrs. Ballard and I had the devil of a time getting them to burn at all. We had Black build a good fire with logs first and pitched half a dozen books on top."

"And after all our efforts, Prance seems to have lost interest in his *Rondeaux*," Luten said.

"He has found a new enthusiasm. He is the sort who must have something to boast about, and the *Rondeaux*, unfortunately, are no boasting matter."

They drove to Bond Street, where they went on the strut, enjoying the warm autumn sunshine and the bustling throng of polite London. Dandies in glossy curled beavers, tight-fitting blue jackets, and buckskins, their Hessians gleaming; ladies in poke bonnets of all heights, many ornamented with fruit to celebrate the harvest season. A sprinkling of red and gold uniforms darted in and out of doors—postmen making their appointed rounds. The grander scarlet regimentals and black shakos of army officers strutted at a prouder gait. A few urchins in rags darted to and fro, hoping to win the honor (and tuppence) of holding a buck's reins while he alit for a moment to greet a friend. One lone black-robed priest hurried by, looking out of place amidst the gaiety.

A steady stream of equipages clattered over the cobblestone

paving. Stylish landaus and capacious barouches, each with its coachman and some with liveried footmen riding postern, tilburies, phaeton high flyers with towering wheels, bucks in yellow varnished curricles, and more sedate passengers in closed carriages, both with and without a noble crest on the panel. Carriage horses bucked and shied as a pair of Corinthians streaked past mounted on glossy blood nags, their manes flying in the wind. The riders bent tensely over their nags' necks were obviously taking part in a race. Their anxious, determined faces suggested a high stake. It might even be the man's entire fortune or estate that was at risk. The bucks were mad gamblers.

The air carried that undefinable aroma of the city. Here the milder country smells of leaves and earth gave way to urbanization. Oil from carriage wheels and smoke from chimneys and stoves blended with whiffs of perfume and men's toilet water as pedestrians brushed shoulders. Food smells were adrift too: tempting coffee, the yeasty delight of freshly baked bread—and beneath it all, the unmistakable stench of horse.

After seven years, London still held a fascination for Corinne. She enjoyed stopping to exchange a few pleasantries with friends, and of course, examining the shop wares. She had written home to Kate that one could buy anything in London, and she was not far wrong. Fine food from all corners of the kingdom was available: ham and cheese, fresh butter and milk and eggs, bread, fruit and vegetables, fish and mutton. There were also spices from the East, sherry from Spain, smuggled brandy and silks from France, muslins from India, furs from Canada and Russia. It was like a giant, civilized bazaar, for all the goods were displayed in tidy shops, each with its hanging shingle, or more recently its name and product emblazoned in gilt over the storefront.

"I'd like to buy you an engagement present," Luten said. He had been watching her to see what excited her interest. "I wish I had stopped at the abbey to get the Luten engagement ring out of the vault. Let me buy you something. Emerald eardrops, to match your eyes?" he suggested.

"You're becoming maudlin, Luten," she said, but she was

pleased with his new sentimentality. "You once informed me that my eyes were nothing like emeralds but closer to the inferior peridot. Buy me peridot eardrops, if you want to give me something."

"You have an excellent memory for an insult, madam. You once called me an egregious ass, but I have long since forgotten it."

"So I see."

"The trouble with ladies nowadays is that they don't know how to take a compliment," he scolded.

"Perhaps it is for lack of receiving them," she retorted.

"Have they not heard of compliments in Ireland?"

"Indeed we have, and if you had told me I trotted over the bog with the lightest toe in the country, I would have known just how to smile and simper my thanks."

He was happy to see they were back on their usual footing of friendly argument. "A high standard of coquetry to keep up with."

"You English lack the silver tongue of my countrymen. We blame it on those silver spoons you are born with in your mouths. They cripple the tongue forever."

"What we require is liberal lacings of poteen to free it. Unfortunately, we prefer to lead some part of our lives in sobriety."

"Pity."

He spotted a tea service in a shop window. It was snowy white and scattered with shamrocks. Without a word, Luten drew her into the shop and bought it, to be sent to her house on Berkeley Square.

"You will remember to make the tea so strong a mouse can tiptoe across the surface," he informed her, when she thanked him very prettily. "The way you used to serve it when you first came to England."

Corinne noticed he never said, "When you were married to deCoventry." Did he dislike the notion so much? "Yes, I have drowned several mice since making it the way you like it," she said.

Luten gave her a disparaging look. "Appetizing!"

* * *

As soon as Coffen finished his breakfast, he went across the street for a word with Prance, who was seated in his study, perusing the morning journals.

"Did Luten talk to you last night?" Coffen asked.

"Yes, he told me why he was seeing Yvonne. I am vastly relieved, especially since he no longer plans to visit her. Mea culpa, I fear. I told her of his engagement."

"Just as well. I'm going with them to Boisvert's place this afternoon." He looked into the cold grate. "I see you haven't got your fire going yet."

"It is warm today."

"Noticed smoke coming from Luten's chimbley. Corinne's as well. Not the kitchen chimbleys."

"Chimney, Pattle. Chimney."

"Eh?"

"Your pronunciation is execrable. You speak like an ostler."

"There's nothing wrong with my pronounciation."

"Q.E.D."

"Eh?"

Prance tossed his white hands into the air. "*Quod erat demonstrandum.*"

Fearing this strange tongue was a forerunner to the *Rondeaux*, Coffen quickly returned to his subject. "The odd thing is, I was at Luten's earlier on. The grate in his breakfast parlor wasn't lit. Nor the saloon."

"He's had Simon light a fire in his boudoir. Luten likes his creature comforts."

"That must be it. Odd, though, this time of year."

"It gets chilly at night," Prance said.

"That's because you open your bedroom windows. I wouldn't if I was you."

"If I ever become you, I shall bear that in mind."

Coffen frowned, but could make nothing of this statement. "You mean if I ever become you."

"That's what I said."

"No, but when *you* say it—"

"Oh, never mind."

"Right, demmed foolishness. I'll never be you. I haven't the stamina for it. Let us go on the strut."

Prance set aside the journal and rose. "Yes, I must buy a little *quelque chose* for Yvonne. A diamond bracelet, I believe, is the customary token for the first favor."

"I'll go with you to see you don't get carried away."

"A wise precaution. When I relive last night, as I do—constantly—I feel I ought to send her a bushel of diamonds. She was sublime, Coffen. We mated like tigers. Twice."

"It might be best to keep that sort of thing to yourself, Prance."

"Oh, but you must let me boast a little. I have never had this sort of purely physical relationship before. I now comprehend the power of lust. I find it has much to recommend it. It jars me out of my usual emotional turpitude. I am an intellectual at heart, you know. And I owe this new vista to you."

Coffen frowned, wishing he had never suggested that visit. "What you ought to buy is a chair and a whip for when you call on her. That's what they use for tigers, I believe."

"Only when one wishes to tame them," Prance said coyly. "I do not."

"Behave yourself, Prance. You're talking like a lecher."

He uttered a long, luxurious sigh. "Soon I shall be behaving like one."

"Tarsome fellow."

Chapter Sixteen

"I'm worried about Prance's fondness for that hussy," Coffen said to Corinne. He had called on her for a consultation before they went to Boisvert's. "I'd give the skin off my back to help him, but there's no getting any sense out of him. As well try to get an oink from a hen. You ought to see the bracelet he bought her this morning. Paved with diamonds, with a big black one in the middle, to match her eyes. You'd think a dirty diamond would be cheap, but it ain't. It cost more than a real one."

"It is real, Coffen. Colored diamonds are rare; that's why they cost more."

"I thought it was pretty ugly myself. It might be enough to turn her off, but there's no counting on it. What we could do is tell him about her stunt with the *Rondeaux*, giving the book he gave her to Marchant."

"It was an honest mistake. Marchant picked it up in error. Reg would have noticed if she didn't have her copy in her saloon."

"He'd never notice if she had an elephant in her saloon. Too busy fighting the tiger off. Not that he does fight her. He says she jumped on him like a dog on a bone. The minute he sat down, she was all over him. Says she makes love like a tiger." He shook his head in disgust. "French."

Corinne had a moment's anxiety about Luten's former acquaintance with Chamaude. How long had he been friends with her? If it had been more than a week, then they had certainly made love. She doubted that her own expertise in that area could match the tigerish efforts of Chamaude. When he said Yvonne had not been his mistress, that didn't necessarily mean he had never made love with her. Corinne knew he had had mistresses in the past. One could hardly expect a bachelor of thirty years to be chaste. She didn't mind the others; she knew they were history. It was only the beautiful Lady Chamaude who got under her skin in this unsettling way.

The trouble was, she didn't really feel she deserved Luten. Until coming to London, she had never met anyone remotely like him. So debonair, intelligent, handsome—and a rich marquess besides. It had been understandable that deCoventry should want her. He had been three times her age, but that such an eligible bachelor as Luten should offer for her still seemed like a fairy tale. Half the ladies in London were throwing their bonnets at him. Her dowry was insignificant compared to his fortune, and she was a widow of twenty-four years besides. Gentlemen usually preferred well-dowered debs.

"Let us hope Luten can prove she's a criminal," she said. "I believe Prance is too fastidious to consort with a known felon."

"And anyhow, she'll be locked up. He'd never go to Bridewell for his courting." He looked into the grate and noticed no fire was laid. "No fire, eh?" he said.

"On such a warm day as this? No, are you chilly?"

"Can't say I am. Just wondering about that smoke coming out of your chimbley this morning. Luten's as well."

"That was in my bedchamber. It was chilly."

"Have you got damp in your attics?"

She hesitated just an instant before replying. "Yes. I should have the roof looked at, I expect."

"I mind deCoventry saying it was a new roof when he bought you this place a few years ago."

"Newish. Shall we go?"

"I'll be driving my own rig, in case you two want to do something else after. Don't mean to make a pest of myself at this time, when you two want to be alone. Together, I mean."

She saw Coffen's plain black carriage standing in the road. Luten's carriage had not been brought around yet, but she hustled Coffen out the door to distract him as he kept frowning at her grate. He was like a bulldog when something was bothering him. They waited at Luten's house until his hunting carriage arrived. Coffen employed the time by looking across the street to examine her roof with his forehead corrugated in confusion.

"That what you're driving?" Coffen asked.

"In case anyone is watching," Luten explained. "One plain black carriage is much like another. We'll get out at the corner of Curzon and walk the last bit. You'll follow us, Pattle?"

Coffen's coachman, like the rest of his servants, was incompetent. He had been known to get lost going around the block.

"I'll not let Fitz lose you. Follow that carriage, Fitz," he ordered.

Luten's groom set a leisurely pace. Fitz managed to keep sight of the rig as they drove through the polite West End. The passengers dismounted at Curzon Street, walked around the corner and on to Shepherd's Market. As Boisvert's studio was on the corner, they just slipped into the alley leading to the back door without attracting any attention. Boisvert had not even bothered to lock the back door. It opened with a simple turn of the knob.

"Pretty lax for a fellow with paintings worth thousands in his studio," Coffen muttered. "I wager he's left someone to guard the shop." He listened a moment at the open door. No sound came from within.

"You two hide around the corner, and I'll give a shout inside," Coffen said. "If anyone comes, I'll let on I'm looking for someone else. We'll have to come back later."

Luten said, "If there's anyone there, then the front door will likely be open, too. If you get an answer, keep the fellow occupied. We'll go in the front door and search the studio."

Luten and Corinne darted around the corner to listen. Coffen opened the door and shouted, "Hallooo. Anyone home?" When he got no answer after three shouts, he beckoned the others forward and they all went inside. The door opened into a sliver of kitchen, where the remains of a simple lunch of bread and cheese were still on the table. In fact, the teakettle was still spouting a faint column of steam. As they continued down a narrow, dark passageway with two doors leading off it, they were assailed by the familiar reek of oils, turpentine, and food. At the end of the hall was a doorway into the studio.

The room was as they remembered. The only difference was that one of the easels was empty. Luten wondered if Boisvert had removed the Watteau he was working on before leaving. He went to the spot where he had discovered the original Watteau resting against the wall the day before and began lifting the canvas that had concealed it. The Watteau was gone.

Coffen began a systematic examination of the canvases stacked two and three deep against the wall. He saw landscapes of points of historical interest in London. Saint Paul's, Buckingham Palace, the Houses of Parliament. Dull stuff, but well enough done if you had a taste for buildings. He preferred dogs and horses and people himself.

Corinne decided to take a look in the bedroom, thinking there might be a desk there with some incriminating note from Chamaude. There were two doors in that narrow corridor. She went back and opened the first one. It was indeed Boisvert's bedroom, but she never got around to searching it. As soon as she entered the dark, cramped little room, she felt a frisson run up her spine. It wasn't just the fetid air, or the mess left behind by a bachelor without a servant to tidy up after him. It wasn't the bare wood floor underfoot or the tumbled pallet he obviously used for a bed.

Even before she saw the dark hump on the bed, she sensed the presence of something awful. She quelled the scream that rose in her throat and took a step closer. It looked like a heap of old clothes. His smock, was it? She thought Boisvert must have changed into his good clothes to go to the elegant Clarendon. Then she saw the arm dangling over the edge of the cot and the lifeless hand, with the fingers frozen in a curved position, and the scream could no longer be restrained.

The banshee wail caused Luten and Coffen to leap, stare a moment at each other in alarm, then run down the hall to the open doorway. Luten just touched Corinne's shoulder in passing, as if to ascertain she was all right, before he hurried on to the bed. She watched as he lifted the lifeless arm and stared at the corpse's face. His own face looked very much the same—all rigid and gray—as he stared at the remains of Boisvert. Then she turned away, feeling faint.

Luten took a long, hard look at the lifeless form. Were it not for the crinkly, tawny gold hair and the smock, he might not have recognized the artist, for his face was discolored and distorted in horror. The head rested at an odd angle, the neck obviously broken. There was no sign of a weapon or blood. This ruthless murder had been performed with the bare hands, which told him that the comtesse had not done the job herself.

"Is that Boisvert?" Coffen asked in a hushed voice, as he peered over Luten's shoulder. Luten nodded. Coffen leaned over and lifted the lifeless arm. "I notice the arm moves easily. He ain't rigor mortified yet. Can't have been dead long. Strangled, from the color of his face, poor blighter. We'd best call Bow Street, eh?"

"Yes."

"Let's have a look for clues before we go."

Luten looked around the room. "Where's Corinne?"

"Straggled down the hall. Studio, I believe. Or maybe outside, retching. Not a pretty sight," he added, his gaze flickering to the truckle bed and the sad relic of humanity on it.

"Would you mind taking her home, Pattle? I'll go to Bow Street."

They went to the studio, where Corinne stood beside the empty easel. Luten drew her into his arms. "Are you all right?" he asked gently. She nuzzled her head into his shoulder a moment, then lifted it.

"She did this," she said, in a small, angry voice. She drew back and stared at him. Her eyes glowed like coals in her pale face. "She killed him. She came here and discovered we had been here."

"He didn't know who we were."

Corinne detached herself from his arms and said angrily, "He had our description. She would recognize it. She knows you are on to her, and she killed him to prevent him from testifying. You must go to Bow Street and tell Townsend everything, Luten."

"Let's see if she left any clues first," Coffen said, and began looking around.

"Yvonne didn't kill him. It would have taken a strong man," Luten pointed out. "He was strangled."

"She wouldn't have done it herself." Corinne's face was stiff with grief and anger and determination. "She probably hired that Frenchman who broke into Coffen's house. He always does her bidding. You ought to make an effort to find him. And search Boisvert's desk, too. She might have sent him a note that she was coming."

"There ain't no desk in his room," Coffen said.

"If there's anything here, Bow Street will find it," Luten said. "I'm calling there immediately. Coffen will take you home, my dear. You're upset."

"Of course I'm upset!" she cried, in a voice edged with hysteria. "It's our coming here that caused that poor man's murder!"

"We don't know that," Luten said, trying to assuage her remorse and his own. "We don't know what else he might have been mixed up in."

"We know the Watteau has disappeared. She took it back so there would be nothing to connect her to Boisvert. I wager the copy was on that easel that's now empty."

A small table stood beside the empty easel. It held a palette, some pigments, brushes, and rags. It also held a watercolor sketch, about sixteen inches by twenty, of a country estate. The sketch was marked off in squares for enlargement, obviously in oils as oils were Boisvert's medium. The mini palace, standing in the middle of a parkland of grass and stately oaks and elms, had its name in Gothic script at the bottom of the watercolor. Gresham Hall.

Coffen took up the sketch. "I don't think he was painting the Watteau," he said. "I believe this is what he was going to paint. The oils on the palette are gray. He's got greens for the grass and trees, blue for the sky as well. It's this big house he was going to paint."

He handed it to Luten, his index finger pointing at the words "Gresham Hall." Corinne looked at the sketch.

"Gresham! We know how he happened to hire Boisvert," she said. "He's Chamaude's friend. She sent him here."

"It looks that way," Luten agreed. A grim smile pulled at his lips. "Brougham will be interested in this. It would help if I could find some evidence she was having the Watteau copied. Let's have a search before we call Bow Street."

A hasty search revealed no trace of the Watteau, nor further copies of Coffen's Poussin either. As they hastened back toward the carriages, they discussed the matter.

"Not really much to tie Chamaude to it," Coffen said. "Who's to prove she sent Gresham to him? Even if she did, it ain't against the law to have a picture painted of your house. You have half a dozen of the abbey, Luten."

"Boisvert is not well known," Luten pointed out. "How would Gresham, a man from Manchester, have discovered him? Yvonne certainly sent him there. She's Yarrow's mistress—"

"Was," Coffen amended.

"Was, and may still be for all we know. In any case, she was Yarrow's mistress when the rocket contract was given to her friend Gresham. There has to be a way to prove it. You take Corinne home, Coffen. I'll see Brougham after Bow Street finishes up here. He's looking into the awarding of that rocket contract."

He assisted Corinne into Coffen's carriage. "I'll call on you as soon as I've finished. Try not to let this prey on your mind, sweetheart."

"You have to prove she did it, Luten," she said, clutching at his fingers. "The woman is a devil."

"A silver lining anyhow," Coffen said. "Always is, so the saying goes. Prance. This'll kill his passion for her. Pity he'll have given her the bracelet before we can tell him."

"It's a small price to pay for opening his eyes," Corinne said grimly.

They drove home, and Luten drove posthaste to Whitehall.

Chapter Seventeen

No sooner had Coffen delivered Corinne to her doorstep than Prance darted across the street to join them. He wore his best afternoon jacket and a cravat of such intricacy that it had obviously taken aeons to arrange. A wanton lock curled artfully forward over his lean, greyhound face, but it was his petulant expression that his companions noticed first.

Coffen directed a questioning look at him. "The tiger made quick work of you this time," he said. "It's only half after three."

"I didn't go," he said. "She put me off. A note arrived just as I was leaving my door. Her ladyship has the megrims. She might at least have come up with a convincing excuse! A megrim named Yarrow, I warrant."

"No, a megrim named Boisvert," Corinne said, and led him into the room, where he lifted his coattails and perched on the edge of a wing chair to hear the explanation.

Black, aware that his beloved was in the boughs, hastened in to inquire if she would care for tea.

"Brandy is more like it," Prance snorted.

Black ignored him. "Wine, your ladyship?"

"If you please, Black, and tell Mrs. Ballard I am home."

"Mrs. Ballard is having a lie-down. Shall I call her?" His look at Prance suggested he required no chaperonage. Black poured the wine and handed it around.

"No, let her rest," Corinne said, grateful for the privacy.

"Pray, what has Boisvert to do with anything?" Prance demanded, when Black had retired to his listening post beyond the doorway.

Corinne briefly related what had happened, with plentiful interruptions from Coffen.

Strangely, Prance was mollified by the tale. After expressing his shock and concern over Boisvert's murder, he said, "At least it was something serious that put off our rendezvous. I feared she was through with me—had found me inadequate as a lover. That would have been a catastrophic blow to my pride, for I put forth my best effort. I shall just dart around now and see if Yvonne is all right."

"Reggie! Have you not been listening?" Corinne asked. "She is a murderess."

He quelled down the frivolous urge to say, "No one is perfect," and said instead, "This so-called evidence is highly circumstantial. Boisvert is dead—well, murdered. Who is to say he was not killed by a burglar, or some lifelong enemy, or as a spy for that matter? In any case, she has no reason to murder *me*."

"She gave your *Rondeaux* to Marchant," Coffen said. "The copy you signed for her. That copy Marchant asked you to sign for him—'twas the one you signed for her. I have it at home."

Prance was vexed that Yvonne had not noticed the exchange but decided to forgive her. "An innocent mistake. Marchant took his copy with him when he visited her and picked up the wrong book when he left."

"Does she still have a copy?" Coffen asked.

Prance gave a smirking grin. "I was otherwise engrossed on my last visit. I shall tell you when I return from my call. *Adieu, mes amis. A bientôt.*" He finished his wine, set the glass down, made a graceful bow, and left.

"He'll not get a toe in the door," Coffen said. "I've half a mind to follow him and see. My carriage is still outside."

"I'll go with you," Corinne said. The little house on Half Moon Street held a dreadful fascination for her. To explain her eagerness, she added, "I cannot like to sit home alone, thinking of poor Boisvert."

"Come along then. I wouldn't mind the company. It'll stop me from thinking about him as well. Terrible sight on an empty stomach."

Corinne ignored the hint for sustenance. They had to wait a quarter of an hour before Prance's carriage was brought around. They let him get around the corner before leaving.

"Half Moon Street, Fitz," Coffen ordered. "And make sure you don't overtake Prance's rig. Go by Berkeley Street and make a right-hand turn at Piccadilly."

"Right hand?" Fitz asked, frowning.

"The hand you shave yourself with." He stared at his coachman's whiskered face. "When you bother to shave," he added.

Fitz began a pantomime motion of lathering his face. "Right hand. I've got it now," he said, and held up his left hand.

"The other one."

It was not to be expected that Fitz could negotiate the shorter route via Charles, Queen, and Curzon Streets, which would require the prodigious feat of remembering three street names and three tricky turns.

"I hope Prance doesn't give her the bracelet," Corinne said, as they clipped along.

"He's so besotted he'll leave it off at the door when she don't let him in, gudgeon."

After making a right turn onto Curzon when he should have turned left, and having to turn the carriage around in midstreet, Fitz finally reached Half Moon Street. It wasn't Prance's carriage standing outside the door that caused Corinne to stiffen like a shirt left out in an icy wind. Of Prance's rig, there was no sign. It was Luten's infamous hunting carriage just leaving the door that turned her to ice. As the carriage turned the corner, two heads were visible at the window. One of them was Luten's; the other was a lady's head, with a capuchin hood drawn over it to conceal her profile. The heads were close together, giving an air of intimacy. The small trunk tied to the roof indicated an overnight journey.

Corinne's heart pounded so violently in her chest she feared it would break her ribs. Her lungs collapsed, hardly allowing her to draw a breath.

"Follow them," she said in a hollow voice to Coffen. Her hands clenched into white-knuckled rigidity.

"That I'll not," he declared. "It ain't what you think, if you're thinking what I think you're thinking."

"It is exactly what I think, and you obviously know it, or you would do as I ask. You're just trying to protect him. If you won't take me, let me down and I'll hire a hackney."

"There ain't a one in sight. I wonder if Prance saw them. Must have seen the hunting carriage parked in front of her house. Dash it, we'll have a duel on our hands. That would suit Prance down to the ankles."

He paid no heed to her protestations but just lowered the window and hollered out, "Home, Fitz. And spring 'em."

The carriage picked up speed until they were jostling along so swiftly that it proved impossible for Corinne to leap out the door as she was sorely tempted to do when she spotted a hackney cab going the other way. Within minutes, they were back at her front door.

"I'll never forgive you for this, Coffen," she said. Her eyes blazed like green fire in her pale face.

He knew it was Luten she was angry with and felt sorry for her. "A glass of wine will settle your nerves," he said, and just shook his head at Black's questioning gaze as the butler admitted them.

Black was speechless with excitement to see his beloved so distraught.

"Bad news, madam?" he inquired in Lord Blackmore's most solicitous tone.

She lifted her chin. "Certainly not. Bring us brandy at once."

"The brandy is already there, your ladyship. Sir Reginald is awaiting you in the saloon. He requested it most forcefully."

"Is Mrs. Ballard down yet?" Corinne asked. It would really be the end if she had to smile at Mrs. Ballard and pretend nothing was the matter at this moment of crisis.

"Yes, milady. She has gone to visit the deCoventrys."

"Good."

Sir Reginald was pacing the small saloon, with a glass of brandy in his left hand, his right hand shading his eyes, which were moist with delighted grief. He looked at Corinne and said in a dying voice, "Betrayed, and by one we loved like a brother."

"Are you being more than one person again?" Coffen demanded. "Thought you was over that foolishness."

He gave a sympathetic glance at Corinne. "Ah no, Pattle. Methinks I am not alone in my agony. It was the 'brother' that led you astray. I meant only one close to our hearts."

"If you are referring to Luten's betrayal of me—of us both," Corinne said in a voice rough with emotion, "you need not mince your words. We saw him driving off with Chamaude and her trunk. I daresay Simon is rushing Luten's trunk to the love nest in his other carriage. Pour me a glass of brandy, Coffen. A large glass."

Coffen poured a glass for them both.

"Then we can speak frankly," Prance said, and lifted his coattails to perch on the edge of a chair. He crossed his legs and leaned forward eagerly. "You must know, dear heart, I share fully in your feelings. I, too, have loved and lost. I didn't go to her door when I saw Luten's hunting carriage there. I was desolate. Well, you know the feeling, as if the sky—nay, a mountain—has fallen on your poor head. Odd he went, when he thought I would be there."

"That's it, then. It was Prance he was after," Coffen said to Corinne.

"Why would he need Prance? It was Bow Street and Brougham he said he was after," she retorted. "He went flying straight to her to warn her of danger. He has smuggled her out of town for safekeeping. He's certainly bought a love nest for her. Why else did she take a trunk? That is why he agreed to drive me past that house on Grosvenor Square. He knew we would not see anything incriminating. He had already set her up somewhere else."

Prance was much struck with this ingenious perfidy. "Such a sly deceiver! One ought to have known that when Luten set out to confound us, he would do the thing to the hilt. I feel it is in part my own fault. I sensed his indignation last evening when I was regaling him with how Yvonne and I had—" He gave a missish smirk. "You know."

"We know. Twice," Coffen said, with a look of deep loathing. "You're making a mountain out of a mole hole. He could be taking her anywhere—to visit a sick friend, very likely. Anything might be in that trunk. Food, or medicine, or some of her pictures. And you needn't go thinking he's taken her to that country inn again—" Prance coughed sharply. Coffen turned red as a beet. "That is—"

Corinne turned on him like a virago. "*Again?* You mean he has taken her there before? You, my best friends, knew it and didn't tell me?"

"Dear heart! We didn't know the whole," Prance said, leaping up and hastening forward to put an arm around her shoulder. "Though I did try to give you a tiny hint in my note. Your *true, faithful* friend." She looked at him with a wildly distraught eye.

"When did he take her to an inn?" she demanded.

"Yesterday. Last night he explained that he was just leading her on, trying to discover something about Gresham."

"And I, for one, believe him," Coffen said. "Innocent till proven guilty," he added, when two hostile pairs of eyes skewered him. "This is England, after all."

"Patriotism, the last resort of the scoundrel," Prance sneered. "What, pray, has English jurisprudence to do with all this?"

"We're all English, ain't we?"

"I happen to be Irish," Corinne said coldly.

"So you are. Forgot. Still, they don't hang a man without a trial in Ireland, do they?"

"You have obviously never read a history book," Prance said. "Don't try to defend him, Pattle. He said last night he would not call on Yvonne again. He lied to us all. That, in my humble opinion, puts him beyond the pale. He need no longer be treated as a gentleman."

"You never had a humble opinion in your life," Coffen said, but he knew he was outnumbered and outargued, nor did he have much heart to defend Luten. Dashed shabby behavior. "Well, I warned him," he said.

Prance gave Corinne's shoulder a last consoling pat, then sauntered to the fireplace and drummed his fingers on the mantel. "I wonder if he even notified Bow Street. We ought to do it, if he hasn't."

"He might have done," Coffen said. "Mean to say, there was time. We came back here, had a glass of wine, waited a quarter of an hour for your carriage to come and go."

"Were you following me?" Prance asked, pleased but pretending to be annoyed.

"We was the second time you went, but Fitz—you know. There was plenty of time for Luten to go to Bow Street and take them back to Shepherd's Market before calling on Chamaude. Boisvert's place is only a step from Chamaude's. Likely Townsend was with them in the rig."

"There were only two people. He didn't go to Bow Street," Corinne said. "He went to warn her, before Bow Street learned of the murder."

"Don't see why he'd have to warn her if she did it, or had it done," Coffen said.

"Warn her that the body had been discovered, I mean."

Prance thought for a moment, then said, "He's smuggling her off to safety, then he'll report it."

"There's no knowing the ins and outs of it," Coffen decided, "but we ought to run down to Bow Street in case it slipped his mind. I hate to think of poor Boisvert, rotting on that truckle bed. There might be rats about."

Prance shuddered. "Please, spare us your overwrought imagination."

"It ain't right. I'm off, Prance. Are you coming with me?"

"I cannot leave poor Corinne alone. Misery likes company. Odd how one falls into cliché at moments of tragedy. We shall comfort each other in our distress."

"I'd as lief be comforted by a tiger," Coffen muttered.

"Much liefer!" Prance said, with a twinkle that suggested he was rather enjoying his tragedy.

"I know a Job's comforter when I see one. You're coming with me, my lad. Let Corinne have her cry in peace."

She clenched her jaw and said, "Cry? I hope I am not such a ninnyhammer as to cry over Luten and that hussy. Good riddance."

"That's the spirit!" Coffen said bracingly. He put a hand on Prance's elbow and drew him from the room by main force.

"I pity Luten when he drops in unwittingly at the full meridian of her wrath," Prance said sotto voce as they left. "She'll attack him, tooth and nail. There'll be nothing left but bones, hair, and blood on her nice carpet."

Black saw them out, then darted upstairs and brought down the softest blanket he could find, to place lovingly over his mistress's shoulders to quell her trembling. He had overheard the whole conversation from his listening post in the hall. At such moments as this, he was in his glory, tending to her needs, supporting her, planning how he could bring the lovebirds together again. His love was so pure he would happily endure the agony of seeing her marry, if that was what she wished. He would admit no callers this day save Luten, whom he would inform how the land lay in advance of announcing him. He would keep even the servants from pestering her with their petty problems.

He would order soup and an omelette for her dinner, to save her the labor of cutting up and chewing mutton. He was entirely confounded in his intentions when she called for her carriage five minutes later and said she would join Mrs. Ballard at the deCoventrys. His mistress seldom called on her in-laws, and with the exception of Lord Harry, they never called on her.

Lord Harry featured somewhere in it, Black figured. Actually young Harry was Lord Gaviston, now that his older brother was dead, and he was the heir. Luten had no love for the handsome young rascal. Jealous as a green cow. Aye, that was what the minx was up to, making him jealous. He admired her dauntless spirit in the face of such adversity.

Chapter Eighteen

As it turned out, Harry was not at home and Corinne had to sit for half an hour exchanging barbs with his mama, whom she despised nearly as thoroughly as the matron despised her. Under a veil of religiosity, the elder Lady deCoventry was a seething vessel of venom. After half a dozen barbed questions and equally sharp replies between the two, the burden of conversation fell on Mrs. Ballard's frail shoulders and from there to the ground. The half hour seemed an eternity, but at last it was over.

"I was surprised to see you land in," Mrs. Ballard said, lifting an eyebrow in question after they left. "I know it pains you to visit there, where you and George were so happy."

"I was hoping to see Harry, but it is no matter. I left a message with the butler."

Mrs. Ballard gave her a roguish smile "Luten won't like that."

"Then Luten may lump it."

Mrs. Ballard was by no means the sharpest knife in the drawer, but she deduced that all was not well with the lovers, and said no more on the subject. She recounted instead the various ailments to which the elderly Lady deCoventry was heir until they reached home. Corinne went directly up to her bedroom. Black whispered a word in Mrs. Ballard's ear. The dame lifted her fingers to her lips, made tsking sounds, and promised she would not disturb the mistress.

"A sup of soup and an omelette in her bedroom for dinner," Black said.

"Of course, and tell Cook the same for me, Black. No need

to set up the table for one." She would gladly have eaten in the kitchen with the servants, for she was one of those ladies who felt she owed the world a debt by the mere fact of taking up a few square feet of it.

Black was astonished when her ladyship came downstairs at the usual seven o'clock, dressed for the evening. She wore a particularly dashing gown of bronze silk with a gauze overskirt and had drawn her hair high on her head. She was ablaze with diamonds and looked like a very angry queen or empress. Her chin was up, her eyes sparking, her shoulders back.

"Was there a message for me, Black?" she asked.

"He's not home yet, your ladyship. I'll let you know the minute he arrives."

"I am expecting a note from Lord Harry—that is, Lord Gaviston. You may bring it to me at dinner, if it comes."

"A glass of sherry while Cook finishes up your dinner?" he suggested, smiling to cover his chagrin.

It was a rare day when Black failed to read his mistress's mind. He had to dart to the kitchen for a word with Cook, then send Jackie, the backhouse boy, upstairs to warn Mrs. Ballard to come down at once; he had to dart back to unlock the silver chest to get out the cutlery. Cook did him proud. The raised pigeon pies she slipped into her oven to reheat, along with a ham and cold mutton, eked out the soup and omelette to provide a tolerable dinner. It hardly mattered; Corinne only played with her food. She was on thorns, wondering when Luten would come.

She was just pushing her spoon around in a dish of syllabub when Black came and handed her a note on a silver salver. She read it and smiled a cold smile.

"I shall be going out with Harry tonight, Mrs. Ballard," she announced.

Mrs. Ballard drew her bottom lip between her teeth. "What shall I tell Luten if he calls?"

"Just tell him I am out with Harry. No need to give him the destination. I don't know where we will be going. Some rout or other, I expect."

She had invited Harry to Drury Lane and had a fair notion

that Luten would seek her out there when he heard who she was with, but she didn't want to make it easy for him. Harry, her favorite in-law, arrived just before eight o'clock. His manner had assumed some tokens of the dignity that now rested on his young shoulders, since the death of his elder brother made him heir to the deCoventry title and estates. His enlarged allowance had also improved his toilette. The deep cinnamon jacket he wore fit him marvelously well. In the folds of his immaculate cravat, a largish diamond in a claw setting sparkled. He wore his dark hair à la Titus and looked every bit as handsome as Luten, though not so distinguished.

When he spoke, she saw the old devil-may-care Harry still lurked somewhere inside him.

"I got your message, Corrie. No need to smuggle notes to me. Mama is not hounding me to offer for you, now that I shan't need your blunt."

"My fear was that she would think I was chasing you. She asked me quite pointedly if I was still single at my age."

"She don't know us very well, does she? What's up, that you are sunk to seeking my escort? Has Luten gone partridge hunting?"

"No, he is after other game this season."

Harry lifted an eyebrow. "I see! There's a rumor afoot that you two were getting shackled. I've been watching the mail for my invitation."

"Don't waste your time. There will be no wedding."

"On the outs, eh? What is my role, to make him jealous? I'll end up with my daylights darkened and my cork drawn."

"You needn't worry. Luten has a new lady these days."

"Anyone I know?" he asked with a flash of interest.

"I sincerely hope not. A Frenchwoman—an older woman, much too experienced for you, Master Harry."

"I'll be the judge of that." He draped her mantle over her shoulders. "Who are we going with?"

"Reg and Coffen might be there. I don't know for sure. It might be just the two of us. It is my box, in any case."

He proudly led her out to his carriage, another symbol of his elevated status. She looked a question at Black as he held the door for them. He gave a minute shake of his head and a commiserating look. They knew each other well enough to know the messages had been received, understood, and appreciated, without a word being exchanged. Luten was not home yet.

The box was empty when they arrived at the theater. Corinne had no recollection, after the play was over, of what they had seen. She had a vague notion it was something by Shakespeare. Presumably a comedy, as everyone in the audience seemed to be laughing. The roars echoed in her ears like thunder. She opened her lips and laughed along with them, to keep from crying. Between the noise and the stifling miasma of a hundred perfumes and her anger, she soon developed a ripping headache.

She remembered that Prance and Coffen had arrived at the first intermission. As they were not surprised to see Harry there, she knew they had spoken to Black. Prance, who prided himself on his exquisite manners, had scolded Coffen into discretion. The name Luten did not arise throughout the evening, but his absence cast a long shadow in the box.

During the second intermission, Prance whispered to Coffen, "We'll go out for supper afterward to tire her out. The later we get her home, the better. Her poor pillow will be drenched this evening."

Coffen screwed up his eyes, blinking away a tear. "Brave little soul," he said in an unsteady voice.

"Luten ought to be horsewhipped for this stunt." Prance was beginning to think that as Luten had stolen his mistress, he had every right to steal Corinne. And she was in just the mood, at the moment, to be stolen away by someone. Of course, she was just using Harry to annoy Luten. He was like a brother to her. She often said so, but Luten didn't quite believe it. Wouldn't he snarl and lash his tail if he came home to find Corinne engaged to himself? It would nearly be worth the trial of having a wife for the pleasure of seeing Luten bested.

"It's beginning to look as if Corinne's right," Coffen said. "The bounder has taken Chamaude off to a love nest somewhere."

"I console myself that she went for the title and, of course, the greater fortune."

"It ain't you I'm worried about. You're always thinking of yourself."

"Someone must think of poor me," he said with a sniff. "Men have hearts, too, Pattle."

"Well, they don't talk about 'em, unless they have heartburn. If you was sick, it would be all right."

"Oh, I am sick at heart and would lie down."

"Then go on home."

Through it all, Corinne smiled gaily and said she thought it a wonderful idea to have supper at the Clarendon after the play. Half a dozen eligible melords, any one of whom would have been happy to replace Luten in her affection, stopped at her table. She flirted outrageously with every one of them. But when she was at home in her bed, the tears Prance had prophesied came gushing out to scald her cheeks, as the imagined intimacies of Luten and Chamaude scalded her heart.

She knew it was only Luten she wanted, yet she wouldn't lift a finger to fight for him. Pride prevented it. There was a rumor in her family that the Clares were descended from Spaniards who got ashore to Ireland during the sinking of the Armada. Her coloring suggested it, and her pride was of the best Spanish quality, strong and rigid and sharp as a Spanish blade of tempered steel.

If he treated her like this, she would ignore him. She would not betray by so much as a blink that her heart sat like a ton of lead in her chest. When they met, and of course, they were bound to meet, she would act as if their engagement had never existed. She would not mention the words *engagement* or *comtesse*, or ask where he had been. She would be civil but cool. Meanwhile, she would go on the strut tomorrow and smile at everyone she met—and come home again and cry alone in her room.

Around four o'clock, emotional exhaustion lulled her into a restless sleep. She awoke at eight, to see pencils of light shimmering around the edges of her window blinds. A green glow came through the green lutestring hangings, giving her room the appearance of being underwater. She had no instant's reprieve of not remembering all her troubles. They came storming over her the moment she opened her eyes. She was tempted to stay in bed for the next few weeks but again pride was her goad. She reached out and pulled the cord by her bed.

Within minutes, the maid was at the door with her morning cocoa, served in a delicate white china pot with a matching cup and saucer. She thought of the tea set with shamrocks Luten had bought for her—it seemed a year ago. She'd send it back this very day, without a word of explanation.

"Shall I open the curtains, milady?" the maid asked.

"Thank you, Mary." She glanced at the tray, hoping to see a note from Luten. There was none. "Send Mrs. Ballard up in ten minutes, if you please."

Mary bobbed and left.

Corinne drank up her cocoa hastily. She usually admired her pretty bedchamber with the elegant white furnishings trimmed in gilt while she enjoyed this morning treat. On that day her eyes stared unseeingly at the far wall. When Mrs. Ballard came, Corinne selected her outfit for going on the strut on Bond Street. The violet worsted suit she had had made for half mourning after George's death suited her mood and the autumn weather, and still looked well on her. The waist pinched in to the same twenty inches of her girlhood. The feminine swell above and below had increased a little, however.

When she went belowstairs, Black stood waiting for her. He held no note in his hand but a flash of keen interest lit his obsidian eye.

"He got home at six this morning," he announced. Not "his lordship," not even the more familiar "Lord Luten," but "he." Black knew there was only one man of interest to his beloved at this time.

Corinne's heart began to palpitate. Not even to Black would she reveal her eagerness. She didn't ask if there was a message for her. If the flush on her cheeks betrayed her, that was nature's fault.

"What were you doing up so early, Black?" she asked.

"I had trouble sleeping, milady," he replied, with an arch

smile that told her he had been on guard all night. "He had changed his team. It wasn't his own nags drawing the carriage. He was alone," he added, piercing her with a meaningful look. "Wearing his blue jacket and fawn trousers. Driving all night, it looked like."

"Gracious, Black," she said, blushing at her duplicity, "one would think I had set you to spy on Lord Luten."

"I'll keep you informed, milady," he said with a leer that he imagined to be the soul of discretion.

"I shall be going out at eleven with Sir Reginald and Mr. Pattle, if anyone calls for me."

"Home for lunch?"

"I'm not sure. Something cold will do, if I return."

"You must keep up your strength, milady. We don't want you going into a decline."

Again she found it impossible to discipline Black. "Will you bring me the morning journal, if you please. Oh, and you might return that tea set to him, the one with the shamrocks. I shan't be needing it," she said, and walked quickly into the saloon.

Chapter Nineteen

When Luten called on Lady Chamaude, he had no intention of spending so many hours with her. She said she was in mortal danger, and it was his job, as well as his instinct, to protect her. Brougham had suggested it.

"She's our only hope of getting Yarrow," he had said, when Luten took the news of Boisvert's death to him, immediately after reporting it to Bow Street. Brougham, a thoroughly political animal, considered the murder in light of how it affected party politics.

"She'll not bite the hand that feeds her—or fed her, in any case," Luten objected. "It would only incriminate herself. And Yarrow is a spiteful old bird. She'd feel his wrath."

"She was not the one who really profited on the Gresham deal, Luten. I have a 'source' at the Royal Exchange who has reported some havey-cavey goings-on there with regard to Yarrow's financial dealings. To call them Byzantine doesn't begin to describe his chicanery. He is senior partner in a real estate company that recently bought a large share of the copper mine that will provide the tubes used for directional guidance of Gresham's rockets—but not Congreve's. Congreve uses a different supplier."

Luten lifted his eyebrows. "I see!"

"That's only the beginning. A rocket has many ingredients, and Yarrow owns a healthy share of companies that provide most of them. Chile saltpeter, for example, features largely in the production of the rocket. You get the idea."

"Yarrow would arrange for Gresham's tender to win, providing Gresham used the materials from Yarrow's companies."

"That's it. No money actually changed hands, so far as we know. It was not a direct bribe, nor does Yarrow have any share in the Gresham Armaments Works. I wasted a deal of time tracing bank accounts, but that is not the way it was done. Yarrow's investments look innocent enough on the surface. He is wealthy; it's natural that he would be investing in various commodities. It was only when I began to look into the production of the rocket that I realized the significance of his recent investments. All since the beginning of the year, when he began to talk up the need for rockets in the Peninsula."

"I think we've got him, Henry," Luten said, and looked for Brougham's opinion.

"It is certainly a conflict of interest, but then there is so much of that sort of thing going on in the House that it will be difficult to round up support to go after him. Even our own members' hands are not entirely clean."

"Is Gresham's rocket reliable?"

"I could find no glaring flaw in the design. It should work."

"You mean to say it's never been tried!"

"Thus far, he's still working on the prototype. No one has seen it in action."

"Is it supposed to be superior to Congreve's? We know it is more expensive."

"Not half as good, but try to prove it. The Tories can rally a quorum of scientists to say it is better. You recall Lord Peck, another good Tory, got the contract to provide poor woolen uniforms for the army sweltering under the Spanish sun, and at a vastly inflated price. No fuss was made of it, even by the Grits. I daresay this Yarrow business is more of the same but with the potential for disaster if the rocket doesn't work. My science is a little rusty, but even I could suggest some improvements. Putting on my other cap, as a lawyer, I can tell you that without something in writing to prove Yarrow's intention, we shan't get far with hounding him."

"He's too cagey to have anything in writing."

Brougham hunched his shoulders. "A chain is only as strong as its weakest link. Gresham is less experienced in double-dealing. He never left Colchester for the first half of the year. I've had men there looking into it. So how was the deal arranged?"

"Yarrow must have gone to Colchester."

"He's more cunning that that, I think. If he went, he covered his tracks well. Of course, the initial approach was made by Yarrow. Such a large undertaking would be outside Gresham's thinking, but I doubt it was done in person. Yarrow would not want to run the risk of being seen in Gresham's company."

"If not by letter, and not in person, then how— Ah, Chamaude!"

"Chamaude's daughter is being raised by a woman in Colchester, a Mrs. Yonge, on Wrye Street. Chamaude is there, from time to time. We know she is acquainted with Gresham. I believe she was used as intermediary. She might be the one who made the initial approach to Yarrow. Gresham is not well known. I don't see how Yarrow would ever have heard of him otherwise. She is up to all the rigs. If any proof exists, she is the one with the wits to hang on to it. We have her in a tight corner now, with this murdered-artist affair. Go to her, and see if she's willing to bargain."

"We have no proof she arranged Boisvert's murder."

"She can't be sure of that. We'll pick up the handsome young Frenchie who calls on her, the one you think killed Boisvert for her. His name is François Lachange, by the way. No visible means of support, but he lives fairly high off the hog. Doesn't have a carriage. He and his mama share a flat on Upper Grosvenor Square. Townsend has been keeping an eye on him. I'll ask Townsend to arrest him on some charge or other. Tell Chamaude we have him in custody, and he has told us some interesting things. See what she says."

"It's worth a try."

"If she's willing to cooperate, see that nothing happens to her. Yarrow would put a knife through her as quick as he'd blink—and through you, too. For God's sake, be careful of yourself. We don't want to lose you, Luten. We know she's murdered once already to save her skin."

All thoughts of his social life and obligations fell from Luten's mind as he anticipated the triumph of catching Yarrow.

Yarrow had been a thorn in his side from the first day he became active in the House. He was one of the Tory stalwarts who profited hugely from his position at Westminster and held a dozen sinecures at court. He blocked any Whig attempt at reform of Parliament. If he could be publicly branded with corruption, it would go a long way toward discrediting Mouldy and Company.

The common Englishman might not have a direct say in running his country, but by sheer force of numbers, he had considerable power, and that power was focused in London. In a city of one million souls with no real police but only the Horse and three regiments of Foot Guards to maintain law and order, a mob could instill terror in the heart of any politician who displeased it. Even the Prince Regent had felt its wrath. Yarrow's carriage would be overturned in the street, and its owner pelted and pummeled. If he made it home in one piece, brickbats flung through the windows, a torch to his front door, and a screaming mob thousands strong in the street would be enough to turn him into an honest man. And nothing was more likely to incite the mob than a suggestion of skullduggery in supplying their lads in Wellington's army.

Luten did remember that Prance was visiting Yvonne that afternoon. It even occurred to him that Prance could help him sequester Yvonne in some quiet country cottage, safe from Yarrow's wrath. Murder, he assumed, would cool Prance's ardor for the wench. But when he stopped for a word with Winkle, he was told that Sir Reginald had not called. The comtesse had received a note delivered by hand by a servant, but the man was not wearing Yarrow's red livery. The comtesse had sent her footman off to deliver a note. Winkle had thought it was a reply to her message, but it now seemed it was to Prance, canceling her meeting with him.

Luten found Yvonne alone, trembling and frightened to death, or trying to give that impression. She clutched her hands to her breast and said in accents worthy of the Comédie Française, "Dear God, if Yarrow ever suspected me of helping you, he would kill her."

"Her?"

A tremolo entered her voice. "Do you think I have put up with the beast all these years for my own sake? It is my daughter, Sylvie, who must be protected."

Luten decided to quiz her about her daughter, to see if she told the truth about anything.

"Where is she?"

"In Colchester, with a Mrs. Yonge. A friend of Yarrow's. Yarrow arranged it for me some years ago, when we were . . . friends."

"Some years ago" suggested to Luten that Yvonne had had plenty of time to remove her daughter elsewhere, but at least she told the truth about where Sylvie was quartered.

"Do you have information that could help us indict Yarrow?" he asked.

"A few notes and letters I purloined from his wallet one night he stayed here. He had been out carousing and came here drunk. I had Boisvert make copies of the letters—and kept the originals. Boisvert is—was a very good forger. Not checks! Just personal letters. He did a profitable business in forging personal letters supposedly from Bonaparte to Josephine. Surprising what people will pay for that sort of thing. Boisvert no longer did his forgeries, since he was becoming a little known as an artist."

"Pity you had to murder him," Luten said, fighting down the anger.

Her eyes turned to fire. "I? You think I had him killed? He was my friend. It was that fat fiend—Yarrow."

Luten pretended to believe her. "I doubt Yarrow did the job himself. Who would he use?"

"One of his servants. He has a few who would do anything for money."

"Is François Lachange one of them?"

Her shoulders squared and her eyes flashed dangerously. "Certainly not! François is my friend. Why do you mention him?"

"I understand Bow Street picked him up in connection with Boisvert's death. They'll get the truth out of him," he said blandly, and watched for her reaction. She was certainly worried.

"Poor François," she said. "But they can't prove he did anything wrong when he is innocent."

"You have no need to fear—if he is innocent." Luten adopted a sympathetic pose to put Yvonne in humor with him. He could see no reason for Yarrow to have the artist murdered. It was Yvonne who was having her paintings copied. "If he has an alibi, for instance . . ."

"I'll say he was with me, if needs be."

Luten pinched back the sneer that came so easily to his proud face. "Let me see the letters," he said.

After a moment's hesitation, she drew them out of her pocket and allowed him a quick glance, but she didn't let him hold them.

"When I have got Sylvie safely out of Yarrow's clutches, then I will give them to you. Word of a lady—and an old friend," she said, and returned them to her pocket.

"What do they say? I didn't have time to read them."

"Notes from Gresham outlining what materials were required for the rockets. Quotations in Yarrow's hand from various companies that supplied the materials, with notations of how much profit he would make on each. Also an apologetic little note from Inwood stating that Yarrow's offer was tempting, but he could not agree that Gresham was the better manufacturer. Inwood had discovered some flaw in the design. He was interested in science. His letter was written the afternoon of Inwood's attack by 'footpads.' Unfortunately, it does not say what the 'offer' consisted of, but Marchant was just made an equerry. His occasional attendance on the prince pays a rather handsome emolument. Yarrow let slip that Inwood was so unwise as to use the word 'bribe' when the offer was made." She gave a dismissing shrug. "He was very naive, Inwood."

The glimpse of the letters Luten had been allowed seemed to jibe with her story. "How did he get on to Gresham?" he asked, with an air of innocence.

"I expect Mrs. Yonge approached him. She and Gresham are

old friends. I have met him at her house a few times. Dreadfully common little man."

Luten considered this. There was really little point in quizzing Yvonne. She had a plausible answer for everything. She might even be telling the truth.

"Pack up what you need, and I'll provide footmen to escort you to Colchester to get your daughter."

"Yarrow doesn't let me keep a carriage. I'm practically a prisoner here. I wouldn't be safe on the public coach."

"I'll lend you my unmarked carriage."

"Come with me. You want to publicly prove Yarrow is a villain as badly as I do. Therefore, I can trust you. It might prove a hazardous journey, Luten. Yarrow is having me watched."

"I didn't see anyone lurking about."

"Yarrow owns that brown brick house across the street. A Mr. Willet occupies it. He seldom goes out. Only when I do. Interesting, is it not? If we leave at once, he won't have time to get his rig here to follow us. He's already sent his footman off to call it. He recognizes you from the other day, when we escaped for a few minutes. I have a small trunk packed, ready to take advantage of the first opportunity that offered. I feared I would have to wait until after dark. As I shan't be coming back, I could not leave without taking the few valuables I have collected."

Luten hesitated only a moment, before deciding he should go along with her plan. "Have the trunk brought down and put on the carriage. We'll leave right away."

She pulled the cord and told her butler to have the trunk brought down.

Chapter Twenty

They left at once. Luten noticed Yvonne glancing at the house across the street, but he didn't see anyone watching them. He felt she was trying to whitewash herself into a victim and went along with it in an effort to get the notes and letters.

They both kept a sharp lookout for any carriage following them as they wended their slow way out of London traffic into the countryside. No one followed them, not on the fifty-mile journey north through the autumn countryside of Essex either, where thinner traffic would reveal a following carriage, but she was either really anxious or an extremely good actress. A hundred times she lowered the window and pointed out anyone on the road. The rig always turned off or stopped before he took alarm. They stopped often to change horses, to allow a good pace.

At one stop Luten said, "I was surprised to find you alone this afternoon, Yvonne. I understood Prance was to call on you."

"He was. Half an hour before he was due, I had a note from . . . a friend, telling me of Boisvert's death."

"Lachange?"

"Yes, as a matter of fact, it was Françoise. He stopped at the atelier to visit Boisvert. He took time to send me a note before going to tell Boisvert's sister the horrible news. The Boisverts and Lachanges are good friends. I was in no state for company after hearing of the death. By the time you arrived, I had determined to get away at the first opportunity. You came most opportunely, Luten. It is possible you have saved my life."

He weighed her story and could find no inconsistency in it.

It might have happened as she said—or it might be a carefully contrived tissue of lies.

At evenfall they were halfway to Colchester. They stopped at an inn at Chelmsford for a hasty dinner and a change of team. The comtesse nibbled a piece of bread and gulped three glasses of wine, which did not have the effect of loosening her tongue or her grip on the papers Luten wanted but only made her sulky.

It was after ten o'clock when they passed through the ancient city walls of Colchester. This busy garrison town was noted as an agricultural center as well, but at that hour, there were few carriages or pedestrians about. They drove to an ancient half-timbered inn on High Street and dismounted. Their conversation took place at the front door, with the carriage standing by.

"You can hardly go to Mrs. Yonge at this hour and have Sylvie taken out of bed," Luten said.

The comtesse looked surprised. "I doubt she would be in bed yet." A blush colored her pale cheeks. "She is no longer a child, Luten."

"How old is she?"

The arch smile she directed at him was a travesty. Yvonne suddenly looked old.

"That would be telling," she said. A bit of arithmetic told him the "child" must be in her late teens. "I shall call, but I must go alone. It would look odd to Mrs. Yonge if I went with a gentleman. She would be bound to send word off to Yarrow. I know she spies on me. I stay at the Red Lion here in town when I come to visit. Sylvie has spent the night with me before. I shall go now and fetch her. Perhaps your driver could see if the inn has a carriage for hire?" A frown grew between her brows. "She won't be able to bring any of her lovely gowns with her. No matter, I shall buy her new ones when we are safely settled—somewhere."

"I'll wait for you here." He called to John Groom, who darted into the inn and came back to tell them a whiskey would be around presently.

"No, dear Luten," she said, putting her two hands in his.

"Your job is done. Here are the letters." She handed them to him. He studied them eagerly a moment. "They are genuine," she said. "I hope you make good use of them and put that wretch behind bars for life. Unlike France, there is no hope of England executing a peer of the realm."

"Where will you go? Where can I be in touch with you?"

"If I read in the journals that you have Yarrow under lock and key, I shall go to London to testify against him." Her face clenched and her eyes glittered with determination. "I'll say anything you like, to see him get what he deserves."

This statement did much to give Luten a disgust of her and confirmed that she was perfectly willing to perjure herself. Was she lying to him now? Were the notes and letter from Inwood some sort of hoax? Would they be revealed as forgeries if taken into court? Mouldy and Company would have a field day!

"Very well," he said, but he knew he would have to remain in town and discover where she was going. When she left in the whiskey, he set his coachman to follow her at a discreet distance.

To pass the time until he returned, Luten enjoyed a plate of the famous oysters from the River Colne and a glass of ale.

Over an hour later, John Groom returned. "She went to that boardinghouse on Wrye Street right enough, but she never come out, your lordship. I waited an hour."

"What did she do with the whiskey?"

"It dropped her at the door and left."

"You're sure she didn't slip out the back door?"

"I couldn't watch two doors, could I? Did the whiskey come back to the inn?"

"No. And no, dammit, you couldn't watch two places at once. I should have gone with you instead of indulging myself in ale and oysters."

He rose at once from the table. "Take me to the house," he said.

His team had not been unhitched. It was waiting at the inn dorway. Luten got into the carriage, and his coachman turned off the High Street to continue for two blocks along a residential street. He drew up in front of a respectable-looking stone house. There were lights burning downstairs. The upper story was in darkness. Luten left the carriage and went to the door. On the second knock, a weary female servant in a cap and apron answered.

He adopted a friendly smile and said, "I would like a word with Miss Sylvie. I know it's dreadfully late, but it is a matter of some importance." He didn't know what surname the daughter used, but the servant didn't seem to find it odd that he used only her first name.

"Miss Beaudine has left," she said.

"Out for the evening, is she?"

"Oh no, sir. She's left for good this very day. She's not coming back at all."

"I see. How long ago—"

"She got a letter from London this morning. Her mama sent a carriage for her in the early afternoon."

"Any idea where she's gone?"

"Why, to London, sir, to visit her mama."

"I see. Thank you."

He tipped his hat and returned to the carriage. Chamaude, the wily witch, had outsmarted him. Sylvie had been spirited away from Colchester hours ago. Why had Yvonne led him this merry dance? Was it just to get him out of London for the day? What was afoot there? A memory of Boisvert's lifeless body rose up in his mind. And young Inwood, murdered as well. Was she busy arranging another death? Whose? He doubted very much he would find her or her daughter in London. Yvonne had made an arrangement to meet the girl at some other place. She had probably ducked straight out the back door of Mrs. Yonge's house, darted to the nearest coaching stop, and gone to meet Sylvie. He now felt fairly sure the letters he carried were useless. They might land his party with a libel suit if they used them in the House.

"Back to London," he said to his driver, and crawled into the rig, fatigued from the long drive already endured and the prospect of another long haul before he could lay his head on a pillow.

His thoughts were black as the team ate up the miles. Bad

enough to be outwitted but to be bested by a woman! God, he'd look a fool when he took this story to Brougham. And where the hell was Chamaude? If anyone could finger Yarrow as a villain, she was the one. That, of course, was why she had run off, no doubt on Yarrow's instructions. And she had used himself to engineer her escape. The air was blue with his curses.

He was fifty miles from London. Fifty miles of dark, nearly deserted roads. Yvonne—or Yarrow—might have hired assassins anywhere along the route. Perhaps that was the very reason she had lured him to Colchester, to have his murder occur well away from London. His watch and money purse would be taken to make it look like the work of a highwayman. No one knew he had left town with Yvonne except her butler, who was part of the plan, of course. Even Brougham didn't know he had gone, though he would suspect foul play.

He pulled the drawstring and directed his coachman to take a circuitous route back to town. It would make the trip a few hours longer, but at least he wouldn't have to fear for his life every minute of the way.

During that long, tedious journey, he remembered he was supposed to have taken Corinne to the theater that night. She'd be furious with him. If she ever discovered he had been with Yvonne, he could forget his engagement. What convincing story could he tell her? A sudden death in the family? She didn't know all his relatives—but she could smell a lie a mile away. He'd take her flowers first thing in the morning, along with his humble apologies. Better make that diamonds. Flowers weren't going to get him out of this mess.

Chapter Twenty-one

Luten reached London at six the next morning, dog-tired, bewhiskered, rumpled, hungry, and extremely out of sorts. He planned to be up and about at an early hour, but as neither Brougham nor a jewelry shop would be available before nine or ten, he had a few hours to rest. He pulled off his jacket, his Hessians, and his trousers and fell into bed.

It was there that his valet, Simon, found him at his usual rising hour, eight o'clock. Seeing his master's disarray (and the mess he had made of his bedchamber), Simon refrained from drawing the curtains. He tiptoed from the room and sent an order below that the upstairs maids were not to begin their duties until notified. Simon was extremely out of curl when he was greeted with curses at ten o'clock.

"Why the devil did you let me sleep so late?" Luten demanded.

"Why, you looked so fatigued, your lordship. Surely two hours can make no difference. The House has not yet convened."

"I have more in my dish than Parliament. Prepare my shave at once. Bring me some coffee—and call my carriage."

Simon's eyes wandered about the room, where trousers lay on the floor, jacket had been thrown over the desk, and a cravat hung from the post of the canopied bed. "Would that be your regular carriage, sir, or—"

"Of course my regular carriage."

The tardiness of his rising meant he had to visit Brougham before calling on Corinne. He sensed that his visit with her might require some considerable time. He thought of sending her a note, then decided against it. He would go to Love and Wirgams to select a large diamond ring for her engagement and deliver it in person. Simon made him presentable and brought him a cup of coffee. Luten drank it and left, still frowning and muttering under his breath. Simon was out of sorts all day after this unaccustomed harshness from his master.

"These look genuine," Brougham said, studying the notes and letters Luten handed him after he had discussed his trip to Colchester. "I'll send them around to that handwriting specialist on Bridge Street. We'll need something written by Yarrow for comparison."

"And Inwood. That letter is a telling document. The comtesse mentioned Inwood had discovered some flaw in the rocket design. If we could find his research and have it checked, we might get the contract recalled, even if these notes are forged."

"Now we know why the Tories were in such an almighty rush to clear out Inwood's office. His notes have been burned long ago. I've a drawerful of notes from Yarrow. We can check on his handwriting. Nothing from Inwood. I wonder who would have."

"Marchant, but I don't like to tip him off. He's in Yarrow's pocket. I'll drop around to the rooms where Inwood lives—lived." A frown creased his brow to think of that young life cut off before its time. And of course, it would have to be the better young man who was dead. He would have been a fine addition to the Whig ranks. "Marchant mentioned the address. Craven Street, just around the corner from Whitehall Street. Inwood's family will not have cleared his things away yet."

"Better get on to it right away. If by any chance the note is genuine, you may be sure Yarrow won't waste any time rounding up every word the fellow ever penned and burning it. Oh, by the by, the Melbournes are having a do this evening. Are you invited?"

"I am, but I hadn't planned to attend." He had hoped for a quiet evening with Corinne.

"Yarrow will be there. Melbourne is halfway to being a

Tory, you know. He always admired Canning. They hope to reel Melbourne in. No matter, I can attend myself."

"Then I pray you hold me excused. I do have a life beyond Whitehall, you know."

Brougham gave him a glinting smile. "So I hear. When is the big day?"

"Never, if I don't find a moment for my fiancée soon."

"Best look sharp, then. I hear she was out with young Lord Harry last night. I shan't bother you again today—unless an emergency arises, of course," he added with a twinkle.

Luten felt a spasm of alarm at hearing the name Lord Harry. The handsome rascal had been a special friend of Corinne's for years. He consoled himself that she had only gone out with Harry to make himself jealous. He went straightaway to Inwood's little flat on Craven Street. When he told the landlady he was there to recover government documents from Mr. Inwood's rooms, she did no more than cast a glance on his crested carriage before letting him in.

"He was a great one for working at home," she said, smiling in fond remembrance as she led him upstairs. "Such a nice young fellow. Here we are, then." She unlocked the door but didn't follow him inside. She knew a gentleman when she saw one. No fear of this lad pinching any of her goods. His house would be inlaid with gold and silver, to judge by the looks of him.

The flat was only three rooms—a parlor, bedchamber, and study—all of them modest. Inwood was obviously not from a well-to-do family. MPs were not paid, and he was too honest to have provided himself with any lucrative sinecures. His landlady cooked and cleaned and did his laundry. Inwood didn't even have a personal servant. From the quantity of books in his study, all tumbled over tables and chairs, Luten deduced that he had been a bookish fellow and with a bent for science. His papers appeared to be intact. He had made copious notes on rockets, but they appeared to be preliminary notes. If he had discovered some serious flaw, Luten could find no sign of it. As Luten knew little of the science of rocketry, he gathered up the notes to take along for Brougham to look into. He also scooped up other samples of Inwood's penmanship. The writing certainly looked like the writing in the note to Yarrow. A good forgery would have similar writing but even the paper was identical.

When he took the papers back to Brougham, he decided to tend to a few other matters while he was there, to obviate having to return later. It was past noon when he finally got around to visiting a jeweler, where his vague feelings of guilt goaded him into purchasing a gaudy emerald-cut diamond of ten carats, which would look like a platter on Corinne's dainty finger. He put it in his pocket, stopped to buy a large bouquet of flowers from a vendor on Piccadilly, and drove off to Berkeley Square.

Prance and Pattle had arrived at Corinne's house at eleven, as arranged the evening before.

After exchanging greetings, Prance said, "I have had a reply from my letter to Sir Vance Dean, my old tutor at Cambridge. He tells me he has not put my *Rondeaux* on the reading list for his class on medieval literature, but if I would like to send half a dozen copies, he would be happy to include them in the reference library."

"That'll get rid of six more of them copies you bought," Coffen said.

"And another six to Oxford. But I still do not know who the rabid fan who purchased one hundred copies can be. An intriguing mystery, is it not? Prinney, I wonder, planning to give them to visiting dignitaries?"

"Very likely," Corinne said, as she wished to avoid talking about the *Rondeaux* and discuss other things.

"He'll invite me to Carlton House to autograph them. A signal honor."

Coffen just nodded and turned to Corinne. "Have you seen Luten yet?" he asked. Her strained face suggested she either had not, or had seen him and fallen into an argument.

"No. He hasn't called—though Black tells me he returned at six o'clock this morning."

"Six o'clock this morning!" Prance exclaimed, signal honor forgotten at this hint of scandal. "Where was he all night?"

Her delicately carved nostrils flared. "Where do you think?" she asked, in a rhetorical spirit.

He lifted his fingers to his lips. "Oh dear. Sorry I asked." He extracted a billet-doux from his pocket and waved it before her eyes. She recognized the violet ink from the inscription on the *Rondeaux*. The handwriting was spidery. "Dear heart," he added, patting her fingers, "I have excellent news for you. He has not spirited Yvonne off to a love nest. *En effet,* she has invited me to call this afternoon at Half Moon Street. Says she had the megrims yesterday. I shall chide her for that plumper—and try to discover where Luten took her."

"Double dealer." Coffen scowled.

Prance tossed his curls. "I saw her first!"

"I don't mean you, Prance. Her. Cheating on Luten behind his back." When Corinne's nostrils pinched to slits, he realized he had been indiscreet and tried to cover his gaffe. "Not to say she's running around with Luten. No such a thing."

"I don't know about that," Corinne said. "Luten went dashing out of his house at ten-thirty this morning as if the place were on fire. He didn't come here."

"Was he driving his hunting carriage?" Prance asked eagerly.

"No, his crested carriage."

"Then you needn't worry he's with her," Coffen said.

"I am not in the least worried. The only reason I want to see Luten is to tell him our engagement is off."

Coffen considered this a moment, then said, "A good idea, before he tells you. Mean to say, a bit of satisfaction in giving him the boot at least."

"It is all very sad," Prance said, subduing the smile that wanted to peep out, "but don't be overly hasty, dear. Wait and hear what he has to say. Would Yvonne want to go on seeing me if she had a carte blanche from Luten? Methinks not."

"It appears she found Luten unsatisfactory, Prance, and has chosen you over him. There is a feather for your cap."

"Call me a macaroni!" he said. "Shall we go to Bond Street?

I like to buy myself something exquisite when I have been embittered by love. It exorcises the demon, jealousy."

"Hers don't need any exercising. It's strong enough," Coffen muttered.

Prance sighed. "Exercise it to death," he said, to avoid lengthy explanation. "I had thought I would be buying myself a new snuffbox or cravat pin this morning, but as events turned out, I shall help you choose yourself a bibelot instead. It must be a luxury, to make you feel better. I recommend the new foaming soap from Vienna, if you haven't tried it yet."

"Rubbish. Soap ain't a luxury," Coffen said. "Dashed insult."

"Your ignorance is immaculate, Pattle. I do not refer to the cleansing quality. Foaming soap is sybaritic, like covering oneself with whipped cream." He gave a shiver of remembered bliss. "But perhaps you have a point. Losing Luten requires a more extravagant pampering. Perfume, a bonnet. No, I have it—jewelry! There is nothing like gemstones to cure a wounded spirit. I saw the prettiest little butterfly brooch at Rundell and Bridges, gold filigree with diamonds spotted on the wings. Only ten pounds. I coveted it but could think of no place to wear it."

"It sounds delightful," Corinne said, though she did not for a minute think a diamond butterfly would assuage her pain and anger. She went for her bonnet and pelisse.

She didn't buy the diamond butterfly, nor the foaming soap, nor anything to assuage her sorrow. She didn't want things. She wanted Luten.

Prance's French chef, André, prepared a light luncheon for the group. Prance was so enthralled by all the excitement of the day, he ate half a serving of chicken ragout, which was the largest meal he had taken in months.

"And now I must be horrid and ask you both to leave," he said when the meal was over. "I must make a grand toilette for my afternoon rendezvous." He added waggishly, *"Tu comprends, n'est-ce pas?"*

He accompanied Corinne home. "I shall try to discover what was afoot with Yvonne and Luten yesterday," he assured her.

"Don't do anything rash until you hear from me. Luten is too good a *parti* to cast off for some paltry reason."

"I do not consider infidelity a paltry reason. I think you just fear the competition, Reggie."

"Too cruel! But I forgive you. I was feeling in just the same savage mood myself yesterday, and today I am chirping merry. *A bientôt!*" He waved farewell and returned home.

Mrs. Ballard was in the saloon when Corinne entered.

"Did you have a nice morning, dear?" she asked.

"Yes, lovely, thank you. You got my message that I wouldn't be home for lunch?"

"I just had a sandwich in the morning parlor. I plan to go over the linen cupboards this afternoon. The sheets are wearing thin."

"Let me know what we need," Corinne said.

Mrs. Ballard rose and left the room. Corinne sat on alone a moment, wondering what she was to do with the rest of her day, of her life. She was staring into the cold grate when Black came pelting in. A smile split his saturnine face at the good news he was bringing.

"He's coming!" he said. Soon her pale cheeks would be pink with pleasure. "Just hopped out of his rig, carrying flowers. I'll get the door."

Corinne sat frozen to the sofa, not moving a muscle, but inside, she was a seething cauldron of tumult. Far from pleasing her, the flowers were an added insult. They were as good as a confession. Luten never brought her flowers, except occasionally a corsage for evening. If he thought a bunch of flowers was going to make her take him back now that Chamaude had opted for Prance, he was mad.

Chapter Twenty-two

Luten essayed a smile as he entered the saloon; it dwindled to uncertainty when he saw Corinne's squared shoulders and stiff face, her green eyes lit with anger.

"A peace offering," he said, proffering the bouquet. "I am sorry I missed our date last night." She took the flowers without thanking him and set them aside. Her eyes raked him from head to toe. "You may be sure I had a very good reason."

"I am sure you had, Luten."

"Something came up, after I called on Brougham."

She directed a gimlet stare at him and said, "Would that be before, or after, you called on the comtesse?"

His eyes sparkled warily. "Why do you ask that?"

"Because I would like the answer. I know you were with her."

"Have you been spying on me?" he demanded, trying to muster a tone of anger. It proved inordinately difficult. He knew she had him dead to rights.

"Only inadvertently. Actually it was Prance who wanted to go to Half Moon Street yesterday afternoon when Chamaude canceled their meeting. Now we know why! Coffen felt she would not let him in and decided to follow. I went with Coffen. We all saw her trunk stowed on your girl-hunting carriage."

He blinked and drew a deep breath. The infinitesimal twitching of his lips and the strain in his voice when he spoke revealed his unease. "The only reason I took my unmarked carriage was because she didn't want Yarrow to know it was me with her."

"And you, no doubt, didn't want your fiancée to know what you were up to."

"I can explain—"

"Can you also explain why you took her to a country inn the day before?"

"We had tea," he said, in that drawling voice that always infuriated her. His glare of icy hauteur challenged her to disprove it.

"Is that what the light-skirts call it nowadays?"

His guilt was fast hardening to anger at her intransigence. "It was not a love tryst, if that is what you think," he said coldly.

"You read me like a book, sir. That is exactly what I think! A man doesn't hustle a woman like that off to a country inn just for a cup of tea."

"I wanted to quiz her about the Watteau and Yarrow."

"You could have done that at her house. What did you want to quiz her about yesterday that it took you till six o'clock in the morning? Don't bother to invent a story, for I shan't believe a word of it."

"I don't have to invent a story! Brougham felt she had evidence that would help us convict Yarrow."

"Why choose you for this juicy assignment?"

"Because I knew her before."

"Because you were her lover before and still are! Do you expect me to believe that Brougham ordered you to make love to her to discover her secrets? I knew the honorable members have few scruples, but I didn't know they were expected to prostitute themselves for the good of the country. If that is the case, I fear I haven't the stomach to be your wife."

"I didn't make love to her!" he shouted, then took a long, deliberate breath to calm his nerves. "I took her to Colchester to get her daughter. She was frightened out of her wits. Do you think I would take advantage of a lady in that condition, even if I wanted to, which I didn't?"

"I don't know what you would do. I no longer feel I know you, but I am coming to know her uncommonly well after hearing Prance rant about her prowess on the chaise longue."

"It is Yarrow who is the greater villain of the piece."

His defense of Chamaude was the last straw. "It is you who are the fool. Where do you think Marchant got her copy of the *Rondeaux*? She is in it up to her ears. She may pull the wool over your eyes, but she does not fool me. I won't sit still for it—to be made a laughingstock in front of my friends."

"Is that what worries you, what people will think?"

"No, what *I* think—that I cannot trust the man I intended to marry."

"I have done nothing wrong!"

"We obviously differ on what constitutes wrongdoing. You have been seeing that French strumpet behind my back, lying to me! And now you dare to tell me she is innocent!"

"I don't say she is innocent. It was my duty to discover what I could."

"I cannot imagine your duties were so stringent that you couldn't have dropped me off a note telling me you could not keep our date last night. Nor why you went haring off this morning without a word."

"I wanted to give Brougham what I had got and have the rest of the day for us."

"Unless Brougham decides you are required to hold the comtesse's hand again."

"She's left London—for good."

"Has she indeed?" she asked, her head ringing with anger.

"Yes, this is the last place she'd bring Sylvie."

"Liar! Prance had a note from her this very day, inviting him to call at Half Moon Street. He is with her this minute. You had best dart after him, or he will be cutting you out."

"What? That's impossible!"

She saw his concern, and her anger soared even higher. He was furious that Chamaude was seeing Prance. "It seems the comtesse was not so impressed with your attentions as you thought," she sneered.

"She can't be here!"

"She is here. I saw her note to Prance. Perhaps she found the love nest dull without you."

"Something must have happened."

"Yes, like myself, she has had a change of heart, but I'm sure you will soon find yourself another light-skirt, now that you are free. If you had ever bothered to give me an engagement ring, I would have the pleasure of returning it."

"And if you had ever bothered to make the announcement, you would likewise have the pleasure of rescinding it."

"How very remiss of us both. One is led to wonder whether either of us ever had any intention of going through with this farce of a wedding."

"Speak for yourself!"

"I shall. Your actions speak for you."

He drew the jeweler's box from his pocket and slammed it on the table. "One of us intended to go through with it. I bought the engagement ring this morning."

"For whom?" she retorted.

"Go to hell," he growled, then he turned on his heel and stalked from the room.

The little blue velvet box sat on the sofa table. Corinne was sorely tempted to open it, but she was angry enough to subdue the urge. She didn't even touch it, but called Black and said, "Would you please return that box on the table to Lord Luten, Black."

Black had no compunction in opening the little box. "Whew!" he exclaimed, lifting the ring out. "There's a dandy bit of sparkler. Ten carats at least."

Corinne examined it beneath lowered eyelashes. "A vulgar, showy thing," she sniffed. "You may throw out that bouquet of flowers while you are here."

"Happen Mrs. Ballard would like it," he said.

"Throw it in the dustbin."

"Just as you like," he said, and carried it and the ring down to the kitchen, where Cook shoved the flowers into a water jug and enjoyed them while Black retailed what he had heard abovestairs, passing the ring around for the servant girls to try on and ooh over.

"Dandy fireworks abovestairs," he said, "and his lordship hasn't even heard about young Harry yet. There will be another gnashing of teeth and rattling of thunder."

"It's the Irish in her," Cook said. "They never can stand too much peace and quiet. It'll pass. You'll see."

Abovestairs, Corinne sent a note off to Grosvenor Square, asking Harry to take her to Lady Melbourne's ball that evening. Her pride demanded that she be seen out with a dashing buck, enjoying herself, and no one was so likely to infuriate Luten as Harry. She knew she would have a miserable evening, but she would not let Luten think he had wounded her.

When she gave the note to Black for a footman to deliver, he said quietly, "He's had his carriage brought round and left in a hurry. His regular crested carriage."

She knew she should tell him she was not interested in the comings and goings of Lord Luten, but her curiosity prevented it. It saved her a deal of window watching.

"Did you return that box, Black?"

"Yes, milady. He would have had it before he left. That would be why he was in such a pelter."

"Thank you."

She was still in the saloon, reliving every moment of their meeting and thinking of a dozen cutting things she should have said, when Prance was announced. His shoulders drooped.

"That lady's heart is harder than a paving stone," he said. "After sending for me, Yvonne wouldn't see me. She left word with that wretched butler that she had to leave suddenly, but she was there. I could hear her. I don't understand. The woman is a wanton, toying with my love."

"Pity. I was hoping you would cut Luten out. It is only his money she is after, Reg."

"I believe she has settled on Yarrow after all. He was there. I could hear him talking in a loud voice in the saloon, while I was arguing with the butler. Yarrow has managed to get her an invitation to Lady Melbourne's ball this evening. She said something about a girl called Sylvie. Has Yarrow been carrying on with someone else, I wonder? Am I merely a pawn in her game?"

"Sylvie is her daughter. Luten said he took Chamaude to Colchester to fetch the girl. He seemed surprised to hear that Chamaude is back in town."

"I wonder if all this flurry of romantical activity on Yvonne's part has to do with trimming Yarrow into line, forcing him to introduce her more fully into Society, or she would find a patron who would."

She told Prance all about Luten's visit and about the engagement ring.

Prance was a connoisseur of jewelry. The ring diverted his attention. "How many carats? What cut was the stone?"

"Emerald cut. Black says ten carats."

"Magnificent! And not any of the Luten entailed collection either. It must have been a sore temptation to you."

"Not in the least."

"I am a beast to even suggest such a thing, but . . . the ring does not sound like you. Such a gaudy ornament would sit more naturally on another lady's finger. You know to whom I refer, I think."

"Then why give it to me?"

"To make a point, perhaps. Luten's pride dislikes being bested, even in a jilting. He must have the upper hand, always. The ring implies his innocence, putting you in the wrong. He could always buy another for Yvonne." When he saw the tears gathering in her eyes, he rushed into an avalanche of apologies. "Forgive me, my heart. It is mere speculation. I should be muzzled like the rabid cur I am."

She blinked away the tears. "No doubt you're right. Did I mention I am going to Melbourne's ball this evening with Harry?"

Prance pulled a moue. "I had hoped you would go with me."

"Will you be going?"

"It seems it is the place to be this evening. Byron is bound to be there. He and Lady Melbourne are close as inkle-weavers. We ought to have gone together, Corinne, to bear each other company in our gloom. To think of seeing Yvonne with Yarrow, and Byron swanning about, being stroked by all the ladies. I am not sure I am up to it." He looked for encouragement. When Corinne did not urge him to attend, he had to urge himself. "Of course, it will be amusing to see how Yvonne behaves to Luten."

"Do you think he'll go?"

He gave a sly smile. "I wager he will when I tell him Yvonne is going. I'll call and drop him a hint as soon as he returns."

Luten drove posthaste to see Brougham to discuss Chamaude's return to London.

"Demmed odd," Brougham said, frowning. "It was all a hoax, then. Well, I warned you the lady was lethal. Wise of you to take a roundabout way home."

"Has there been any word from Bow Street on Boisvert's murder?"

"A well-known felon by the name of Daugherty was seen in the vicinity. He's for hire for any sort of dirty work, if the price is right. Townsend has picked him up, but we haven't got anything out of him."

"It might be interesting to release him and see where he goes, who he gets in contact with."

"It's an idea. I'll send for Townsend and let you know what happens. You'll be at home?"

"Waiting on nettles."

Brougham gave him a quizzing grin. "As your lady friend lives just across the way, that shouldn't interfere much with your romance."

"What romance? I have been given my *congé*, Brougham."

"It'll pass. The course of true love never runs smooth."

Luten had a good deal to think about as he sat in his saloon, sipping claret to calm his nerves, while he waited to hear from Brougham. The open ring box sat on the table beside the wine decanter, taunting him. He had to devise some plan to win Corinne back. He knew from past experience that her volatile temper flared like one of Congreve's rockets and soon settled down. He admired that openness in her. His own tendency was to nurse his grievances in silence. For four years he had sulked over her rejecting his first offer, made too soon after her husband's death. He had behaved deplorably, snipping and sniping at the poor girl. And she had risen to every barb, giving him back what he deserved. A wan smile tugged at his lips. They had both enjoyed every minute of their little tiffs. But this was different. When diamonds and flowers can't console a lady, the matter is serious indeed.

When this Yarrow business was finished, he'd call on her again and try persuasion. Meanwhile, he pondered Prance's brief visit, announcing in the most casual way possible that Yvonne was attending Lady Melbourne's ball. What was the meaning of that? Should he attend himself, to keep an eye on things?

He only left his study to sit down, alone, to dinner. As soon as he was finished, and he ate virtually nothing, he went back to his study. It was from there that he saw Harry's carriage drive up to Corinne's house. His heart thumped in anger. He waited and watched as the two came out the door together, laughing and holding hands like young lovers. Harry was demmed attractive. She had always had a soft spot for him. When Prance had told him that Corinne was attending Lady Melbourne's ball, he assumed she would be going with Prance and Pattle. Not a word about Harry. They were all conspiring against him. He was suddenly eager to attend the ball himself, but he had told Brougham he would be at home, awaiting word on Daugherty.

It was after nine o'clock when Brougham called in person at Berkeley Square. "Our friend Daugherty went to a tavern and is still there," he announced.

"That's not much help."

"I haven't got to the cream of it yet. He sent a note—to Yarrow."

"By God, I'd like to get a look at that!"

"It might be possible. Yarrow was just entering his carriage with his lady when the note was delivered. He read it and put it in his waistcoat pocket. I mentioned he's attending Melbourne's ball. If only there were some way to read that note." He directed a meaningful glance at Luten.

"I'll take care of it," Luten said. He felt the old excitement pounding in his blood. If Yarrow had the note, he'd get hold of it if he had to knock the bastard senseless and steal it. Really he couldn't think of any other way to do it. It would give him infinite pleasure to knock Yarrow down. If he couldn't strike someone soon, he felt he would burst.

He darted upstairs, called for Simon, and made a fresh toilette. Simon was vastly relieved to be back in his master's favor. He attended most solicitously to cravat and jacket, recommending the new dark green from Weston, with the diamond cravat pin. "To match the pin to the jacket lacks originality," he said.

"If Prance ever heard you say that, he'd commit suicide—or murder."

Before leaving, he picked up the blue box holding the engagement ring. It made a lump in his jacket. He extracted the ring and slid it into his pocket. With luck, it would be where it belonged before he returned.

Chapter Twenty-three

An autumnal mist clung to the ground as Corinne went out to the carriage to join the stream of carriages wending their way through the West End of London, their lamps glowing like earthbound moons in the darkness. At those houses where parties were in progress, lights blazed at every window. The sight had seemed magical to Corinne when she first arrived in London. It excited her still, but on that evening she failed to notice it. When Harry's carriage reached Melbourne House, his liveried footman leapt down and opened the carriage door. Gold-laced footmen in powdered tail wigs lined the steps of the house, ready to offer assistance.

Inside, guests stood in line to be announced before entering the painted ballroom. Below them, the rich sheen of silks and satins glowed beneath the chandeliers. Jewels twinkled on white breasts and wrists; stars and orders decorated the gentlemen's darker jackets. Feathers from ladies' turbans reached ceilingward in an exotic, waving forest. The dying strains of violin and cello echoed below the buzz of conversation, and the miasma of a hundred perfumes wafted on the air.

"Lady deCoventry and Lord Gaviston," the announcer called. Heads turned in interest to view the new arrivals, and conjecture whether a match was in the offing.

"I always feel I ought to sing or do a jig when he says that," Harry said.

He made no secret of the fact that he was there to chase after other women. As a bachelor, he had a great interest in debs. As soon as they entered the ballroom, he said, "I know you only asked me to bring you because Luten is busy, but I don't have to stick like a barnacle, eh? I want to get my name on Lady Eleanor's card before it is filled up." Lady Eleanor Cartwright was the latest in a long line of flirts.

"Go ahead," she said. "I'll join Prance and Coffen. They have just come in."

Corinne was with her old and best friends when the comtesse arrived. They were all surprised to hear her partner announced as Monsieur Lachange. Looking, they saw a handsome gentleman with dark hair. Coffen soon recognized him.

"That's the fellow who called on Chamaude the night we met Yarrow at her place," he said. "Knew he was a Frenchie."

"The one who exchanged your Poussin," Prance added. "Yarrow could hardly bring her himself. This must be the cicisbeo he's chosen for public outings. Handsome! Yarrow is mad, choosing someone so much younger and more attractive than himself. She is looking lovely this evening, is she not?"

Corinne stared across the room and had to admit the comtesse looked very pretty in a burgundy gown, the same one she had been wearing the evening they had met. The jewelry was the same, too. The necklace still looked like paste.

"A tad pale," Coffen said. "I wonder she don't use rouge."

"That is her theatrical training coming out. Those mile-deep eyes look best against pale skin," Prance said dreamily.

Coffen scowled. "Not them sturm dung eyes again!"

"*Sturm und Drang,* ignoramus. It means storm and stress."

"Well named. She does look stressed. If that lady's a day under forty, I am a monkey's uncle."

Prance eyed him askance. *"C'est possible,"* he murmured.

While they watched the comtesse, she was making a visual survey of the ballroom. When she spotted the Berkeley Brigade, she nodded and smiled. Prance made an exquisite bow that acknowledged her presence while suggesting his state of pique, yet still (he hoped) declaring his interest in continuing their affair. It was a great deal to ask of a bow. When he looked at her to see if it had succeeded, her eyes had already turned to Coffen, who gave a curt nod. Then to Corinne, who lifted her chin in the air and looked away.

Vexed as Corinne was with Chamaude, she had caught a glimpse of the lady's expression and felt mean for her own curtness. Prance was right. There were storm and stress in those dark eyes and that pale, haunted face. It could not be easy, living by one's wits and on one's fading beauty. Being French was another barrier to social acceptance. London held so many ersatz French aristocrats that even the real ones, and apparently Chamaude had married a comte, were suspect.

She remembered, too, how the comtesse had winced when Yarrow clamped his sausage fingers on her arm. Coffen said she looked like a baited animal. And now she had, apparently, settled on the fat old toad for her patron. No wonder she had made a play for Luten, when he crossed her path. Corinne could understand, but she could not yet forgive, or forget. She felt the rankling anger would be there so long as Lady Chamaude and she inhabited the same planet.

"They are striking up a minuet," Coffen said. "Shall we stand up and jig it, Corinne?" Corinne scanned the ballroom before answering. "He ain't here," he said, meaning, of course, Luten.

Dancing with Coffen was a trial endured for friendship's sake. He seemed to have four left feet, every one of them attracted to her toes, like iron filings to a magnet. While she and Coffen struggled through the minuet, Prance assumed a dramatic lounge against the wall, one ankle crossed over the other, his quizzing glass raised to watch the comtesse and Monsieur Lachange perform a graceful dance. The glass was a detriment to actually seeing at a distance, but he liked the looks of it. When the set was over, no rush of gentlemen darted toward the comtesse and her partner. They went alone together to sit against the far wall. Corinne and Coffen joined Prance.

"I'm going to ask her to stand up with me for the next set," Prance said. "Look how everyone is ignoring her."

"They don't know her," Coffen said.

"Or worse, they do," Corinne snipped. She saw Lord Yarrow and his fat wife, who did not look at all invalidish but only peevish. They stood with a group of friends, talking.

"Yarrow might acknowledge her, at least," Prance continued. "He could introduce her to some people, or see that Lady Melbourne did. What is the point of getting her an invitation if he does not sponsor her a little?"

Harry came to Corinne for the second set. "Might as well get our duty dance over," he said. "I caught Lady Eleanor for the first set. I cannot stand up with her a second time or the quizzes will have us engaged."

The comtesse seemed grateful to Prance for dancing with her. She also seemed very sad, almost frightened.

"I'm sorry I had to cancel our meeting this afternoon, Rezhie," she said, peering at him with her soulful eyes. Tonight they looked navy-blue, with gold flecks.

"Postponed, surely, Yvonne?" he cooed.

"It is over," she said. "You must forget me."

"Tell me to forget the sun or moon, forget music, poetry—all else that is worth living for—but never to forget you."

She acknowledged this high-flown compliment with a sad smile. "You left out art—paintings, I mean. That was my undoing."

Her wistful voice, the faint wobbling of her bottom lip, inflamed him to folly, even while he noted that she had been up to some chicanery with the sale of her paintings.

"Let me see you tonight, after the ball," he implored.

"It is too late for that, Rezhie. Let us just enjoy this last dance."

Prance could only do as the goddess commanded. He did enjoy the dance, with a sort of bittersweet, mournful contentment, fully aware, as he sighed and gazed, what a handsome picture they made. Their parting, he now admitted to himself, was for the best. Yvonne was beginning to show her age, and if she had chosen Yarrow over him, she did not live up to the promise of her eyes. She was hopelessly mercenary.

Unwilling to give up his histrionics so soon, he invited her to the refreshment parlor for a glass of wine after the set. He felt a spurt of alarm when he saw Corinne there with Harry. There was no counting on Corinne's Irish temper to behave itself.

Unfortunately, Harry saw him and beckoned him over. He went warily, bringing Yvonne with him.

"Harry," he said. "How are you enjoying being the elder son?"

"It helps with the ladies," Harry said, smiling.

Prance then turned to Corinne. "You have met Lady Chamaude, Corinne." Corinne nodded coolly. He introduced her to Harry. That Harry displayed not a jot of interest in the comtesse told Prance the lady was past it. Her charms were best enjoyed in a darker room.

After a moment's edgy silence, Prance turned to Harry and began to discuss politics. "When are you going to take your seat in the House, cawker?"

Corinne looked at the comtesse and felt again a stab of pity. "A nice party," she said.

The comtesse's face softened to gratitude. She turned away from the gentlemen and spoke in a low voice, which was either full of genuine agitation, or wonderfully simulated.

"Forgive me, Lady deCoventry," she said. "I didn't know about you and Luten, the first day you called. I am in some distress at the moment. I needed someone I could rely on to help me. My daughter—"

"Sylvie, I believe?"

"Yes."

"How old is she?"

"Eighteen."

"That old! Oh, I'm sorry. I—"

The comtesse shook her head. "It is no matter. I just want you to know that what I have done, I have done for her. One needs someone she loves more than herself. I am sorry we could not have been friends, Lady deCoventry, but lady friends were never possible for someone like me. I hoped you would be different, as you are too young and beautiful to be jealous of me."

Corinne was insensibly flattered and wondered why the comtesse was suddenly confiding these personal matters to a virtual stranger, practically confessing to some wrongdoing. Uncertain what to say, she reverted to the daughter.

"Your daughter must be a great solace to you. I'm sure she is beautiful."

"No, she has been spared that, thank God. She takes after her papa. Not Yarrow! It happened before I met him. An old friend from France. She is a bookish girl, well raised. I think you would like her."

Corinne assumed that the girl's father was a married gentleman. She sensed that a request was about to be made. Would she sponsor Sylvie into Society? Her spine stiffened.

The comtesse studied her for a moment with those sad eyes, then said in a wary voice, "But this is nothing to do with you. I only wanted to apologize."

Then she turned suddenly and left the room. She looked small and lonesome and terribly vulnerable, walking away with her head high, pretending not to care that no one spoke to her. Corinne thought she had been on the verge of tears. It was cruel of Yarrow to have brought her here if he did not mean to sponsor her. The ton, jealous of its preeminence, could be brutal to interlopers. Why on earth had he done it? Why had she come? Was it to pave the way for her daughter's acceptance into Society?

She turned to Harry. "Dance with her, Harry," she said.

"Who, Yarrow's mistress? What the deuce do you care about her?"

"Just do it—for me."

"Very well, but this puts you in my debt." He hurried off and caught up to the comtesse.

"What was that all about, pray?" Prance asked.

"I don't know. A fit of conscience, I expect. Dance with me, Reg."

They were about to leave when Luten came into the refreshment parlor, with Coffen trotting at his heels in an effort to keep pace with Luten's long legs. Corinne's first instinct was to turn her back on her faithless lover and leave, but she saw the tension on his face, in his whole stiff body, and remained to discover what was afoot. Luten directed one long look at her, but said nothing, not even good evening.

"What's up?" Coffen asked.

"We have a little job to do," Luten said, and moved away from the other guests to talk in private. The Berkeley Brigade followed like lambs.

Chapter Twenty-four

Luten lowered his voice and said, "Brougham tells me Yarrow has a note in his pocket from the man who murdered Boisvert. It's a longish story. I'll fill you in later. The note could put Yarrow behind bars."

"His pocket, you say," Coffen said. "Looks like a job for Corinne. Stand up with him, slip her dabs into his pocket, and snitch it."

"No," was all Luten said, but he said it with that authority that brooked no argument.

"He never dances," Corinne said. "Could someone spill wine on him and help him brush it off? Rifle his pockets while you are about it."

"Spilling wine. Sounds like a job for Pattle," Prance said, glancing to see if his gibe was appreciated. It wasn't.

"It would only alert him we're after the note," Luten said. "We have to knock him out."

"How?" Coffen asked. "Mean to say, can hardly brain him with a blunt instrument in Lady Melbourne's ballroom. Bound to be seen. Anyone got any laudanum we might slip into his glass?"

No one had come supplied with a sleeping draft.

"We'll have to get him out of the ballroom," Luten said. "Any ideas?"

"Tell him you want a word with him in private," Coffen suggested.

"And announce that I am the one who coshed him?"

"Not a bit of it. I'll be hiding behind the door. I'll cosh him, with pleasure."

"I'll still be the one who lured him into the room. I'd be expected to prevent you from escaping, or identify you at least."

"I'll knock you out as well."

"It's early yet," Prance said. "Why don't we just keep an eye on him, and if he wanders off by himself, we slip after him?"

"We can't wait. He might burn the note. Someone keep an eye on him while I try to figure out a plan," Luten said.

"I'll do it," Coffen said. "Nobody ever notices me." He sauntered out of the room. As he said, no one noticed him.

The three who were left behind suddenly fell silent. None of them could think of anything to say. Prance and Corinne were both angry with Luten, and he was fully aware of it.

"I wonder if Byron is here," Prance said, looking around.

"I heard he's gone to Eywood with Lady Oxford," Corinne replied. "Lady Caroline has been sent to Ireland to recover from the grand affair, you know."

Lady Oxford, whose brood of children were collectively known as the Harleian Miscellany due to their various fathers, was an aging but still lustful countess.

"Pity," Prance said. "I had hoped for a word with him about my revolution poem." Luten paid them no heed. He stood deep in thought.

"We'll leave Luten alone to think, Reg," Corinne said. "They are just starting the waltzes. You and I will dance."

Luten shot a dark look at her. "Why not with Harry?" he asked in a tight voice.

"Oh, I have already stood up with him. If we have another dance, folks will say it is to be a match. We're not ready for that—yet."

She led Prance off. Luten said as they left, "Keep an eye on Yarrow."

"I shouldn't be much surprised if Yvonne would help us," Prance said, when they were beyond Luten's hearing. "I was afraid to mention her name when you two were within striking distance of each other. What do you think?"

"She's Yarrow's mistress. She would hardly help us."

They met Coffen at the doorway, big with news, and followed him back to Luten.

"Yarrow just stepped out to blow a cloud," he announced. "We'll not get a better chance."

"Is he alone?" Luten asked.

"Yes. His wife has gone to the card parlor, and he slipped out the French door at the end of the ballroom. We'd best take a different route. That one's too public."

"There's a door from the library," Luten said. "I'll go out that way. I'll go alone."

The others watched as he darted to the library, to find more than a dozen guests resting there by the grate, enjoying champagne. He left in frustration and continued down the hall a few paces until he found a closed door. It opened into a small, unlit waiting room. There was no door to the outside, but there was a window. He raised it, looked down at the ground twelve feet below, and threw one long leg over the windowsill. Luten was just over six feet tall. By hanging from the sill by his fingertips, he managed the drop to the ground without spraining an ankle.

He found himself in a narrow, paved walkway between Melbourne's and the house next door. It took a moment to get his bearings. The French doors at the end of the ballroom gave out on the backyard. He'd have to sneak up quietly and hope the yard offered some concealment. He also needed a blunt instrument. A shaft of moonlight slanted down through the wisps of mist between the houses, silvering the cobblestones. One stone jutted up. He nudged it with his foot and found it loose. He jiggled it out, picked it up, and hefted it. It would do the job. He crept forward quietly.

A stand of lilac bushes concealed the back of the house. He smelled the cigar smoke before he spied Yarrow through the branches. Light from the ballroom illuminated the courtyard in a pearly light. Yarrow was pacing back and forth along its length with his hands locked behind his back and the cigar in the corner of his mouth. He seemed worried.

Luten crept forward, toward the near end of the courtyard. When Yarrow reached it and turned around, he'd strike the back of his head. He should have worn a mask, in case he was seen. He put the cobblestone down, removed his handkerchief from his pocket, and tied it round the lower part of his face, then picked up the stone again. Peering through the branches, he saw Yarrow striding toward him. His brow was furrowed, his eyes narrowed in thought, his whiskers jiggling as he chewed on the cigar. As he reached the edge of the paving and began to turn around, Luten lunged forward and struck the back of his head, gauging the force to knock him out without killing him. Yarrow fell forward with a grunt and lay motionless. The cigar fell from his mouth and rolled over the paving stones.

Luten turned him over on his back and delved into his waistcoat pocket. The first one held his watch. He tried the second and felt a crisp corner of paper. He drew it out and rose to leave. Then he stopped. Yarrow seemed to be completely unconscious—but when he recovered, he'd have a good notion who had done this. Luten felt his inside jacket pocket and removed his purse. A prigger would take the watch and that ruby ring on his little finger as well. He took the watch but couldn't wiggle the ring off his fat finger.

When Yarrow emitted a groan and began to stir, Luten rose and hurried back behind the bush, down the alley to the open window, still wearing his mask. Unfortunately, it was more difficult to enter the window than to exit. He couldn't reach his arms up twelve feet. He worried that Yarrow would rouse up and come after him if he made any noise. He was about to leave and go around to the front door again when a head peered over the window ledge.

"Give us your hand," Coffen said, and leaned out the window. "Did you get it?"

He pulled down his handkerchief. "Yup." He stuffed the note, wallet, and watch into his pocket.

Coffen's stubby arms could not quite make contact with Luten's hands. Prance reared up beside him. His longer arms could make contact, but he hadn't the strength to pull Luten up. Between the two of them, they finally managed it, with Luten digging his toes into the bricks of the wall for leverage.

"Close the window and draw the curtains," Luten said. He

saw that Corinne was there as well, looking a little frightened, which he took for a good sign of concern. Someone had lit one small lamp.

"What does it say?" Prance demanded.

Luten opened a small piece of paper. It looked like a corner torn from a journal. He took it to the lamp and read aloud: "Can't do it tonight. I'm being followed, but a mate will handle it." There was no signature, not even an initial.

"Do what?" Coffen asked.

A frown grew between Luten's eyebrows as he studied the scrap of paper. "I haven't the faintest idea."

"Hardly worth knocking Yarrow out for."

"It must be important. Yarrow hired Daugherty to murder Boisvert."

Luten drew out Yarrow's wallet and opened it. It held a wad of bills but no written notes. He drew out the watch, too, a handsome Grebuet hunter with Yarrow's crest engraved on the back.

"You'd best dump that lot," Coffen advised.

"I can't leave them here. If Melbourne's servants find them—well, we don't want to saddle Lady Melbourne with having to explain it to Yarrow."

"We'll split the loot up," Coffen suggested. "One of us take the watch, one the wallet."

"What foolishness," Corinne scoffed. "No one is going to search us. Give them to me. I'll put them in my reticule."

Coffen considered it for a moment, then said, "Can't. You're a lady."

Luten reached behind the curtains, opened the window, tossed watch and wallet out onto the paved walkway, and closed the window again.

"Let us see if Yarrow has come back in yet," he said. "We shan't all leave at once. Corinne, we'll go first. You two follow us in a moment."

If Luten had not asked her to go with him, she would have been furious. Her Spanish pride did not go without an argument, however.

"You and Prance go ahead," she said. "Coffen and I will follow in a moment."

"It'll look more natural if you go with Luten," Coffen said. "You've already stood up with me once. Nobody would do it twice on purpose."

"Very well," she agreed, and strode out before Luten could put his hand on her elbow.

They went along to the ballroom, where their eyes immediately flew to the French door at the end of the room. It was closed. A quick survey of the area showed them Yarrow had not come in.

"I hope you didn't kill him!" she said.

"No, he was grunting. He's just catching his breath before he returns."

"Let us stroll past the French door and see if he's still out there."

"I'd rather not show my curiosity."

"I'll go," she said, and walked off before he could stop her. A strange nervousness had seized her, and it had nothing to do with Luten's infidelity. She kept seeing in her mind's eye the haunted face of Lady Chamaude.

The music had stopped. Couples and groups moved about the floor; some stood chatting. She worked her way between them. The light from the ballroom fell on the paved courtyard; she could see there was no one there. Luten strolled through the mingling throng at a nonchalant pace and joined her.

"He's gone," she said. "He's not in here, but he's not out there. I wonder if he's called for his carriage. He wouldn't leave without his wife, would he?"

"That depends on where he's headed. Let us find out if his carriage was called."

They went out into the entrance passage, and Luten said to the butler, "I wanted a word with Lord Yarrow. I can't seem to find him. Hasn't left already, has he?"

"He has, your lordship. He called for his carriage a moment ago and asked me to notify Lady Yarrow that he would send his other carriage for her at midnight."

"His other carriage? Then he didn't go home. Gone to his club, I expect?"

"Very likely, though he said he had a touch of megrim. He had stepped out for a breath of air and came in at the front door. He did look poorly."

"Thank you. I'll catch him tomorrow at the House."

Luten and Corinne turned toward the ballroom but lingered outside the door.

"What did that note say, exactly?" she asked. Luten repeated the message. "What is this mate going to handle? Luten, I have a feeling it has something to do with the comtesse."

Any mention of that name between them was bound to cause friction. Luten's jaws locked, then he said grimly, "Surely we have more important things to discuss now than the comtesse."

"She was speaking to me earlier, before you arrived, about her . . . dealings with you."

"How pleasant for you! You mustn't believe a word the woman says. She's a consummate liar."

"Never mind that! I know she is in trouble. My aunt Moira has the sight, Luten. I know you laugh at such things, but I have the most horrid feeling that something is going to happen to her. We've got to protect her."

"Protect her! That's a new wrinkle. I thought you would be happy to see her dead."

"Not dead!" she exclaimed. "I never wished her dead! I feel . . . I don't know. I feel sorry for her, and I'm sure that criminal mate is going to harm her. Let us see if she's all right."

"I'm more concerned to discover what Yarrow is up to."

"Follow him, then. See if he really went home. I'm going to watch Yvonne."

The comtesse's Christian name sounded strange on her lips. Luten was accustomed to hear Corinne speak disparagingly of "Chamaude." It was contrary that now, when his own distrust of the Frenchwoman was at its height, Corinne should suddenly have become her champion. Yvonne had taken him on a wild-goose chase, pretending she was afraid of Yarrow, that she wanted to get Sylvie away from his clutches, yet she went running back to London the moment she had escaped him. As to those papers, he had not heard yet whether they were genuine.

"What did she want with Prance this afternoon?" he asked. "You said she sent for him."

"She didn't see him after all. Yarrow was with her. They were speaking of Sylvie. Arguing, he said. Perhaps they've had a falling out." She felt again that nauseating certainty of danger. "You said she had some evidence that would incriminate him, Luten. Perhaps that's what they were arguing about."

"But why would he bring her tonight if—"

"If he means to harm her, he would hardly do it at Half Moon Street, where he is known to visit daily. Her calling Prance might have been an attempt to flee."

"I helped her flee yesterday, and she fled straight back to Half Moon Street."

"Yarrow must have some hold over her, have her dancing to his tune. She despises him, Luten. She could find another patron if all she wants is money. Reggie would take her on in a flash."

"I'm glad you didn't say Luten would!"

"I don't know about that," she said dismissingly, as if it were of no interest to her. "If you won't help her, then I shall speak to Reg."

She peered into the ballroom but could see neither Reggie nor Coffen. Accompanied by a protesting Luten, she went to the library, to the small parlor where Luten had climbed out the window, then to the refreshment parlor. It was at the wine table that they finally met Prance.

"Punch, at Melbourne House. Who would have thought it?" he said. "And it is not even good punch."

"Where's Coffen?" Luten asked.

"He's gone haring after Yarrow, to what end, I cannot even imagine. Searching 'clues,' he said. He was loitering about the front hall and saw Yarrow call for his rig. Coffen sent for his at once. God knows whether Fitz will succeed in following Yarrow. They are probably both in a ditch by now, or held up by footpads, Coffen's usual fate."

"Reggie," Corinne said, "I think Yarrow means to harm Yvonne. Will you help me watch out for her?"

"With the greatest pleasure, my pet. But surely she and Yarrow are the best of friends. Why should he harm her?"

"I don't know."

"She has a *feeling*," Luten said, smiling tolerantly.

"I don't see what harm can befall her when Yarrow has left, but if it pleases you . . ." Prance's attitude was similarly condescending. "What would you have me do?"

"I don't know," she said again. "Just help me watch her."

"Avec plaisir." He put his hand on her elbow and led her into the ballroom, where the comtesse had finally found a partner, an aging roué, Lord St. Clair.

Coffen returned half an hour later and informed Luten that Yarrow had gone to White's Club and was playing whist with his cronies. When Corinne heard this, her fears were somewhat allayed—but there still remained the question of what job Daugherty's mate was handling that night for Yarrow.

Chapter Twenty-five

At eleven-thirty Corinne saw Monsieur Lachange lead the comtesse from the ballroom. Watching from the doorway, she saw them calling for their carriage. The gentleman put her mantle over her shoulders, then they stood waiting for the carriage. Again, or still, Corinne felt that numbing sense of danger. But what danger could the comtesse be in? She had willingly returned from Colchester, according to Luten. Was it Lachange who meant her harm and not Yarrow after all? She pondered this a moment. Lachange, a friend of Boisvert, angry at his death . . . Luten had said Yarrow arranged Boisvert's murder. Perhaps Lachange was the man he used.

Luten suddenly appeared at Corinne's elbow. "You can relax now. She's leaving," he said, with satisfaction.

"So am I. I'm going to follow her."

"This is nonsense!"

"I'm following her. I'll ask Harry to take me."

Seeing her determination, Luten said nothing but beckoned the butler and asked him to send his carriage around at once.

"Thank you," Corinne said coolly.

She got her wrap, then they stood together in silence, with a row of potted palms between them and the comtesse. From the occasional glimpses the moving fronds allowed, Corinne could see the comtesse was deathly pale. Anxiety pinched her pretty face into a mask of pain. She smiled wanly at Lachange, then reached up and kissed his cheek, which seemed to suggest they were good friends. Or at least the comtesse thought so. When the butler called them forward to enter their carriage, Lachange walked Yvonne to the door but returned again, alone.

"Why isn't he going with her?" Corinne asked, her voice rising in alarm.

"I shouldn't think he gets to a party like this very often. He'll try his hand with some of the debs."

"What's keeping your rig?"

"I can't imagine. It's been all of two minutes," he replied in his infuriating, bored drawl.

Coffen, who spent most of his time in the refreshment parlor, spotted them and came forward. "Are you two leaving?" he asked. "Glad to see you've patched things up."

"Nothing is patched up. We're following Yvonne," Corinne said.

"Ah. Still have that 'feeling,' do you? Prance was telling me about it."

"Yes, stronger than ever."

"I'll tag along in my own rig. Never know, another hand might come in handy if there's trouble."

He called for his carriage, then went off in search of Prance, who decided to remain behind and keep an eye on Lachange. Corinne and Luten had left when Coffen got back, but he assumed they would be following Chamaude to Half Moon Street and headed in that direction, or as close to it as Fitz could manage.

There was still considerable traffic on the street at midnight. Even in the autumn little Season, there was more than one party a night to be visited. It seemed unlikely that anything could happen to the comtesse during the short drive to Half Moon Street. Corinne was on the lookout in case the carriage stopped to allow Yarrow's henchman to enter. She saw no suspicious dark forms loitering about the streets, however. The comtesse was nearly home. When the rig slowed down to make the turn at the corner of Curzon and Half Moon Streets, there was still no sign of a footpad.

Busily scanning the street and roadway, Corinne missed seeing the man. If the man hadn't had to open the carriage door, Luten might not have seen him either, for the comtesse's carriage did not slow down. The opening door of her carriage could only be seen from Luten's window. It flew open and a dark form leapt out, stumbled, then regained its balance and fled into the shadows of the night. When Luten jerked the drawstring, Corinne was momentarily stunned.

"Luten, why did you—"

Before the carriage stopped, he was out the door, chasing a shadow between two dark houses, while the comtesse's carriage continued for a few yards, then stopped. The driver had heard the door banging to and fro and worried for the safety of his passenger. He climbed down from his perch and went to the door. He stuck his head into the carriage, then leapt back. "*Sacre bleu!*" he cried, looking all about the dark street.

Corinne waited a moment, tense in every muscle, her heartbeat pounding in her ears like thunder. Why had the comtesse's carriage stopped? She was certain no one had got into it to harm Yvonne. Why had Luten left his own rig? Had he seen Yvonne running away? Luten's driver clambered down from the perch and came to the carriage door.

"Should I take you on home, milady, or wait for his lordship?"

"We'll wait a moment," she said. As they were stopped, she decided to see if Yvonne was in her carriage and have a word with her to discover what was going on. John Groom assisted her down to the street and accompanied her to the carriage. She was glad for his presence. It helped to control the tightening knot of terror that was growing inside her.

As she approached Yvonne's carriage, she saw the driver standing in the street with a ghastly expression on his face.

"What's the matter?" she demanded.

"Madame—she is *blessée*."

Corinne hastened to the carriage door and looked inside. The comtesse was lounging against the cushioned seat. "Are you all right, Comtesse?" she asked. There was no answer.

As the groom had not put down the step, Corinne braced one foot on the coach floor, put her hands on either side of the doorframe, and pulled herself inside. The groom had lit a lamp and appeared at the doorway behind her, holding the light high. In its flickering glow, she saw the dark stain against Yvonne's white breast, saw the head lolling at an unnatural angle, and knew her worst fears had been realized.

"My God!" she gasped, taking the comtesse's hands.

The dark eyes opened, pale fingers clutched on to hers. "Milady," the comtesse whispered.

"Don't talk. We'll get you to a hospital. Or send for a doctor."

"Wait!" Yvonne held on to her with a strength that seemed out of proportion to her condition. "Yarrow," she said. "He has Sylvie. Save her."

"Did he do this to you?"

"His man—in carriage—"

"He was already here when you got in? Is that it?"

"Oui. C'est ça."

The comtesse breathed out her sorry tale, stopping often to regain her breath, slipping into her native French at times, then rousing herself to try to say it in English. *"Il y a quinze années, j'ai fait sa connaissance à Brighton."*

Fifteen years ago in Brighton, Yarrow had come to her humble little cottage to charge her with selling his wife a forged painting done by Boisvert. The comtesse, in her innocence, had not known Lord Yarrow was an art expert—but she knew he was a powerful man. He had terrorized her with threats of prison. She had used the only weapon she had, her beauty. She had become his mistress. Yarrow knew of the art collection her husband had secreted in France and had offered to smuggle the art to England for her during his official visits to France for the government. He arranged the sales—and kept the money, giving her barely what she required to live on. Even her jewels were only paste.

He told her he was investing the money for her to buy a house. He also arranged to have her daughter raised by Mrs. Yonge, in Colchester. When she realized he had no intention of buying the house or letting her have her money, she had turned again to forgery.

"*Mon bon ami,* Alphons Boisvert—"

"Who killed him, Yvonne?"

"Yarrow's henchman—Daugherty. Yarrow had my house

watched. His man followed Maurice—my butler and friend—to Boisvert's and saw the Watteau. Yarrow feared I would make enough money to be free of him, so he had Boisvert murdered. It was all I wanted, to take Sylvie and run and hide from him. But he got her before me."

"That's why you returned to London?"

"Of course. Find her, milady!"

"We'll find her, Yvonne."

Yvonne tried to squeeze her fingers, but her strength was ebbing quickly. *"Oui, je me fie à vous, madame,"* she whispered.

Tears filled Corinne's eyes. "I trust you," Yvonne had said. "We'll find her," she repeated, and placed her hand tenderly on Yvonne's brow. It already felt cold.

"Tell Luten—the papers. Use them. Catch that devil Yarrow." Madame's eyelids flickered one last time over her dark and stormy eyes. With her last breath, she whispered, "Sylvie."

When Luten returned, he found Corinne, with tears running down her cheeks, cradling the dead comtesse in her arms.

"My God!" he cried, staring at the lurid scene before him. "What happened?"

"Yarrow had a man hiding in the carriage. He stabbed her. Did you—"

"He got away. Is she—"

"She's gone. What should we do? Take her home?"

Luten laid the body gently on the cushioned seat and led Corinne from the carriage to the shadows beyond. He held her a moment tightly against his chest, making soothing sounds until the trembling stopped.

"Yarrow has Sylvie, Luten," she said. "I promised her I'd find Sylvie, get her away from that devil. He has kept Yvonne a virtual prisoner for fifteen years."

He let her anger boil, to keep the hysterics at bay. While he listened to her tale, he began to hatch a plan to catch Yarrow. There was little time; he had to trust people he didn't know; a hundred things could go wrong—but he had to do something. When a carriage rattled by, he realized they were attracting attention and told the groom to drive on to the comtesse's house. He and Corinne rode inside with her body, while his own driver drove around the block, to be back soon if needed.

Coffen's carriage had gone astray and come by a different route. It was just approaching the comtesse's house from Piccadilly as Yvonne's rig arrived. Luten and Corinne got out and told him what had happened.

"The blighter will get off scot-free if we don't do something." Coffen scowled. "He's sitting in his club with a dozen witnesses to say he was nowhere near the comtesse when she was done in."

"Then we'll have to break his alibi for a start. If we could get him to come here—"

"He knows she's dead. You couldn't drag him here tonight with a dozen wild horses."

"I wonder what he'd do if he thought she had escaped. Say I, or Prance, drove her home? If she threatened him by note, he'd come running."

"Send for Townsend, have him land in on them. Or would the driver go along with it? I expect he's Yarrow's man."

"He's French," Corinne said. "I think he's Lachange's friend. The French seem to stick together."

Luten said, "I'll have a word with him."

Before he spoke to the groom, the butler came out, wearing an anxious expression on his dissipated countenance. "Is something the matter, melord?" he asked.

The comtesse's groom ran up to him and began talking in French. The two men spoke rapidly, with many gesticulations in the French manner. Luten, listening, heard the driver say that that devil Yarrow would try to lay the blame in his dish, but they both knew who had done this heinous thing. Satisfied that both men were faithful to their late mistress, he began to formulate the details of his plan.

The butler came forward. "Let us take her ladyship into the house," he said. "It is not *comme il faut* to leave her body in the carriage."

"A word, before we touch anything," Luten said. "We agree that whoever plunged the dagger, it was Yarrow who is responsible?" Vociferous agreement, in both French and English, volleyed forth. "Then let us see if we cannot arrange some rough justice. Coffen, that watch I left at Melbourne's. Could you fetch it?"

Coffen drew it from his pocket. "This one? I decided to pick it up. Planned to throw it in the Serpentine. Mean to say, bound to be discovered in a day or two, there where you left it."

"Excellent. We'll send word to Bow Street to alert Townsend. But first, a note to Yarrow at White's. For that we shall require the comtesse's stationery."

"And her purple ink," Coffen added. "A nice touch. Bound to fool him. Try if you can find a sample of Cham—Yvonne's handwriting."

The butler, listening, began to grasp the rudiments of the plan. "I'll take you to her study. She has notebooks."

Luten interrupted his planning only long enough to suggest to Corinne that she have his driver take her home. She did not condescend to argue, but only said, "I shall stay, Luten, but Coffen should have his rig removed before it's recognized."

"If you insist on staying, then perhaps you could forge a note for me. A lady would do a better hand. The butler will take us to Yvonne's office. I'll tell you what to write." He asked Coffen to remove his rig.

They went inside; she studied some samples of the comtesse's handwriting and practiced imitating it. Her hand moved stiffly at first, but Yvonne's writing was not so different from her own feminine style, and she soon felt the forgery would fool Yarrow.

Luten lit the pages on which she had been practicing and threw them into the grate to remove the evidence. He dictated while she sat at Yvonne's desk. "Dear Yarrow: No, forget the 'Dear.' It is not a billet-doux. Write, 'Yarrow: Your plan failed. I have certain papers re Mr. Inwood and the Gresham Company that I shall discuss exchanging for Sylvie. I will meet you in Hyde Park in the carriage, on Rotten Row, just at the east end of the Serpentine. If you aren't there before one o'clock, I shall give the papers to Lord Luten.' Sign it Lady Chamaude. That should bring him."

"Hyde Park?"

"He wouldn't risk killing her here, with servants about."

"But would she risk meeting him there alone at night?"

"She would if she had the papers hidden elsewhere. He'd not kill her until he got his hands on them. I'll ask her butler to deliver the note to White's."

"You mean to have Townsend catch Yarrow with the body?"

"I do."

"How can you account for calling Townsend to Hyde Park? An anonymous note?"

"I believe Lady Chamaude should write to him on her crested stationery saying she is meeting a gentleman at Hyde Park and expressing some concern for her safety. She'll ask him to have a man there. Townsend will be there in person if I know anything. He's taking an interest in Boisvert's death." He dictated another note and Corinne wrote.

She was just sealing it when Coffen poked his head in at the door, then sauntered in. "My rig's around the corner in the shadows. Was just thinking, Luten. What about the weapon? I didn't see any knife in the carriage. The assassin must have taken it with him. Will this do?"

He pulled a small dagger from his pocket. It had a bone handle and a blade eight inches long. "I could put a bit of her blood on it."

Corinne made a gagging sound. Luten said, "Fine. It doesn't have your inititals on it, does it?"

"No, it's a common sort of knife. You see them everywhere. I keep it in the side pocket of my rig, since I never seem to have a pistol handy when I'm held up."

"Good. And put the watch in Yvonne's fingers, as if she had torn it from his waistcoat. I believe we're all set. What time is it?"

Coffen glanced at Yarrow's watch. "Half past twelve."

"Then we'd best get a move on."

Coffen took the watch out to the comtesse's carriage. He tried to forget she was dead as he wrapped her cold fingers around it and pressed the knife against her bloodied chest. He then placed it in her lap, as if it had fallen, or been pulled out.

Luten gave the butler the note to deliver to Yarrow. The

butler suggested the footman take the other note to Bow Street to indicate that it was from the comtesse. It was explained to Yvonne's coachman that he had driven the comtesse home. No one had got into the carriage. She had told him to wait, gone into her house, then come out and asked him to drive her to Hyde Park.

"What do we do?" Coffen asked, when he had joined Luten and the others. "Can we be there? I'd like to see the old bustard being put into manacles."

"We'll be there early and find some dark spot to watch." Luten looked at Corinne. "We'll drop you off at home." She just looked at him as if he were a moonling. "Oh, very well, but if you have nightmares, don't blame me."

"I blame myself," she said in a wistful voice, regretting all her ill humor toward Yvonne.

If she had been more understanding, if she had helped Luten help the comtesse . . . But the roots of this tragedy were deep. They went far into the past, to a frightened young French girl forced to sell a forged picture to support herself and her illegitimate child. If she had sold that picture to anyone but Lady Yarrow . . . If Yarrow had not been such a lecherous, evil old wretch . . . If, if, if. The past was beyond recall, but she could do one thing for Yvonne. She must rescue Sylvie and help her to some decent sort of life. That was the only atonement she could make, and she felt it was all Yvonne really wanted of her.

Chapter Twenty-six

Coffen suggested they all go to Hyde Park in his unmarked carriage, in case someone recognized Luten's crest entering the park. Hyde Park was well enough known to Fitz that he delivered them there without mishap. He halted halfway down Serpentine Road, and they walked through patches of mist toward the spot Yvonne's carriage was to stop. The moon was dulled to a silver glow, enough to light their path, painting grass and branches with an evanescent light. Their footsteps, though quiet, echoed loudly in their listening ears. When an owl uttered a plaintive, echoing *whooo*, Coffen nearly leapt out of his slippers.

"I knew there'd be an owl," he muttered, and was hushed by Luten.

Luten held Corinne tightly against his side as they waited in the still shadows. She thought of poor Yvonne and was grateful to be alive, to be safe, to be loved. They heard the heavy clop of hooves and grinding of wheels first, then watched as the carriage carrying Yvonne's body drove slowly along Rotten Road and drew to a stop. The coach might have been a hearse, the driver Death. The coachman looked all about but didn't call or leave his perch. It seemed a long time they waited.

Coffen drew out his watch and announced, "One o'clock—and all ain't well. What's keeping Yarrow? If Bow Street gets here first, we're sunk."

As he spoke, they heard the dull clatter of a carriage coming at a fast pace. They exchanged a wide-eyed stare.

"Oh Lord, I hope it's Yarrow and not Townsend!" Corinne whispered.

As it came into view, it was seen to be a crested rig, drawn by a blood team. Yarrow! They drew a collective sigh of relief. The driver drew on the reins, the horses slowed, the carriage pulled up behind Yvonne's and stopped. His coachman alit and opened the door for him. Yarrow dismounted, peered around into the shadows, and walked at a stiff-legged gait to the waiting carriage. They watched with bated breath as he opened the door and peered inside. They couldn't hear what he said, but at least he didn't leave.

"If he takes to his heels before Townsend gets here, we're out of luck," Coffen said. "What's keeping Townsend anyhow? Are you sure that footman you sent for him can be trusted, Luten?"

"No. I didn't have a week to make the plan. It was done on the spur of the moment. There! He's getting into the rig. He's certainly seen she's dead. He won't stick around long."

"He'll make a search for the papers before he goes," Coffen said. "If he sees his watch, he'll take it. He must be wondering how the devil it got there."

Before Yarrow left the carriage, Mr. Townsend of Bow Street came shambling down the road in a jig drawn by one elderly nag. He took up his lantern and leapt down from his perch. The fat little figure in a flaxen wig topped by a broad-brimmed white hat was dressed quite independently of fashion in a straight-cut coat and kerseymere breeches. This famous character had taken more criminals than the rest of the Bow Street officers together. He was in great favor at court and was often to be seen guarding against crime at the better balls, making easy with the great and near great.

Yarrow stepped down from the carriage. "Your lordship!" Townsend said, doffing his hat. "Is Lady Chamaude quite well?" The lantern cast a lurid light on Yarrow's dissipated countenance.

"What the deuce are you doing here?" Yarrow cried in a voice that betrayed his agitation.

"Her ladyship requested I dart along to keep an eye on her. I can't imagine in the world what she is up to. Meeting some desperate fellow, I daresay. French!" he added disparagingly. "But you know that. She's all right and tight, is she?"

"Of course she is. Run along, Townsend. This has nothing to do with you."

"I will, your lordship, as soon as I have a word with her ladyship. All in the line of duty, sir. No word will cross my lips if I have arrived inopportunely. Just ask her to throw a blanket over her nekkidness, and I'll say good evening to her."

"That's not necessary, my good fellow. Run along."

Without further ado, Townsend shoved a protesting Yarrow aside and poked his nose into the carriage. He uttered a loud "Yoicks!" and his rump disappeared into the rig.

"By God, it worked!" Luten said. He was almost more surprised than gratified. There were so many things that could have gone wrong. If Yarrow had chosen to ignore the summons, if he had come and gone before Townsend arrived, if Yvonne's servants proved to be in Yarrow's confidence . . . But the butler and footman had delivered the notes, and as Luten peered through the shadows to see how the coachman behaved, he was fully satisfied that the driver was following instructions.

He crept closer, knowing that no one was paying attention to the periphery when such exciting doings were going forth closer at hand. He saw Townsend climb out of the carriage, brandishing the bloodied knife.

He heard the driver say, "Her ladyship, she was alive ten minutes ago when she asked me to drive her here. No one else has been in the carriage except his lordship."

"Who are you going to believe—a demmed French servant or an English peer?" Yarrow demanded in a rhetorical spirit.

Townsend held up the hand holding the lantern. From his fingers dangled Yarrow's watch. He studied it in the light.

"I believe my eyes, milord, which showed me your watch in the victim's fingers. May I just see your hands, milord?" He reached out and grasped Yarrow's right hand. "Blood! I'll have to ask you to step along to Bow Street with me to explain a few things."

"Don't be ridiculous! She was dead when I arrived."

"Suicides seldom stab theyselves. Poison, now—"

"I'm a bosom bow of the Duke of York!"

Townsend cocked his head almost playfully and clamped his fingers on Yarrow's arm. "I'd not boast of that alliance! Don't make me use force, milord. It ain't fitting to darken a lord's daylights."

Yarrow, blustering and threatening awful reprisals and demanding his lawyer, was taken into custody to be driven in the ignominious gig to Bow Street. Before leaving the park, Townsend ordered the comtesse's driver to remain at what he called "the scene of the crime" until another officer arrived, at which time both Yarrow's carriage and the comtesse's were to be driven to Bow Street, where both would be examined for evidence and the corpse would be examined by the coroner.

"Well, it's done," Coffen said with quiet satisfaction. "Now can we go home and get a bite to eat? I'm famished."

"Yes, we can go home," Luten said, peering through the shadows at Corinne. When he took her hand firmly in his, she felt a sudden easing of tension. Her heart expanded like a balloon. It was all right between them,. and as for the rest, they would make that all right, too.

"We still have to rescue Sylvie," she said. "I have no idea where Yarrow has taken her. He could hardly have her at his own house, with his wife. I promised Yvonne, Luten."

"We'll find her," he said. "But for now I'm taking you home. No arguments, my dear." He placed a kiss on her forehead and walked with her to the carriage.

Coffen followed behind, smiling to see them together.

When they were in the carriage, he said, "I expect we've bent a few laws this night."

"It is a case of the end justifying the means," Luten replied. "The greater crime would be to let Yarrow off scot-free."

It was not until Coffen had dropped them off at Berkeley Square that they could speak of more private matters.

"I'm sorry I was so horrid about Yvonne," Corinne said, as they sat side by side on the striped sofa. "If you had told me the truth—"

"I tried. You didn't believe me."

"You didn't tell the whole truth. You never told me you were taking her to inns and to Colchester."

"You wouldn't have believed it was just business."

She gazed deeply into his eyes. "Was it just business, Luten?"

"Is it ever just that, between a man and a woman? Knowing something of her past life, I felt sorry for her. It is a man's instinct to help a lady in distress." Luten saw the mistrust growing in her eyes and decided that was enough truth for one night. What she really feared was that he loved Yvonne, and he hadn't.

"I'm not sure I can trust you, when you say things like that," she said.

"I don't trust you and Harry, when you're together. He's the first one you turned to."

"He's an old friend!"

"Yvonne was an old friend. If we can't trust each other, then what hope is there for us? We can't go about tied to each other like those unfortunate twins born in Siam. I love you. I had, and have, no intention of being unfaithful to you, unless you are unfaithful to me."

"Marriage is impossible," she said. "I don't know who ever invented such a stupid institution."

"Nor do I, but until someone comes up with a better way of raising children, it seems we are stuck with it. So is it a bargain?"

"How romantic!" She gave him a saucy look. "I'll think about it."

"I'll help you," he said, and drew her into his arms for a scalding kiss and a much more romantic proposal.

When Coffen came tapping at the door later, Black just shook his head. "This ain't a good time, Mr. Pattle. You understand."

"Making it up, are they?"

"They've got over that hump. I'm wondering if I ought to throw a bucket of water over them," he added roguishly.

Pattle gave him a frown. "Mind your manners, Black. You're talking about a lady." On this setdown he returned to his own house to ponder the mystery of romance, which always seemed to elude him.

The next few days were busy ones. Monsieur Lachange called on Lord Luten, whose name did not publicly arise in connection with the tragic case of Lord Yarrow and the comtesse. Lachange proved, upon close examination, to be even younger than Luten had thought.

"I want to thank you for trying to help Lady Chamaude," Lachange said. "I don't know how you did it—I ask no questions—but I cannot believe Yarrow personally killed her. He hasn't the courage, but he is morally responsible. I doubt they will hang him. It is unknown for a jury of a lord's peers to do so."

"He'll spend the rest of his life behind bars at least," Luten said with satisfaction.

"Small enough punishment for the years of agony he has caused. He has held Lady Chamaude a virtual prisoner for years. I know she was deathly frightened of what he would do when he forced her to attend that party."

"Why did he make her go?"

"I thought he just wanted to keep an eye on her. He knew she was desperate to find her daughter. I believe she suspected all along, and now, of course, I realize he wanted to get her away from Half Moon Street to murder her. Yet in his own evil way, he loved her. Dog in the manger. If he couldn't have her, no one could."

"It was Yarrow who removed Sylvie from Mrs. Yonge's?"

"Yes, he became nervous when Lady Chamaude began seeing you and Sir Reginald and hired one of his henchmen to bring Sylvie to London. He told Sylvie her mama wanted her. He feared that, between the two of you, you would help Lady Chamaude escape his clutches. He needed something to keep her in line and knew her daughter was the likeliest thing. But he went too far. When he threatened to harm Sylvie, the comtesse spat out all the pent-up years of hatred—then he knew he must kill her."

Luten just shook his head. When he spoke, it was of other

things. "We've been looking for Sylvie—put advertisements in the journals, questioned Daugherty. Bow Street has him in custody again for the murder of Boisvert."

"Sylvie is with me and my mama," he said. "Yarrow had hired a woman to guard her. He told the woman she was a lunatic. He kept Sylvie locked in a room in St. John's Wood. When the woman read of Yarrow's arrest, she unlocked Sylvie's door and fled. Sylvie came to me. We have been engaged for a year. We shall marry at once. I met her when I began taking the comtesse to Colchester to visit. Her ladyship approved the match."

"You have known Lady Chamaude a long time?"

"Since I was a child. She was a friend of Mama. We émigrés stick together. Lady Chamaude had a few faithful friends, but unfortunately we were powerless against Lord Yarrow. That is why she sold Mr. Pattle that forged Poussin, the one I exchanged for the original. She was desperate for money, you see, and the forgery was very good, but she feared in the end that Yarrow would find it out and make trouble for her. They were bickering over everything by that time. He may have threatened—I don't know.

"He knew Yvonne had used Boisvert in the past. When the Watteau disappeared from her walls, he went to spy on him and presumably saw the Watteau, as he had Boisvert killed."

"Who sent Gresham to Boisvert?"

"The comtesse suggested it, to help Boisvert. Like the rest of us, he was always in need of money. He wanted to remove his atelier to a better address."

"What will you and Sylvie do for money?" Luten asked.

"I make my living as a French tutor and translator. There is still the Watteau—the original—to be sold," he said. "And a few lesser pieces. We don't need much. We hope to set up a small day school in some town far removed from London."

"There is a pretty painting in a small waiting room. A Greuze, I believe, of a young girl."

"A Greuze? Ah no, that is a painting of the comtesse when she was a girl. Boisvert did it fifteen years ago in Brighton. It is good, *non*? He was under the influence of Greuze at the time. I know Sylvie wants to keep it."

"Of course. Let me know if I can help," Luten said.

"You were interested in the Watteau, I think?"

Luten didn't think Corinne would want that constant reminder of Yvonne in their home, nor did he. "I can find a buyer, if you like."

"If you hear of anyone who is interested, I can be reached at this address." He handed Luten his card.

"I might be able to do better than that," Luten said. "I'll be in touch."

His visit with Yarrow's lawyer was unpleasant but necessary. In order to keep certain unsavory facts regarding the nature of his long relationship with Yvonne out of the journals, Yarrow agreed to turn fifteen thousand pounds over to Sylvie.

To suppress the evidence of Yarrow's dealings with Gresham, the Tories agreed to reconsider the granting of the contract for the rockets. Gresham, after careful consideration, decided that his Armaments Works was incapable of supplying the rocket in the quantity required, and the contract was awarded to Congreve.

Sir Reginald, pleasantly embittered by it all, went into a three-day decline, had straw laid in the street to deaden the sound of carriage wheels, wrapped his knocker up in black, wore a black armband, and composed a threnody on lost love. By the third evening, his friends had ceased sending messages and flowers. He became bored with solitude and mourning.

When he saw Luten and Coffen going to Corinne's house, he called his valet and said, "Make me presentable, Villier. I put myself in your capable hands. I require a toilette that suggests my loss, without flinging it in the faces of my friends. The black jacket and striped waistcoat, I think, and of course, the black pearl cravat pin."

"Shall you wear a ring?"

Prance considered it a moment. "No, that would be too joyful."

"Just a touch of talcum on your cheeks, milord?" Villier suggested. He had discovered that Sir Reginald not only tolerated the misnomer "milord," but liked it very well when they were alone.

"Just so, and a hint of that lilac water from France. Now for the cravat. Not the Oriental when I am practically in mourning."

"May I suggest the Carlton? Your patron, the Prince of Wales, particularly admired it."

Half an hour later, a highly polished Sir Reginald duly appeared in Corinne's saloon, where he found the rest of the Berkeley Brigade enjoying a glass of wine. He was warmly welcomed back into the world.

"Finished your epic, have you?" Coffen asked, drawing Prance a chair by the grate, as if he were an invalid.

"Ah no, Coffen. Kind of you to inquire, but no creating was possible in my emotional state, save for a little threnody in memory of *her*." The hushed pronouncement of "her" left no doubt as to whom he meant.

"*Sturm und Drang,*" Coffen said, nodding. "Sorry for your trouble, Prance, but you can't let it get you down."

"I realize I have been self-indulgent. Naughty of me, but really, you know, the way I was feeling, it would have been cruel to inflict myself on Society. And how has the world been wagging while I have been hors de combat?" He darted a coy glance at Corinne and Luten. He noticed she was wearing the ten-carat emerald-cut diamond. It looked quite ludicrous on her little hand. It occurred to him that the black diamond bracelet would make a suitable wedding gift.

"About the same as usual," Corinne said. She and Luten brought him up-to-date on their various doings with Yarrow, Sylvie, and Monsieur Lachange.

Prance gazed into the leaping flames. "The cycle of life goes on," he murmured. "Love, death, marriage—and eventually new birth. I trust you two have not slipped off to visit the archbishop for a special license while my back was turned?"

"Oh no. Luten is not that eager to be under cat's paw," Corinne said, with a smiling glance at her reinstated fiancé.

"Then I am not too late to help you with the arrangements

for the nuptials? You cannot refuse me! It would be too cruel. I need some distraction to ease me out of this melancholia I have been floundering in. All has been disaster for me this spring. The failure of my *Rondeaux*, and of my love for the comtesse. Between the two of them, they have nearly undone me."

"You've got your *Rondeaux* into Oxford and Cambridge. I don't call that failure," Luten said bracingly.

"Now, that is an odd thing, Luten," Prance said, with a questioning look. "It was not the university that bought all those copies of my *Rondeaux*. Nor has there been any word from Prinney. He would have asked me to autograph them if he were giving them to visiting dignitaries. Villier mentioned something about some large boxes being delivered to you the day before my poems appeared in Hatchard's window."

"A few items I had sent from my cousin's estate—the one I inherited, you know. Some books on religion I promised to Bishop Farndale."

"Ah. I have been thinking of that unexplained smoke from your bedroom chimney."

"The rooms were damp."

"Odd that mine were not damp."

"I must have my roof looked at."

"P'raps it was old King George who bought the *Rondeaux*," Coffen suggested.

"Yes, he is mad after all," Prance said, and allowed himself a small smile at his sally. "We must laugh at our own follies, or we become brutes. But enough of this lugubrious chatter. About our wedding, folks, have we decided between Saint George's in Hanover Square and Ireland? Saint George's would be easier for me, right here in London, where I know all the sources for what I shall require."

"Ireland," Coffen said.

Prance frowned. "Southcote Abbey would be an impressive site," he suggested.

"Ireland," Coffen repeated.

"Or your house right here on Berkeley Square, Luten?" Prance said.

"It's to be Ireland, tarsome fellow," Coffen said again.

Prance sighed. "Ireland. If you tell me the bride plans to wear green, I shall disown the lot of you."

Coffen looked alarmed. "Married in green, ashamed to be seen," he said. "That's what my nanny used to say."

"It would match her eyes," Luten said mischievously, and grinned at his jealous fiancée.

"For such a sad occasion, perhaps I should wear black," she retaliated.

"Married in black, you'll ride in a hack," Coffen warned. "I think you ought to wear white, even if it ain't your first time out, Corinne. Married in white, you've chosen right."

"White it is," Luten said.

Coffen smiled contentedly; Prance frowned, and Black, wearing the face of a martyr on this sad occasion, came to the door to suggest champagne.